SCORPIONS IN STILETTOS

Also by Hinemura Ellison & Ted Hughes:

Trinity Trilogy:

Book 1: Sharks with Lipstick

Book 2: Snakes in Suits

Book 3: Scorpions in Stilettos

SCORPIONS IN STILETTOS

Hinemura Ellison

&

Ted Hughes

BACH DOCTOR PRESS

This first edition 1.0 published in 2020 Bach Doctor Press

This is a work of fiction. While many places are real, the events and incidents are products of the authors' imagination. Any resemblance to the behaviour or appearance of actual persons holding positions similar to characters in the story is coincidental and unintentional. For legal reasons, I am obliged to stress that this novel and series IN NO WAY implies that any of the mentioned government departments, people, systems, back handers exist. That would be an outrageously unbelievable allegation.

A catalogue record for this book is available from the National Library of New Zealand.

ISBN: 978-0-473-51334-4

ISBN: 978-0-473-51335-1 Epub

ISBN: 978-0-473-51336-8 Kindle

Cover design by: Michelle Connor, EbookCoversOnline

Acknowledgements:

Amazing work from our wonderful copy editor Joan Rosier-Jones, thanks for the insightful questions. This book wouldn't be the standard it is without your input. Formatting once again completed by the talented Mark Innes-Jones.
Huge thanks also to Michelle Connor for the magnificent cover artwork, your vision for the series has been fantastic.
Thanks again to Darin Dance and his crew at Bach Doctor Press, keep leading the way, you do make a positive difference.

Contents

If someone tells me, "The sky is green," I simply say "okay." I don't need to agree with them and I don't need to prove them wrong or show them "proof" that I'm right if I believe otherwise. I simply go on with my life with a newfound understanding that, to some people, the sky may indeed look green. And I'm okay with that. It keeps external conflicts from disturbing my inner peace. And isn't that where world peace begins - with each of us being peaceful

Timber Hawkeye

Prologue

Clara walks confidently in front of the Jury stand, not noticing the highly polished sheen on the heart-rimu handrail that she trails her fingers across, "May I approach the bench, Your Honour?" she says in a husky voice.

The Judge looks the on-comer up and down, his eyes lecherously taking in her younger curves, "That depends on the applicant's intentions," he rumbles in his deep baritone manner.

Throwing her jacket onto the Court Clerk's table, Clara replies, "Oh my intentions are very, v-e-r-y, naughty." She props a patent leather boot onto the Court Clerk's chair, revealing her black patterned stockings as her skirt rises.

"Well in that case…"

Neither of them noticed the red winking light from the CCTV camera.

Chapter One

Caught in Court While Courting…

All that can be seen from the receptionist's desk, is the complete bird's eye view from the CCTV showing Clara in full flight on top of the Judge on top of the Judges' Bench.

"Despite that being quite an impressive gymnastic display, it brings the whole legal profession into disrepute! Thank you, Agnes, for bringing this to my attention. I trust that this will keep you silent about the matter." Yvonne, the HR manager, slides a particularly fat envelope of cash across the desk, in exchange for the USB stick, "This is the only copy I trust?"

"For that price Ms Wakefield, it is!" Agnes grabs the envelope greedily, "I'll be off now, if that's alright with you…"

"Enjoy the extended vacation Agnes," Yvonne says dismissing her and turning to head to her office.

Damn that woman, Clara has been such a good

employee, the most dedicated Training and Development specialist we've ever had, but she's crossed the line this time, Yvonne thinks to herself, Nothing for it, but to let her go.

*****

"What do you mean, you've been transferred?" a bewildered Clara says into her cell phone. "I don't understand, I thought you had a big trial in Wellington?"

"I did Clara, but I'm at the airport now about to board the Airforce's Boeing 757-200," Judge Jacobsen explains. "Something about an international crisis they need me for and I'll be out of contact for the duration. I'm really sorry we are over, but after nearly getting caught out last weekend at Waiheke, it has to finish. Sorry, but I've got to go now," he says, cutting the call.

"Well I never..." Clara exclaims, as her phone rings again. Not looking at the display she answered it immediately, "Thank god you phoned back..."

"Clara, in my office NOW!" Yvonne barks.

"Ah, yes, sure thing Ms Wakefield," Clara stammers, as she immediately rises from her desk, wondering what has upset her tyrannical boss this time.

*****

"A High Court Judge? Just what were you thinking, Clara? A married man in that esteemed position. Don't you realise the potential disaster this affair could bring?" Yvonne paused for a micro second to draw breath, she had a knack for speaking continuously without seeming to take a break, but if you dared to concentrate hard enough and didn't listen to what she was saying, you would have noticed the miniscule pauses.

Clara unfortunately couldn't muster the courage not to listen to Yvonne's tirade. "If the *Capital News* got hold of this, god knows what damage that grubby little broadsheet would do to the entire Judiciary! Let alone our company's reputation, a reputation that my grandfather established last century. I'll not have our good name sullied by your sordid little affair! You have crossed the line Clara and there is no going back. You have three minutes exactly to clear your desk. Laurie from Security will escort you to your desk, then out the back door. I'll have your lanyard now. Your final pay will be paid this afternoon and you are never to show your face in a courtroom or this office ever again. DO I MAKE MYSELF CLEAR?"

*****

Standing bewildered outside the back entrance of her old office, her black leather hobo bag slung over her shoulder and clutching a plain brown cardboard file box containing the few personal items and mementos she had accumulated over her seven years' employment, Clara blinks back her tears wondering just what the hell has happened and just what does she do now?

Phone Jack, he might be able to pick me up and get me home, she says to herself, fishing for her phone while balancing her file box on her knee.

"Darling, it's me. Can you come and pick me up now?" Clara asks, "I know it's short notice, but I need you right now… what do you mean 'catch a taxi'? I'm your girlfriend in distress and I need you now." Clara tries to understand, "What do you mean you are in Khapaudi? Where the hell is that anyway? Somewhere near Taupō, isn't it?... Nepal! What do you mean? Are you climbing Mt Everest? I need you here now! Oh, this is impossible!" She hangs up and walks towards Stout street, where she frantically waves down a taxi outside the Big Super Ministry building, putting on her best stiff upper lip.

*****

Sitting in the back of the taxi, Clara quickly takes stock. She has no job, her lover has been posted god knows where overseas and her boyfriend is mountain biking in the Himalayas near Mt. Everest, and not many more working days until the sheer debacle that is her family Christmas. What a heck of a Monday to start the week, with Jack out of the picture, only her two closest friends will be able to come to her rescue with some solid advice, or at least come up with some laughs and light relief.

She texts her besties, Sven and Freya, *'Unbelievable news girls, meet you at the Café Astoria for lunch tomorrow, where I'll spill...'.*

That will get them wondering, Clara thinks, as she pays the taxi driver. "Thanks for the ride and keep the change."

Locking the front door to her sanctuary behind her, Clara turns and carefully places the file box, her keys and handbag on the hall table and walks through to her lounge, slowly shedding her stoic exterior. Looking out at the harbour, she feels the tears running unchecked down her cheeks, her mind like the wild Wellington winds a furious storm of emotion.

Chapter Two

Tuesday and Consequences

Clara wakes to a pounding in her head, a series of booms then a small break before it starts again. Slowly she realises that it's someone knocking or rather pounding on her front door and it's not that familiar Saturday morning hangover headache arriving early on a Tuesday morning.

Wrapping her dressing gown around her, she staggers towards the main entrance unsteadily, before unlocking her front door to a vaguely familiar excited young woman.

"What's the urgency banging on my door at this ungodly hour?" Clara asks.

"Clara! Fantastic news. They accepted your ridiculous counter offer and have countersigned the contract! You've sold your house," cries the woman jumping up and down on her front porch – well it was her front porch, wasn't it?

Clara squints at her name badge, "You had better come in, Kirsty, and explain while I get the coffee on." Clara sighs, thinking, *What mess have I gotten myself into now?*

Wrinkling her nose, Kirsty smiles in reply, "I'll get the coffee on Clara, you jump into the shower, it should be ready when you get out and I'll lay the paperwork out on the dining table for you…I hope that's okay?"

"Ah, yeah…sure," Clara says passively as she heads for the bathroom.

*****

As Clara steps out of the cold shower, towelling herself dry, she slowly pieces together the afternoon and evening. She had a glass of wine, cleared the mailbox and saw an unsolicited letter from Kirsty the real estate agent who was currently in her kitchen, making her coffee. On a whim, Clara had phoned Kirsty asking for a ball park value for her house, and surprise, Kirsty just had a gap in her calendar and could be around in a half hour to give her an 'honest' appraisal. Clara, had another glass of wine to steady herself from the morning's series of unfortunate events before Kirsty arrived.

Kirsty plucked a grand figure of $900,000 for Clara's 1940's architecturally designed house by a local Architect of note, to which Clara responded, "Add another couple of hundred onto that and you just might have a deal."

Unbeknown to Clara, Kirsty had a client who desperately wanted a Bernard Winton Johns' designed house at any cost. After a few wines and some to-ing and fro-ing, Kirsty was opening a bottle of bubbles and was drinking a toast with Clara and promising to be back first thing in the morning with the countersigned sale and purchase agreement! Clara then finished the bottle and collapsed onto her bed comatose thinking of lands afar.

"Oh my god," Clara says, looking at herself in the steamy mirror, "what have I done?"

*****

"Let me get this right, I countersigned on 1.3 million and compromised on the settlement date which is tomorrow? I've only got a day to pack and move? Just how the hell am I going to manage that, Kirsty?" Shaking her head in confusion, Clara asks, "What do I do?"

"I know a reliable moving company that still has storage space available, Clara. They will wrap and pack your contents. All you have to do is find somewhere to stay in the meantime and pack the clothes you need until you find your next dream home," Kirsty explains smoothly. "Just give me the go-ahead for the mover and I'll get the ball rolling."

Cradling her coffee in both hands, Clara sip's on the liquid brown lightning, trying to make sense of the situation, "Well, I guess you had better contact the movers and I had best start packing," she says resignedly.

She still can't quite come to terms with the last 24 hours and the absolute total upheaval and chaos that her nice quiet, ordered life has become. Clara then remembers her text message, *Oh no, just what am I going to tell the girls at lunch? I had best phone my shrink and update her; Maggie will have some tools and advice for me.* Clara searches for her phone.

*****

"I must say girls, I've never seen that before!" Clara says, picking up her coffee and taking a sip before continuing, "You both look so funny making fish motions with your mouths open, but nothing being spoken."

Sven is the first to break the silence, "But Flat White, your life is so ordered and well…"

"Go on say it Sven," Clara beckons.

"…well normal," Freya butts in.

"I was going to say 'boring', but even that's too harsh," Sven clarifies.

"Ouch!" Clara says, "But I get where you're coming from Sven. Truth be told, I've lived my life since coming back to Wellywood from Europe, in the most unspectacular way possible, working hard to develop my career, putting in the hours and saving hard for my home. In fact, it was only our weekly catch-ups that have been keeping me sane."

"And Judge Jacobsen… anyone else on the side that us mere mortals should know about Clara, like the Big Super Minister or a diplomat by any chance?" Freya asks.

"No, that creep of a Minister is shagging his EA, if I'm not mistaken," Sven interrupts.

"Well, a girl doesn't spill all her secrets Freya," a red-faced Clara says.

"But your adorable little Bernard Johns' house sold? In this market, what with the housing shortage due to the Poms and Chinese buying up large, as well as the earthquake red stickered homes and apartments, what can you replace it with?" Freya queries.

"You might have to move up the Coast," Sven says brightly, "Imagine us on the 'Kiwi Con' commuting each day?"

"It might have to come to that, as I have to be out tomorrow. Have either of you got space for a couch surfer?" Clara sips on her coffee, "Just until I find something?"

"What about your Mum's or your sister's?" Sven queries.

"Oh, you're joking Sven. It's bad enough when we all get together for a 'happy family Christmas' and that's only once a year. There's no way I could put up with the whinging, back- stabbing, psychological abuse from Mum," Clara explains.

"There's space at the family bach at Waitarere," Freya invites generously, "You are more than welcome to stay as long as you want, as I'm at Zita's in the Bay now."

"I'm not sure the Merc will be safe parked at the Levin Railway Station all day though," Sven thinks, "No, you will have to stay at mine in Waikanae and share the couch with fluffy Edward. Besides, it will be an easier commute."

"Are you sure Sven?" Clara asks.

"Absolutely, that's settled. Now the packing," Sven says, "Shall we pop around this arvo, I'm sure we can knock off early and help get your essentials ready. Then we can load the Merc up with your stuff and maybe even miss the traffic."

"Oh my, here I go again," Clara says, blinking back some tears. "That's why you girls are the best. It's definitely my shout though, even after the bank has taken their cut, I'll have a nice nest egg."

"Well, you deserve it after all your scrimping and saving, Flat White," Freya comments.

"And I second that." Sven agrees.

*****

"Freya, can you start packing those clothes and shoes into these two suitcases, and Sven I'll be back with your cases in a mo'," Clara explains.

"These are impressive lists Flat White," Sven answers as Clara exits the room. Sven is sorting through the wardrobe for clothes and piling them onto the queen-size bed, "When did she get the time to write these detailed lists Freya?"

"That's our OCD buddy for you."

"My god, I think I'm going to need these two cases just for her shoe list!" Sven exclaims.

"Imelda Marcos has got nothing on our girl, Clara," Freya laughs, "She will be sooo over-dressed for the Coast."

"I can just see her at the bar at the Citizens Club in this slinky black number, ordering a glass of Sav," Sven joins in.

"…and being asked did she want a red or white Chateau Cardboard?" Freya completes the sentence, laughing so hard she sets Sven off with her peculiar nasal snorting giggle, which then sets Freya off again and they both collapse onto the bed in a giggling frenzy.

Carrying some extra bags, Clara walks back into the room, "Here you go, Freya, I've got the makeup bag and… Oh girls, we don't have time for this mucking about." Clara starts welling up. "We only have an hour before the movers arrive and we have to be packed by then."

Sven gets up and rushes over to give Clara a hug, "Don't you worry, the Trinity Trio can achieve anything. Now dry those tears and find some more cases or boxes. I've no idea how we are going to get all this into your Merc, but we WILL manage it."

Wiping her tears away Clara replies, "You girls are just the best!"

"Oh Ho, Jackpot!" Freya exclaims, "Geez, this one would make your eyes water, girlfriend," Freya pulls out a huge black vibrator from the bedside table.

"We might be besties girl, but you're not borrowing mine," a red-faced Clara replies, laughing. "Pop that one in the make-up bag, please, Oh and the red one, too, please."

*****

"Well after unpacking that little car load, Sven, I think we need a little bubbles to celebrate," Clara declares.

"Sure thing Flat White, one small problem though, I'm out of bubbles," Sven replies as she starts to rummage in her handbag for some cash. "if you can pop down to the supermarket and get a couple of bottles...damn I thought I had a $20 note in here..."

"No drama Sven, it's my treat. We need to have a proper celebration for my house sale." Clara grabs her car keys.

"No Flat White, we always go halves," Sven rejoins.

"None of that now, girl. You're putting me up, just think of it as a small contribution to the rent," Clara says as she heads out the door.

*****

Sitting on the deck looking out over Waikanae towards Kāpiti Island, Clara and Sven soak in the peace and quiet of the sleepy village below.

Sven hesitantly asks Clara the question that has been nagging in the back of her mind, "Flat white, please don't take this the wrong way, I'm asking this out of genuine concern..."

"Sven darl, I know we can have the occassional fireworks moments, but both you and Freya are my rock. I simply don't know what I'd do without you in my life," Clara pats Edward who is sprawled out full length on the cane two-seater beside her, purring.

"Thanks, so please remember that, girlfriend once I've asked you this... Okay? Clara do you actually know what you're doing with your life?" Sven puts it bluntly.

Looking shocked, Clara asks, "What do you mean, Sven?"

"Well, where to from here, Flat White? I mean, you are cashed up—well the money will be in you bank account in the next few days once the lawyers and agents have taken their cut. Your lover has ditched you. Your mother is a psycho. Your boyfriend, Jack, well I should say, good-looking, kind-hearted ex-boyfriend is overseas. Your 'stuff' is in storage. You have no commitments like a job, club, family or business. I guess what I'm trying to say is that the world is your oyster. What does the real Clara James actually want?"

Clara sips on her wine and thinks for a moment, "You know, Sven, I find it hard to get real with myself. I've tried to surround myself with a career, house and boyfriend, who by the way, I know I've treated Jack appallingly. But I've had those so-called solid things to create a structure for my life, so I have something to hang onto. Does that make sense?"

"Yeah, I can see that now you've explained it, but go on..."

"What I don't understand is my, well, I don't know

what else to call it, but my self-destructive behaviour. Who in their right mind, would have an affair with a High Court Judge in a small town like Wellywood, where you are going to be seen by your boyfriend's mates?"

"I see..." Sven responds.

"And to top that off, getting caught on camera getting down with the judge in a court room... just where was my head?"

Sven puts her glass down on the glass-topped cane outdoor table, taking a moment before replying, "Now that's a really good question, Flat White, but you will have to find that one out for yourself. Can I give you a small bit of advice?"

"Please do!"

"How about taking a leaf out of Freya's book?"

"What do you mean? I'm not sure I want to start a business."

"How about taking your trusty journal and working out what your inner dreams and desires really are? I mean, it might help clarify what sort of job you really should be applying for, where you want to live, who you want to be with... just try it for a few days and see what you come up with."

"Hmm, I'll give that a go. That's what my therapist suggested. I mean I'll have a bit of spare time until I find a job.

Come on drink up flat mate," Clara laughs.

Chapter 3

Wednesday Job Seeker

After waving goodbye to Sven at the BS Ministry, Clara weaves around the corner into Lambton Quay, armed with a list of agencies to call on in the hope of finding her next job.

Intrigued by a quirky sign, she follows it towards a stairwell leading down to a basement café called *Munamuna.* Taking in the quietness of the place, and admiring the funky furniture, she thought to herself, *Oh, this looks like a great place to have a quiet rendezvous. I must tell Sven.*

She orders her favourite coffee, and spies, a table in the far corner, partially screened by potted plants. She takes a seat there, and opens her hobo bag to set up her temporary workstation. First up her tablet, checking her smart phone, punching in the café Wi-Fi code and with pen and her journal, Clara sets about locating the employment agencies and their addresses so she can door knock in an efficient circuit.

"One triple shot large flat white, no sugar, will there be anything else?" the barista enquires as she places the coffee in front of Clara.

"Thank you so much. Just the coffee this morning thanks, but I will be back with my friend this afternoon. She will just love this place." Clara smiles. "Do you mind me asking, what does *Munamuna* mean?"

"It's Māori for underground, but secretive."

Clara nods. "Wow that's the best name. Thank you Jasmine," as she looks at the girl's name badge.

Taking a sip from her coffee, Clara thinks, *Ah nice and hot, I'll definitely be back*. Then she focuses on her task mapping addresses.

"Good there's no one here." A male voice comments as he enters the café. "Two Americano's over here, and make it quick," he barks at the barista, as he and the woman with him take a seat close to the door.

How rude… Clara thinks. She peaks through the fern frond at the couple, noticing the purple pin striped jacket the woman is folding over an adjacent chair. *Oh my god, that's Margaret Johnson, Bernard's wife! But who is she with?* Without thinking Clara picks up her smart phone and zooms in on the couple, taking a couple of quick photos before anyone notices.

Then emailing the photo to herself, she pulls the image up on her tablet. Clara starts searching Margaret on the internet, looking at the google images and sees lots of Margaret and Bernard, but none of Margaret and the man seated in the café.

Intrigued, Clara peaks through the fronds again and catches the man passing what looks like a small bottle to

Margaret. As Margaret takes the bottle, the man clasps both his hands around Margaret's saying in a slightly raised voice, "Are you sure about this, darling?"

"Stop being so wet, man," Margaret says as she shakes his hands off hers and carefully puts the bottle into her purse.

"It's just that there is no going back after this, Margaret."

"There's too much riding on this for that little tramp to upset the apple cart. She has to go, and I know just when to deliver this." Margaret pat's her purse, "You just keep a watching brief and make sure it stays under wraps."

"Well that I can do. I've already had one judge sent off-shore to delay a trial, so that the developer can get on with that Petone job we have a stake in," the man boasts.

"Good, I'll be needing the profit on our investment for my own nest egg. Then I can be free of him," Margaret explains.

"And then we can finally be together, darling."

"When the time is right, we can and not before." Margaret stands grabbing her purple pin striped jacket and purse.

"Did you not want your coffee?"

"You have mine, I've got to get back to work for an important meeting," Margaret answers as her stilettos click across the tiled floor.

*****

Slowly finishing her coffee Clara completes an efficient agency list before waving thanks to Jasmine and heading back out into the pedestrian chaos that is the government quarter of downtown Wellington.

Public servants, dressed in black, white and various shades of grey, criss-cross the streets, looking equally interchangeable, except for the different coloured lanyards telling the observer one ministry from another.

Intermingled with the shades of grey are the colourful loud tourists from the cruise ships, normally overweight older couples or foursomes wearing brightly coloured cross-trainers, beige fanny packs and a jacket tied around their waist. Always at least one of the group carries an expensive camera around their neck, with a telephoto lens that a photo journalist would be proud to use.

With her smart phone in one hand, Clara follows the map apps directions to her first destination, dodging between the tourists asking directions to see the Hobbits, and the public servants intent on making it to their next vitally important meeting.

Walking down Brandon Street, Clara finds her first target sandwiched between the Norwegian Consulate General office and a lawyers firm Russell, Whitaker and Prendergast.

The last surname triggers a memory for Clara, *Whoa, I think this is the guy Martin and I avoided at the Queens Wharf restaurant last week, Prendergast and that developer Church that Freya is battling with.*

Then it hits her. *OMG that man with Margaret said he had sent a judge overseas about a property court case. Oh, I'm so thick. That has to be Martin! Who is he to be able to send Martin overseas?*

She quickly texts Martin the photo she took of Margaret and her mystery man this morning: *Martin, who is this man? Is he the one who sent you overseas? He is somehow tied up with the developer CHURCH that I was telling you about last weekend. Call me, I might be able to help. C x*

Taking a deep breath, Clara steadies herself for another rejection from Martin, her recent lover who had broken their affair off on Monday morning. She knew deep in her heart, that it wouldn't last but hadn't wanted to admit it to herself. Only finally accepting the truth, after many deep and meaningful conversations with her besties Sven and Freya, while staying at a bach on Waiheke Island last weekend.

Her phone beeps and she looks frantically at the reply: *Clara although we are over, can I call you in 20 minutes? Please don't show ANYONE that photo! M*

Without thinking Clara replies: *I'm not trying to get back together Martin. I'm just trying to help C x*

Okay Clara James, time to pull up those big girl panties and get on with what you came here for, a job. She strides confidently into the employment agency, smiling her best at the bored receptionist who has her nose in a glossy fashion magazine.

*****

Feeling a bit more confident after successfully chatting briefly with the receptionist and having her CV accepted, Clara strides down Lambton Quay towards the short cut through to the Terrace to see the next agency on her list.

The familiar ringtone pings and not recognising the number, Clara answers hesitantly, "Hello Clara James speaking…"

"Clara, it's Martin. Thanks for the photo, I don't have much time. Who is the woman the Police Commissioner is with?" Martin asks.

"Wow the Police Commissioner! Why is Margaret Johnson meeting with him? Sorry, that's Bernard Johnson's wife. She's DCE for some government department." A shocked Clara replies.

"Thanks, I'll get her details. Now, what's this about that ratbag Church?" Martin asks.

"I heard something about a stake they had in a property deal with Church, oh and he passed her something, I don't know what it was, but he seemed concerned about her, I think they might be having an affair," Clara spilled, "Does that help you?"

"Like you wouldn't believe, thanks Clara. Don't tell anyone, but I'm back in Auckland and should be back in Wellington today, I'm at the airport now," Martin replies.

"A new phone?" Clara queries.

"Yes, for many reasons. Thanks again Clara I really mean that, you have just saved my career. Please don't contact me again. It was fun, but it's over. Sorry got to go," Martin apologises as he disconnects.

Turning into Woodward St, Clara looks at her phone in disbelief. *There you go, I save his career and... and... oh what's the point.* She puts the phone back in her hobo bag and looks up in time to see an old man with a cane, emerge from an office building.

A look of terror masks her face as she recognises the man who she knew as a child. Stopping in her tracks, those old feelings of helplessness and vulnerability wash over her.

To her horror, he looks up and sees her. Clara sees the look of recognition in his eyes as he licks his lips. Frozen in place with her past fears and conditioning, she hears him speak, "Ah, there you are young Clara..."

His voice breaks the spell she finds herself under. She stammers in a quiet fearful voice, "St… st… stay away from me you bastard!" Then turning she runs back the way she came, her heels clacking on the pavement as she puts distance between herself and her former tormentor.

*****

Rounding the corner into Willeston Street, Clara finally slows down, leaning against a parking ticket machine, breathing hard, trying to catch her breath.

Fucking bastard, why of all people did I have to see him today? Clara thinks, then noticing the strange looks she is attracting from the pedestrians nearby, she straightens herself up and walks purposefully towards Frank Kitts Park.

At Jervois Quay, she walks towards an empty bench, blinking back the tears that are now running unchecked down her face.

Taking a seat, she finds a tissue in her bag to wipe her tears as she sits staring out across the harbour, striving to make sense of her internal thoughts. Trying some deep breaths to steady herself, her jumbled mind gradually starts to slow down.

Clara shudders as she remembers one of the childhood incidents, where Fred let her stay up late to watch TV while her parents were out.

Then flashing to another memory of her sitting upright in her bed, her knees drawn up towards her face with her hands clasped tightly around her ankles, rocking herself back and forth, tears flowing down her face from the repeated nightmares she suffered as a consequence.

Mixed with that, are the heightened emotions of selling her home – her sanctuary against the unsafe world. Her recent failed relationships and sacking from her job all jumbled in her head.

Oh my god, how on earth did I get myself into this mess? I really am floating up shit creek now in a waka without a paddle. Who is going to save me now? My knight or knights in shining armour? I've gone from two to one, to zero. Yes one big zero. Who is going to take a look at me now? I am on the wrong side of 40, with no prospects and nothing to blame but myself. Holy shit, Clara, you've done it this time?

Clara didn't exactly like, let alone love herself. She had always been incredibly hard on herself and today was no exception. She had just lost, by her own doing, everything and anything and anyone that was slightly important to her. Her mother would be really pleased. She could just hear the bitch saying… *I told you so, Clara. I told you and your father and your sister numerous times you would amount to nothing and you have.*

Clara felt alarmed and overwhelmed. *Where do I begin? I don't really trust myself at the moment, every decision I have made recently hasn't been that flash. How do I know that the next one won't be equally as bad, in fact oh my god, life could get worse?*

If only I hadn't seen fucking Fred. I was just starting to feel like the day might turn out okay.

Oh dammit, where do I start, with the job, or the house? They kind of go hand-in-hand. I can't buy a house unless I have an income to either pay off the mortgage or to pay the rent. But then I can't get a job if I don't know where the hell I want to live. And the bloody shrink says don't go and do anything rash at this time, Clara. There is too much unsettlement in your life so don't go and be impulsive and be rash and get the first place you can find.

But my god I am incapable of making an informed decision, I need my besties. I can't decide what the fuck to do. What comes first the house or the job or…?

Picking up her phone she finds her friend's number and pushes the contact to connect, *Oh my god Sven hurry up and answer.*

Sven being permanently glued to her phone answers almost immediately. "Hey girlie what's up?"

"Oh Sven, please help, I'm having a bit of a meltdown, I just saw someone from the past and that triggered a panic attack."

"Where are you?" Sven demands.

"Frank Kitts Park, but…"

"No buts, Flat White, I'm on my way… sorry Nigel, family emergency gotta go…"

Sven walking briskly along Queens Wharf, rounds the corner of the TSB Arena, recognising Clara immediately and breaks into a run towards her.

Clara seeing her friend running, stands up and greets her with a grateful smile, tears welling up in her eyes.

Sven pulls her friend into a warm hug. "Oh Flat White, what's happening to my bestie?"

Clara blinks back tears. "Th-Thanks Sven, I don't know what I'd do without you at the moment."

They sit on the bench, Sven looking worryingly at Clara, "Come on Flat White, tell me how I can help."

"I don't know where to start Sven. Life is far too overwhelming for me right now. With everything that's happened, and I know I'm at fault, but I just don't know where to start, like getting a fucking house or a job. I don't know what comes first? Everything just caught up with me…" Clara tries to explain, not willing to reveal her encounter with Fred just yet.

"Flat White, thanks for ringing me. Seriously it takes one brave woman to stay put and face the reality of everything that is happening. All three of us seem to be at a cross roads at the moment, aren't we? Trying to work out what it's all about. Sometimes life, well, it's just not that easy."

"I knew I could rely on you to make me feel just a tad better. Somehow it makes it easier when you know someone else is down Shit Street as well and we are all just bumbling on the best we can. I know you and Freya all have your own shit to contend with at the moment so I don't really like ringing, but I really needed to see a friendly face."

Sven chips in, "Look how is it going with your shrink, are you connecting with her? That's the main thing, it's really important you see someone you connect with?"

"Yep, I think she's okay for now. She's got me doing these reflective journals and I am starting to write down how I feel. It's all a bit too heavy for me, as I'm not like you and Freya, I'm not into writing, well a bit of poetry every now and then, but she'll do for now. You know how overloaded the health system is, I'm lucky to see her fortnightly. Look Sven just quickly as I know you have to get back to work. I can't decide which is most important, getting a flat, or buying a new house, or scoring another HR job. To be honest I can't work out where I want to be, or what I want to do. In fact I feel like I'm having a mid-age crisis, I don't even know who the fuck I am anymore?"

Sven replies, "Yeah darl, it's hard eh. One minute life is fine and dandy and you have your whole life ahead of you and the next it comes crashing down, all four walls, your spiritual, mental, physical…"

Clara interrupts, "Look if you don't mind can you not give me that spiritual and Māori Health wellbeing model, that Tare Ra…"

Sven chips in, "It's Te Whare Tapa Whā, and it's okay. I get you are not connected to the Māori world like Freya and me. I wasn't trying to ram it down you. It's just that at times like this you can't really address just one side. You can't have physical pain without mental/emotional etc. Anyhow, I know you didn't bring me down here for a lecture. So look are you up for going for job interviews? I know it takes a lot to send off your CV, get all tarted up, and go through all the questions. Mind you, you have been on the other side doing the interviewing for so long, you would be able to do the whole interview process in your sleep. So where are you at with jobs?"

"I've started with a list of agencies. Been to one so far. Then I thought I would tap some of my old contacts. You know the recruiting, HR world is pretty small, and we all move on from one place to another. It's just what do I do when they ask me what I am CURRENTLY doing and then I have to drop that bombshell of being out of work and due to being dismissed and the reason why. I mean it's not as if half of Wellington doesn't already know. You know sometimes I just want to be anonymous and escape all together."

"What do you mean escape all together? You're not thinking of doing anything rash, are you? I mean even more rash than you have been?"

"No, no, I'm not going to top myself. Well not yet. I mean just skip the country and go back to the UK or Sweden and get a role over there. You know how much they love us hardworking Kiwis. But that's just day-dreaming."

"Just keep up the journaling and see what you come up with. Hey listen Flat White, maybe we should have another girl's weekend? I'll talk to Freya about it. I'm sure I can tear her away from Portobello, maybe we can go up to the bach at Waitarere Beach," Sven suggests.

"You know what Sven, that's a great idea, I've always felt welcome and safe up there, all through our school holidays," Clara replies enthusiastically.

"Right, I'll get onto it when I get back to the office, how are you now, Flat White?" Sven asks looking intently at Clara.

Clara takes a deep breath. "Much better now, thanks Sven. You really are one in a million."

Checking her phone and Fitbit, Sven slyly comments, "You better get moving, Flat White. I'm 3000 steps ahead of you."

"Oh you bitch! I'm going to blitz you today, I've got some more agencies to door knock," Clara fires back, good naturedly.

They stand together and as they hug again, Clara says, "Thanks Sven. Hey I've found a great little coffee shop called *Munamuna*. Shall we meet there this arvo?"

"Text me the details. Catch you later." Sven waves as she strides back towards the BS Ministry building.

Chapter 4

Wednesday Arvo

Successfully seeing four of the six recruitment agencies on her list, Clara finds herself walking back on the Waterfront Walk, purposely avoiding the main CBD thoroughfares so she doesn't bump into any old work mates. She decides to stop by the Museum of New Zealand - Te Papa to enjoy the sun.

Being very diligent, Clara tries to remember and practice everything that Maggie her psychologist has been teaching her.

Insomnia was what she had gone to her doctor for, hoping for a quick remedy of some more sleeping pills. Little did she realise what a can of worms she was about to open.

One series of questions later, and her doctor had referred her to see Maggie to explore a proper diagnosis, after explaining that Clara couldn't stay on sleeping pills forever, especially if she was drinking alcohol regularly.

He then recommended a local psychologist to see if that would help.

Maggie had a waiting list the size of Africa, but due to Clara's doctor being very persuasive, he managed to get Maggie to see her at short notice. Clara had seen Maggie several times and wasn't really enjoying the process. She, unlike her two friends, had never believed in wearing your emotions on your sleeve, and felt if she had got to this age without having to be so brutally honest, why start now? However, Sven especially swore by the process, so she had stuck it out, that and the fact that she was hoping to fool Maggie into giving her more sleeping pills.

Clara hadn't even been honest with herself about significant events that had happened in her past, thinking *I don't have to regurgitate my past, the past is the past and that is where it lives. There is no point opening up about this and that. I mean I am fine, I have a perfectly good man, good job, lovely house...*

She then broke down and cried when she remembered; all of those things were in the past, the very recent past.

Recalling their last session, Clara hears Maggie's words, "Look Clara, the two main things for you to prioritize on right now is 1. Self-care and 2. Feeling safe. And remember to 'Drop the anchor'."

Well Clara James, let's try that anchoring technique out. Closing her eyes, Clara listens for four things she can hear. First the seagull cries, then the waves lapping against the wharf, followed by a couple talking as they walk by, then the beeping sound of a truck reversing.

Then trying her other senses, Clara notices the smell and taste of sea salt in the wind, the waft of curry and spices from a food vendor.

Feeling calmer and more centred, Clara wipes her eyes and pulls her journal out of her hobo bag to record her mindful observations for her upcoming session with Maggie scheduled for next week.

Checking her Fitbit step count and the time, thinking, *Ha, there is no way Sven will catch me today! Hmm, nearly time for that afternoon coffee.*

Finding the *Munamuna* café on Google, Clara emails Sven an appointment invitation with the café's address.

Packing her journal away, Clara heads back along the Waterfront Walk towards the government quarter, soaking up the sun with a smile on her face.

Her phone pings, looking at the screen, she sees that Sven has accepted the invitation. Then the phone rings, startling her as she wasn't expecting it. Seeing the caller ID flash 'MOTHER', Clara's stomach drops, *What does she want?*

"Hi Mum…" Clara starts, being immediately cut off.

"CLARA JAMES! JUST WHAT WERE YOU THINKING?!"

"Geez Mum, no need to yell…" feeling the words hit her like physical blows.

"I'M NOT YELLING! YOU HAVE UTTERLY DISGRACED THE FAMILY – YET AGAIN!"

Immediately Clara's familiar childhood feelings of shame, humiliation and embarrassment come flooding back, wondering just what she has done now to upset her mother.

"WELL, WHAT HAVE YOU GOT TO SAY FOR YOURSELF?" her mother spits down the phone.

"Ah… Mum… I don't know what you are talking about," Clara ventures.

"You know EXACTLY what I'm talking about young lady. Poor Fred was HUMILIATED when you snubbed him today."

"What…" Clara starts before being interrupted.

"CLARA JAMES, YOU know perfectly well that he is an old family friend. WHERE were your manners? WHY didn't you talk to him? WELL I'M WAITING FOR YOUR EXPLANATION."

"Mum, this is the man who…" Clara starts to explain.

"STOP RIGHT THERE YOUNG LADY. I'LL NOT HAVE YOU REPEAT THOSE LIES."

"But…" Clara tries again.

"YOU made up those fanciful stories, just to stop your father and I from having a night out. YOU are so selfish Clara! Fred is a perfect gentleman. And your behaviour tarnishes my good name."

Shaken Clara tries once more, "Mum, you weren't there, he was going for sis …"

"STOP IT CLARA. You are making it all up. Your sister said nothing ever happened. I want you to come around tonight and apologise to Fred and me. I'm having him around for dinner to make up for your actions. Now of course, I'll be expecting you at six sharp. I know you're working, so there is a nice Italian restaurant down the road. You can order some of their *Gnocchi di Patate*. I simply love their rocket and walnut pesto."

Stunned at her mother's commands, Clara responds, "Sorry Mum, I'm already booked ton…"

"YOU WILL BE HERE YOUNG LADY. You have some serious apologising to…"

Mustering all her courage, Clara hangs up on her mother. Stunned, shocked and appalled at the conversation,

Clara walks towards the café in a daze.

*****

Syncing her Fitbit to her phone app, Sven approaches the new café to meet Clara, wondering, *I hope Flat White has had a good day. Hang on, there she is…*

She calls out, "Flat White!" and attracts the odd look from the occasional distracted public servant, and other pedestrians.

Clara stops in her tracks, startled at her name being called out, she turns and seeing her friend, her troubled frown breaks into a beaming smile.

"It's so good to see you Sven, you wouldn't believe the call I just had from my bitch of a mother."

"Not our Maude, the fraud? Oh, you poor girl! Come on, it's time for an afternoon tea sweet treat to get our blood sugar levels all out of whack!" Sven laughs.

"Great idea." Clara leads Sven down the steps and into the café. "Now, what do you think of this place?"

"I love how it's not obvious, kinda like a special place hidden down these secret stairs," Sven replies enthusiastically.

Approaching the counter, Clara smiles at Jasmine, the barista. "I said I'd be back with my friend."

"And here you both are. Look the cakes are half price at this time of day. Now it's one Flat White, no sugar and…" the barista looks at Sven.

"Great memory, this might just have to be my new favourite café!" Clara responds.

"Make that two flat whites please," Sven adds, "and I think I'll have that custard square."

"And, I'll go for that apple, oatmeal and coconut muffin," Clara orders. "Come on Sven, over here," as Clara leads the way to her hidden table she had in the morning.

Sven took a seat. "Come on then, spill, what did Maude want?"

"OMG, I'm still trying to process just what happened."

"I thought you were in a daze, when I saw you outside."

"Yeah, look Sven, I don't want to go into all the messy details, as I know you've only got limited time before you have to get back to work. In a nutshell, Mum phoned to have a crack about how I'd sullied the family name by not acknowledging a family friend. And I have to apologise over dinner tonight."

"Hardly a biggie really."

"I know right. Well, the kicker is that she also wanted me to order and pay for the dinner!" Clara finishes.

"Bloody Maude! Fuck, she sure knows how to put the boot in." Sven shakes her head in amazement.

"I know right, well this time I'm damn well not going, she can sort her own dinner out! Mum's always been weird, but I don't really know what her problem is."

"Well, I'm a bit detached from your family, and god knows every family is unique and perfectly dysfunctional, but just humour me and tell me a bit about your family dynamics," Sven encourages.

Clara acknowledges the barista, as she delivers their coffee and cakes, "Thanks for that." She thinks, then before replying to Sven. "Okay, I've always been used as a scapegoat and Mum has blamed me for everything that ever went wrong in her life."

"And what about your sister Sabrina?" Sven asks gently.

"Oh, the fabulous Sabrina that can do no wrong. Whereas everything I do is a constant embarrassment to her. You know Sven even when I do something good or achieve something, it's just never good enough, or she takes credit for it." Clara continues.

"Oh, that's right, I remember when you won the school prize for poetry at boarding school. Good old Maude, made a spectacle of herself at the prize giving, protesting to the Principal, claiming you had stolen her lines," Sven recalls.

"That was so embarrassing!" Clara exclaims, "But why would she do that?"

"Flat White, I can't answer that. I only took a couple of Psych papers at Uni, but tell me, how is your relationship with Sabrina?"

"I've always loved my sister and tried to protect her, regardless of how Mum always treated her as the golden child, or tried to set us against each other." Clara pauses. "It's just a shame that Sabrina was too young to remember when most of the shit went down. I got packed off to boarding school and could only have a superficial relationship with Sabrina from then on."

Sven's phone peeps. She glances at it quickly, "Oh mate, look. Can we continue this when we get home tonight? I really want to explore this, it might help you understand your family dynamic better."

"Something up at work?"

"Looks like all hell is breaking loose with Nigel and the Recruitment team. News of Cathryn Tennyson's upcoming restructure before Christmas has just broken. Bernard wants me to intervene and help calm things down," Sven explains, "sorry Flat White but I have to go. See you at the station at 4:45?"

"Sure will flatmate, I've got a couple more agencies to see before then," Clara smiles, as Sven beats a hasty retreat back to the BS Ministry.

*****

Gee, that interview went really well, Clara thinks as she rounds the corner from Atholl Crescent into Boulcott Street. Feeling positive and with a little bounce in her step, she overhears a couple of male students who are vaping outside the Victoria University Boulcott Hall residence.

"Check her out man," the blonde student comments to his mate, breathing a huge noxious cloud of second hand vape into his face.

"I can't see anything dude," his dark-haired mate replies frantically waving his arms to clear the cloud so he can see where to perv.

Laughing to herself, Clara crosses the road, deciding to give the teens a treat, she ever so slightly exaggerates her walk showing off her shapely behind in her tight mini skirt.

Hearing the teen's cries of, "Wow!" and "Dude!" Clara smiles with satisfaction, thinking as she heads downhill towards Willis Street, *Still got it!*

She walks, deep in thought. *I wonder if Jack would still be interested? I know I've stuffed things up by having an affair, but I wonder…*

Her phone rings breaking her train of thought.

"Hi Clara, it's Bianca here, I've just seen your CV come through from one of the Agencies. We are needing someone to start a project ASAP, would you mind coming in for an interview tomorrow morning?" Bianca asks forthrightly.

"Wow, sure thing! Thanks for the opportunity, Bianca, do you mind emailing me an appointment request and I'll be there bright and early tomorrow," Clara enthuses.

"It will be sent through, as is best practice within the next hour. Bye," Bianca abruptly replies, disconnecting the call.

A huge smile breaks out on her face, and Clara decides to skip the last agency and head for the Railway Station bar 'The Green man' to celebrate.

*****

"… ko te Ao," Sven finishes singing, as she puts the finishing touches to her Rongoā brew.

"That's a beautiful song Sven, what does it mean? And why do you do it when you are making your concoction? And what is this brew for?" Clara asks.

"Thanks Flat White, well this brew can help people sleep a bit better at night…" Sven starts.

"Oh, so I can have some instead of sleeping pills?" Clara interrupts.

"Only if you take it easy on the alcohol, girlfriend!" Sven laughs, "But seriously, this one can also help you start to process some past trauma."

"Like a bitch of a mother perhaps?" Clara jests.

"Yes, and other, deeper stuff too, and the reason I sing when I'm making my special brews is to… now don't laugh… is to ask for a blessing from the Atua or gods to make the brew more potent," Sven explains.

"Really?" Clara raises an eyebrow, "Well, it's a lovely song and you sing it well, and the only thing I know about medicine is what the doctor tells you."

"What like… *take two tablets and call me in the morning?"* Sven jokes.

"Oh, don't get me started, Sven, *call me in the morning, p-lease… more like, finish the prescription and if it hasn't worked, make another appointment.* Then he can charge you another consultation fee," Clara snorts, and pats her bottle of wine. "Sometimes I think I'm better off with this medicine. Are you ready for a glass now?"

"Now I've finished my brew. I'll have a glass, but I'm having a night off tomorrow because no doubt with the three of us together again for the weekend, our livers will take a pounding."

"Yes, good idea Sven," Clara agrees, pouring a second glass. "Shall we join Edward on the deck?"

"I swear that cat just sleeps all day. He knows just where to find the sunniest spots," Sven adds as she takes the offered glass and walks outdoors to catch the evening sun.

"This is such a good flat, Sven. Thanks again for having me." Clara takes a seat next to Edward, on the cane two-seater.

"Well here's to my new flatmate scoring an interview," Sven toasts, raising her glass to Clara, *"Skål!"*

"Cheers," Clara replies.

"Flat White, can we pick up from our conversation this afternoon, about your family?" Sven asks.

"Sure, damn where did we get to… I'm always the scapegoat, Sabrina can do no wrong, Mum takes credit for everything and she is so self-absorbed, you should hear some of the stories she tells of how she accomplished this or told someone how to do things. Yet when I run into that someone and get talking, they have a very different take on what happened," Clara explains.

"Have you got an example?" Sven asks.

"Too many. You know Wellington is such a small place, you can't help but run into people from the past..." Clara pauses, thinking of her encounter with Fred today, and standing her Mum up for dinner. Dismissing it, she continues, "Mum always said that she started the Wellington/Ruapehu Ski Club as a teenager, organising the vans and accommodation and that she is a life member and was the first President."

"I do seem to remember her talking about lots of ski trips when we first met her at boarding school," Sven recalls.

"God, didn't she just bore us with those stories?" Clara rolls her eyes. "The one time she took me, the weather was so bad, we stayed at the Chateau and I played in the lift all day."

"Why did you stay at the Chateau? Wouldn't you stay at the ski club lodge?" Sven asks.

"Ah, good question, no doubt she wanted to stay in style at the Chateau, rather than slum it at the lodge," Clara says. "Anyway, I ran into Patricia Bentley in town a few months back. She's an old skiing friend of Mum's, and we got talking. I was shocked at her reaction when I mentioned Mum's old position as President." Clara pauses to take a sip of wine.

"You can't leave me hanging there," Sven exclaims.

"Let's, see if I can get her posh accent down... 'President! What utter codswallop! Your mother was nothing but a hanger on, and a tramp. She never organised a thing. In fact after one particular trip to the lodge, where she was found in *flagrante delicto* with not one but two different men, she was banned from the lodge and kicked out of the club. God knows why your father stayed in the marriage as long as he did.' Then she stamped off down Lambton Quay." Clara shakes her head.

"What! Your Mum having an affair! Wasn't that what she accused your Dad of before she kicked him out?" Sven asked.

"I know, right! I was blown away, I haven't had the courage to ask her that yet, I'm not sure if I want to. But the point I was making, was you hear one grandiose story from Mum, but the reality is something quite different."

"Her nickname we gave her all those years ago, 'Maude the fraud', is starting to ring true, isn't it?"

Clara shakes her head. "I know Sven. It's like I've been living my life in a fictitious family history. Do you think I should ask Dad about this?"

"Well, if you want to get to the real story, you might have to. Where is he these days?" Sven asks.

"I'm not too sure. He broke my heart when he left the family all those years ago. And was only very occasionally in contact, like when he came to my graduation. Mum always said he was a loser, running around with lots of different women and that he never paid child support," Clara recalls.

"I remember all the tears at boarding school, I just didn't know how to help you, except to listen. Freya had a knack of getting you to smile."

"I know she made me laugh with her quirky poems. You were both so good to me back then. Here's to the Trinity Trio." Clara raises her glass in a toast.

"*Skål!*" Sven joins in, taking a sip.

"I remember talking to your Dad at your graduation,

which was the last time I saw him. Such a kind man. He has a real soft spot for you. I remember seeing him well up with pride when you walked on stage to receive your diploma," Sven recalls.

"Mum was so furious that he showed up and then disappeared so quickly after the ceremony. I can still hear her saying how dare he show up and then disappear without paying child support."

"But you two did see each other before he left, didn't you?"

"Dad came over as I was leaving the stage to find you guys, gave me a big hug, gave me a small present, told me how proud he was of me and said he had better scarper before Maude caused a scene."

"Wow, so many questions left unanswered! First up, what was the present?" Sven asks.

"Well, I didn't open the present until I was alone, in my bedroom, as I didn't want it spoilt by Mum…" Clara starts.

"And..?" Sven demands.

"The present was this antique ruby necklace that I always wear, and remember that was just before we headed overseas on our OE," Clara coaches.

"Yes, it was, I had just completed an internship at the *Petone Herald* to get the cash together. Fun times!" Sven reminisces.

"I haven't told anyone before, but also in the present was $3000 cash. That's how I could afford the ticket so we could all go together," Clara reveals.

"Wow. Thank you Mr. James! Here's to your Dad." Sven raises her glass in a salute.

"Yeah, he came through for me then, but I wish he was still around. I still miss him," Clara admits.

"Hey, well, what's stopping us from tracking him down?"

"I just don't even know where to start. He hasn't been in contact since then, no contact address, phone number nothing." Clara answers, "And besides, if Mum finds out, she will no doubt get IRD and the police involved and have him arrested for not paying child support."

"Do you really think Maude would do that?" Sven asks.

"Mum has always drilled into both Sabrina and I that if we ever hear from him, we are to tell her so she can go to the authorities. So, yeah, I believe she would." Clara admits.

"Fuck, she is such a bitch. What a lose-lose situation."

The girls sit quietly, Clara patting Edward who is sprawled lengthwise across the two-seater, taking up as much room as possible.

Sven breaks the silence, "Flat White, do you really want to see your Dad?"

"You know what? I've always thought I was protecting him from Mum by not trying to find him. But right now, I could really use a hug from my Dad and maybe some sage words of advice," Clara concedes.

"Well, there's nothing stopping us from looking. You never know what we could find."

"If you had stayed engaged to Charlie, he could have used the police database to track him down," Clara laughs.

"Knowing Charlie, he would have done that too!" Sven joins in, "But shall we call it a night and talk more about this on the train tomorrow?"

"That's a great use of commuting time," Clara agrees, "And besides, I'll need to be up early to get my war-paint on for that interview. Thanks Sven, you are the best.

Chapter 5

Thursday Interview

The light is so bright in the interview room next to reception, that Clara can hardly make out Bianca's facial expressions. So she is finding the interviewer hard to read.

"So Clara, tell me a time when you had to overcome a hostile situation that you weren't expecting with a client," Bianca leans on the desk with a hand on her chin.

"Well, there was this one time when an acquitted murderer was…" Clara shares one of her prepared answers, as she shifts her chair slightly to finally catch an expression on Bianca's face – this time one of shock, followed by awe as Clara finishes her story. She wonders when the pathetic 'tell me a time' questions would finally finish. She knows that they are behavioural questions designed to see if the candidate is a good fit with the company. But they only work if the interviewer is highly skilled and has a degree of empathy. As Clara knows from her past HR experience, often the interview degenerates into a tick box exercise where the unskilled interviewer is frantically recording the conversation and never even looks at the candidate's body language and non-verbal expressions. Let alone be able to make a valid hiring decision. "Thanks Clara, well that about wraps it up. Just one more question. If you are successful, can you start on Monday morning?

"Yes, I can start on Monday Bianca," Clara enthuses, "That is of course if I am the successful candidate."

"That's great. Well, that will be all. Thanks for coming in at short notice." Bianca stands and offers her hand, drawing the interview to a close.

"Thanks Bianca," Clara shakes her hand and leaves the meeting room. She heads to reception and returns the 'Visitor' lanyard, waves and heads back out into the hurly, burly that is the government quarter.

She stops by a neighbouring building to send a text to Sven, *'Aced the Interview, see you at the café in 10, C x'*

Looking up Clara sees a woman in a purple pin-striped jacket with her back to her, arguing with another woman in a red suit, who looks familiar and is clearly in tears. The woman in red turns and walks briskly in the opposite direction, towards the BS Ministry. Before Clara recalls where she has seen her before, the woman in the purple jacket turns and walks towards Clara, who she instantly recognizes as Margaret Johnson, her new boss. Not wanting to draw attention to herself, potentially losing the opportunity for a job, Clara crosses the road and ducks into a bookshop. Glancing back, she sees Margaret enter the building she has just had her interview in, recalling the rumours about Margaret and Bernard, when they were all working in Sweden, Clara thinks to herself, *Geez, I wouldn't want to cross that woman!*

*****

"Nice tattoo Jasmine, is it new?" Clara asks her new favourite barista, admiring the entwined design of a flowering plant.

"Thanks Clara. Yeah, it's my namesake, a flowering jasmine. It flows over my shoulder and trails down my back. I didn't want it on my neck, I think neck tattoos are the new tramp stamp."

"I have to agree, they do look trashy."

"Do you have any ink art?" Jasmine asks.

"Not me, but I believe my friend Sven has one. You have to appreciate that it's only the last couple of decades that they have gotten so popular in New Zealand. They weren't so much in Europe, which is where we were doing our OE at the time. I kinda missed the boat," Clara explains.

"Well, it's never too late. Oh here's your Scandi friend Sven, two flat whites coming up!" Jasmine pre-empts their order.

"Ata mārie you two! It's another stunning day out there," Sven breezes in.

"Nice pronunciation Sven," Jasmine comments.

"It should be, te reo is my native tongue," Sven shoots back.

"But, you're a blonde with a Scandi name…" Jasmine looks confused.

"Aroha mai Jasmine, it's a common mix up. I'm part Swedish and part Māori but 100% Kiwi!" Sven laughs. "Seriously, my iwi is Ngāi Tahu, and most of us southern Māori's are well a bit paler and fairer than our northern cousins."

"There you go, never judge a book by its cover, eh? You take a seat and I'll bring your coffees over soon."

There are a few patrons at nearby tables, but Clara sees her favourite table is free and leads Sven over behind the fern planter.

"So how was the interview?" Sven asks enthusiastically as she takes a seat.

"Too easy Sven. Bianca asked all the usual 'tell me a time' questions, didn't look at me for most of the interview as she was taking notes on my prearranged answers."

"So predictable! God, when are job interviewers going to break out of so-called 'best practice', which is 30 years out-of- date and get into the 21st century?" Sven asks rhetorically.

"I know, right!" Clara agrees, "You'll never guess who my potential new boss is."

"No idea, go on spill…"

"Margaret Johnson."

"No way! Too funny. We'll be able to compare notes on Bernard and her marriage," Sven laughs.

"Oh the scandal and gossip from husband and wife bosses," Clara winks.

"So what's next on your to do list for today?" Sven enquires.

"There is one more agency I missed yesterday and I googled a couple more while I was waiting in reception for my interview, so I'll drop my CV into them today, just to cover my bases in case the interview doesn't check out."

"Nice work, but do you think you will get the job?" Sven asks.

"Let's just wait and see. But I did see Margaret Johnson

having an argument with another woman as I was leaving the office," Clara confides.

"Wow, your potential new boss, having a cat fight in the street? That doesn't sound like the Margaret Johnson we got to know in Stockholm," Sven replies.

"Well, don't be so sure of that," Clara advises.

"What do you mean?"

"It's just that when I was working at the Swedish Prime Ministers' office on that English speaking gig with the British Institute, I heard a few things about Margaret," Clara explains.

"Go on," Sven prompts.

"I don't know all the details, but Margaret was always the keen networker. Always at the diplomatic cocktail parties, trying to be seen with all the 'right' people. I bumped into her a few times at the Prime Minister's office, where she was meeting with various trade officials…" Clara continues.

"And…"

"Well, she always ignored me, but as I was saying her reputation was chequered," Clara pauses as Jasmine arrives with their coffee.

"Thanks Jasmine." Sven takes the coffee from the barista.

"Two medium flat whites, nice and hot! I hope that is kakato," Jasmine replies.

"Mmm, this smells mōkarakara." Sven enjoys the aroma.

Jasmine leaves smiling, looking pleased with herself.

"Now what do you mean, 'chequered'?" Sven asks, getting right back to business.

Looking around to make sure she couldn't be overheard,

Clara confides, "I heard that she wasn't above the odd sexual favour to close a deal."

"What!" Sven shrieks.

"With either sex…" Clara adds.

"No way!" Sven looks absolutely shocked, "But the story I heard from Katarina was that Margaret dragged Bernard back to New Zealand, so she could be closer to her family."

"When was that?"

"About nine months ago in Stockholm. It was right before Katarina followed Bernard out here to be his PA."

"Well, as you know, I left about seven years ago. Of course, I have no evidence, it was all rumour in our off-the-record 'conversational English language' sessions," Clara says.

"Yeah, but it does make you wonder…" Sven ponders, "If that's true, then no wonder Bernard and Katarina carry on together. I mean they were discreet in Stockholm, and always denied it, but I was always sure they were having an affair."

"Is that why she came out here? To be with Bernard?" Clara asks.

"I get on with Katarina really well, always have. Officially, Katarina is out here on her OE, but I suspect it's because they haven't broken the affair off," Sven surmises.

"Are you going to ask Katarina?" Clara asks.

"Well, I might do, it's about time I had coffee with her," Sven replies, as her phone pings. Glancing at her notification, she says, "Damn, they've shifted the Incident Management meeting time, aroha mai Flat White, I've gotta go. E noha rā."

"Ka kite āno," Clara farewells her friend, trying one of

her few te reo phrases.

Sipping her coffee, deep in thought, she recalls some of her favourite 'students' in Stockholm, when she used to teach conversational English, breaking down the formality of the language and highlighting the nuances and contemporary slang. Remembering that she used to feel so alive and full of energy back then. *Geez, what happened to that Clara?* Then shaking her head, she finishes her coffee. *Come on Clara James, time to get cracking, on to the next agency.* She tells herself convincing herself it is the right thing to do.

*****

Walking into Lukes Lane for the first time in many years, Clara sees her next destination, the Stellar Staff Specialists. Her concentration is broken by her phone ringing.

Glancing quickly at the caller display, her stomach drops as she answers, "Sis, what's the emergency?"

"Well hello to you too, Clara. Now why do you think there's an emergency?" her sister asks snippily.

"Because Sabrina, the only time you ever phone me is because of some imagined emergency of Mum's or it's to tell me off because something I've said or done has upset Mum."

"What rubbish!" Sabrina says defensively.

"Do you want the real truth? Or a half-hearted apology Sabrina?" Clara demands.

Pausing for a moment, Sabrina asks, "Do I really?"

"Sorry Sis, but yeah… you do," Clara gently replies.

"Wow, that hurts…"

"Look are you in town? Can we catch up over a coffee? Just us two," Clara asks.

"My turn to apologise Clara, I've got to go around to Mum's with dinner, her oven is on the blink again and she has Fred coming around," Sabrina explains.

"Not again, Mum wanted me there last night to see him, anyway that must be the tenth time this year Mum's pulled the oven story. I guarantee there's nothing wrong with her oven, I swear she is abusing your kind nature, Sis."

"It does happen often alright, but Mum wouldn't fib about it, would she?"

"Well, if you're up for it, I've just had an idea."

"Oh, one of your naughty plans, Sis? Come on, what is it?" Sabrina asks eagerly.

"When you take the dinner around, ask to heat it in the microwave. And when you're in the kitchen, turn one of the elements on and test it," Clara says. "Anyway, why is Fred, the bastard, visiting again?"

"Well, that's what I was phoning you about. I don't know why you always call him a bastard, he's always been kind to me," Sabrina states.

Clara shudders as another incident involving Fred, flashes across her mind. Quickly blanking it out, she replies quietly, "One day I might tell you, Sis. Just believe me when I say he can't be trusted."

"What, one day when I'm old enough? For fuck's sake Clara, we're adults! Stop treating me like your five-year-old kid sister!" Sabrina angrily replies.

"Sabrina, please trust me. You know I've never, ever lied to you."

"Okay, okay, yes, I know, you have always been straight with me. Not so much with Mum. Boy you've told her some porkies over the years," Sabrina concedes.

"Thanks, Sis. Now, what was the call about?"

"Well, Mum's really upset that you were evidently really rude to Fred in town this week and she wants you to apologise to him, tonight," Sabrina explains.

"Ain't happening Sis. Sorry, but I plan to never see him again ever in my life. Besides, I'm tied up until next week."

"Well, I know your work with the judges is really demanding. So no doubt you are busy with their professional development," Sabrina acknowledges.

"Ah, yeah, about my job…" Clara begins.

*****

Strolling down Manners Street from Lukes Lane, Clara's phone pings. Glancing at the notification, she sees a text from Sven.

Hey C, text me your Dad's full name and I'll see what I can dig up at work. See you at the station later. S x

She replies with the details, thinking, *I wonder what she can access at the BS Ministry?*

She looks up and recognises a large round man in a navy- blue suit, waddling out of a restaurant while putting a large cigar into his mouth. *That's, ah Mr. Prendergast, the one that Martin and I avoided at the Waterfront a couple of weeks back.*

Ducking into the lee of a nearby shop, she sees Prendergast turn to talk to his companion, billowing smoke after lighting his cigar.

Clara could hear parts of his conversation.

"Well how was I to know that Judge Jacobsen was going to perform some magic act and return miraculously?

We had our man Chute all lined up for the job, ready to rule in our favour," Prendergast explains.

A grey-suited man, obscured by billowing cigar smoke, emerges from the restaurant into Clara's view, saying menacingly, "If you and your lawyer mates can't win this case, then we are all screwed, Prendergast."

"Look man, it's early days and at least we're all remanded at large. That was no small feat I managed to pull off," Prendergast explains.

"And just what does that mean? It was still highly embarrassing being arrested," the grey-suited man says. The smoke clears, revealing his hook-nosed face, Clara recognises the property developer, Donald Church. The very man who is trying to steal Freya's inheritance from under her. Listening closer, Clara hears Prendergast explain, "Remanded at large, means that we are free to come and go until our next court appearance next week. It also means that the prosecution has a weak case as they don't have enough evidence to keep us locked up, or to set bail for our remand. In short, it means we should be free men this time next week!"

"And you're sure the Police Commissioner can cover up that incriminating evidence?" Church asks.

"What, the bank records? Of course, don't worry. We've paid him enough, and as the banks are Australian owned, they can conveniently hide the records in question. Besides he and his fancy woman now have a substantial stake in your Petone development."

"Okay Prendergast, you better be right on all this. I'll see you next week before our 'appointment'," Church turns and walks towards Clara.

Quickly ducking into the drycleaners, whose sign she

was hiding behind, Clara manages not to be seen by the men as they leave.

"Can I help you, Miss?" the dry cleaner asks.

Putting on her best bimbo voice, she asks, "Can you dry clean my hobo bag?"

"Well we can try, but it's not recommended, Miss," the man answers.

"Oh, why is that?" Clara asks, knowing the answer but buying time before she heads back outside.

"Because Miss, the leather texture just won't be the same and the leather will probably shrink."

"Oh well, there goes that idea. Thanks all the same."

Looking to make sure the coast is clear, she exits the dry cleaners and sends Martin a text, *OMG, I just overheard a conversation that relates to a case you're hearing, ring me C x*

*****

Leaning against the door frame at the back entrance to the Supreme Court, Martin says, "Thanks Clara, this is highly irregular, but it will mean justice will be done. I've been trying to expose Chute for a while now, as his decisions have been rather questionable. But the Police Commissioner? Are you sure you heard that right?"

"I'm sure it's tied up with my friend Freya's building, I'm sorry, but that's all I heard."

"I know you want to help your friend and I'll do what I can, legally. But you can't reveal this to anyone else, Clara. These are dangerous men, especially that developer, Church. He has his own gang, 'The Choir Boys', ruthless murdering thugs. And the Police Commissioner has a handful of cronies close to him. This has to be handled right. That's why I asked for a Palmerston North detective to run the investigation in Petone, even though I know the Commissioner is getting a copy of his reports. So, for you and your friend's sake… for the safety of your lives, please keep this quiet."

"Geez Martin, how is this possible?"

"It's always about money in these cases. And the more money involved, the more people higher up the food-chain get involved. Stamping out corruption and greed Clara, that's been my mission since I was first admitted to the bar," Martin replies shaking his head.

"So are Freya and I safe?" Clara asks.

"As long as you keep quiet until I can get them behind bars, you all will be. These crooks play for keeps and are not beneath threatening you and your family. They just don't care about anyone except themselves," Martin continues, then looking at his watch, "Look Clara, I have to get back. Thanks again, you have been a huge help."

"Thank you for taking me seriously, Martin, and not dismissing me as a rejected girlfriend trying to get us back together," Clara replies gratefully.

"Clara, I've always taken what you said seriously, you are lots of fun, but you've never been frivolous," Martin states, "Now I must go. Take care, Clara."

"You too, Martin," Clara replies, watching Martin disappear through the back door to the Supreme Court.

She pulls her sunglasses down and walks quickly down the alleyway that empties onto Ballance Street and heads for the Railway Station to meet Sven. Her mind is a whirl with the new information from Martin. *Wow, Martin is a great guy and I can see what I saw in him. Hmm, he's clearly well and truly over me...*

*****

"Well, young lady, you had better pack your togs for the weekend," Sven tells Clara as she takes her seat on the Kiwi Con.

"Really? Where are we off to?"

"The Trinity Trio are off to Freya's bach at Waitarere," Sven declares.

"Yay! Freya too? Can she get away from Portobello?"

"Yes, I just got off the phone with her. Zac said he would keep an eye on Portobello, so she can make it. In fact all three of us will be catching this very train tomorrow," Sven replies enthusiastically.

"God, when is Freya going to make a move on Zac?" Clara asks.

"It will have to be soon, Flat White. A good-looking guy like Zac could have his pick of the ladies."

"Okay, let's see if we can't talk some sense into her this weekend," Clara declares.

"Oh, look out, here comes the loud one again," Sven warns, as a dark-haired woman, in a red suit with a leopard skin overcoat folded over her arm, enters the carriage.

"Ah, there you are, Sven. Skipped off early did we? Not much *'coaching'* to do today was there?"

"I've just sat down, Cathryn…" Sven starts, but doesn't finish as Cathryn walks straight passed her.

"What an absolute bitch!" Clara exclaims. "Are you okay, Sven?"

"She's such a nasty piece of work," Sven fumes.

"A real 'Shark with Lipstick', is that…" Clara asks.

"Yep, the one and only Cathryn Ann Tennyson, our BS HR Director. Currently everyone is under the threat of being restructured out of their jobs. We find out on Monday who gets the chop," Sven explains.

"Everybody? But you've only just started there," Clara states.

"Oh, I'm okay at the moment, because I report directly to Bernard. And she hates that! That's why she sticks the knife in every chance she gets," Sven smiles.

"That is still so unnecessary."

"I know, but hey, let's forget about it. Do you want a coffee before I share my good news?" Sven asks.

"Sure, I'm flagging after today's hiking around town. Best sync your Fitbit girlfriend. I think I'm going to beat you today!"

"Will do, but I doubt you have. Back soon," Sven retorts.

*****

Sven returns with two flat whites and a couple of cookies, declaring, "I thought these would keep us going until we get dinner cooked later."

"Good idea. Now tell me Sven, what did you find out about Dad?" Clara demands.

"Well, take a look at some of this," Sven invites as she pulls a wad of A4 printouts from her shoulder bag, handing half to Clara.

"What's all this?" Clara asks.

"I managed to get one of the temps in the SHIT team to help me out," Sven starts.

"The SHIT team, what's that?" Clara looks confused.

"Sorry, in-house acronyms. The Science, Health & Safety and IT teams were merged a few months back and have been landed with the funniest acronym I've seen ever," Sven laughs.

"How unfortunate," Clara joins in, "But you will still need to explain how they fit in with Dad."

"Well, I got this IT temp Emily, to do an unofficial search for me on anything we had on your Dad. With five government departments merged into one, you just never know what random stuff we might have. I certainly wasn't expecting this much paperwork!" Sven explains.

"Wow, this one shows a business Dad tried to start in Marton fifteen years ago."

"Look Clara, before we start reading through them all, I thought if we took notes, maybe highlighting the relevant information, we might get a picture of where he has been and if we are really lucky, where he is today," Sven advises.

"Good thinking, I've got a pink highlighter in my bag somewhere." Clara fishes in her hobo bag.

"Great, I've got a notebook from the stationery cupboard," Sven joins in, writing *Marton* and *business* on the first page.

"Wow, this is like a real detective mystery," Clara says, continuing, "Hey Sven, if we get stuck, I saw a Private Eye sign on a door in the Railway Station while I was waiting this afternoon."

"Really? I had no idea. Did you catch the business name?" Sven asks as she sips on her coffee.

"Not really, but it was something like… *White Rabbit Investigations*, Tom somebody-or-other," Clara recalls.

"I think we might just find your Dad ourselves," Sven surmises. "Look here's something about a patent application for a machine – was your Dad an engineer?”

"Sven, I have no idea. He left when I was so young and Mum just banned us from talking about him," Clara explains.

"I think we need to put dates in the book, too," Sven adds.

"Yeah, oh this is so fascinating!" Clara exclaims, "This one says…"

Chapter 6

Friday Confrontation and Celebration

Bianca leads Clara passed reception, indicating a vacant pod. "Congratulations, Clara. You start on Monday. Now, after you sign in at Reception and get a visitor's lanyard, make your way over to this desk and start your online induction training."

"Okay, that sounds good." Clara looks at the empty desk. "Will there be a laptop available on Monday?"

"Of course, as it's Taylor's last day on Tuesday, her laptop will be available on Monday." Then turning to the three women seated at the pod, she announces, "Girls, this is Clara. Clara this is Claudia, Taylor and Megan."

Claudia stands and after giving Clara an in-depth look up and down, shakes her hand, "Welcome aboard Clara. Haven't I seen you somewhere recently?"

Clara studies the woman and suddenly remembers, "Hi Claudia, yes, I've just started catching the Kiwi

Connection, perhaps there?"

"Yes, you're probably right, I guess I'll see you this afternoon then," Claudia replies.

"Kia ora Clara. Excuse me I won't stand." Taylor indicates her wheelchair as she reverses backwards.

"Tēnā Koe Taylor, no worries," Clara says.

"Welcome to our little front-line family. I'm Megan the fun one." A bright-eyed teenager bounces up to Clara, carrying a half laden plate. "Fancy a gluten free, sugar free, dairy free muffin?"

Taken aback, Clara quickly responds, "Ah, no thanks Megan, I've just eaten."

"Knock it off Megan. Come on, girls back to work," Bianca commands. "You'll have plenty of time to talk next week." She looks at her phone, and takes Clara by the arm. "Apologies, but I have another back-to-back meeting scheduled with Mrs Johnson, I'll see you out."

"See you next week pod-mate," Megan calls out.

A bit surprised, Clara allows herself to be led back passed reception, then turns to Bianca, "Thanks again for the opportunity."

"I'll see you Monday at 8:30 sharp," Bianca replies.

As Clara walks back out into the sunshine, she thinks, *Well, that was an odd half hour. Bianca was so friendly, but seemed to change when she was in company, I wonder what's going on there…*

Her thoughts are broken by her phone ringing, without looking at the display, she answers.

"CLARA JAMES! JUST WHAT WERE YOU THINKING?!" It's her mother.

"Fa…"

"DON'T YOU USE THAT LANGUAGE YOUNG

LADY." Maude admonishes.

"Mum, you gave me a fright. You shouldn't yell like that," Clara attempts, her anxiety starting to mount.

"I'M NOT YELLING! I can't believe that you gave up your job. Now what are you going to do to support me in my elder years?"

"Well, about that…" Clara starts, her breathing getting shorter and sharper.

"NO! I don't want to hear about it over the phone. You WILL come around tonight and tell me what your plans are. I've invited poor Fred around again, so that you can apologise to him for your abysmal actions earlier this week. I'm still waiting for that meal you promised me. My stove is on the blink, so you will have to pick up a takeaway meal. Now there's a lovely little Cambodian Restaurant down the road and they do a nice *Babong* and also get a large *Mee Goreng*. I'll see you at six o'clock tonight." Maude pauses, finally taking a breath.

With her anxiety intensifying, Clara musters up her remaining courage, and says firmly, "Mum, I have other plans."

Trying another tack, Maude softens her voice in that manipulative tone that Clara knows only too well, "But Clara… you promised."

Clara recognises the tactic her mother is trying on, the sweet little old lady routine. Clara starts to regain her poise and queries, "What exactly did I promise, and when was this?"

A quietly spoken Maude replies, "You promised me, Clara, when your Dad ran off with his fancy woman and left us paupers all those years ago, that you would always look after me."

"Mum, I was nine years old, and you were crying for weeks. Of course I would say that, I'd have said anything to get you out of bed. You had pulled me out of school to help at home. Sabrina and I were surviving on baked beans, toast and corn flakes. That's all I could cook." Clara's confidence is growing.

"Oh, now you are making up stories, Clara, just like those awful stories you made up about poor Fred. Your father left us penniless and skipped the country so he didn't have to pay child support."

Suddenly feeling confident with the latest information that she and Sven have uncovered, Clara feels she can now take her mother on. Pulling the notebook that Sven and her had started filling in last night, Clara verifies before answering, "Mum, that's not what is in the records at the BS Ministry. According to them, Dad was paying twice the child support rates he was legally obliged to pay, right from the start."

"What utter rot Clara. I never received a penny from him," Maude counters.

"Mum, I've even got the bank account number from the records. It's the same one I've been sending you money to, ever since I first started work. The paperwork doesn't lie." Then seeing another fact in her notebook, she asks, "Didn't you say that Nana had to buy our house off the bank?"

"That's right Clara, your father skipped off owing thousands on the mortgage payments. The bank was about to foreclose and kick us out into the street, and Nana used the last of her retirement savings to rescue us. The bank had already taken both Sabrina and your money from your accounts for the debt."

"Yeah, I remember you telling me that about the bank. I've never banked with that bank again," Clara recounts. "But that wasn't the case, at all, was it Mum? According to the records, Dad left you a freehold house. In fact, the ministry report from the child support investigating officer noted that Dad; and I quote, '...*had gone above and beyond in supporting his children and estranged wife, but was continually denied access to the children'*. Can you explain that report Mum?"

"What? Where did you get this poppy-cock from? That was clearly written by a male trying to put the knife into a poor solo mother," Maude objects.

"If only it was Mum, if only it was. The report is signed by Jennifer Goldstein." Clara notices the quietness on the phone and continues, "So all those stories we grew up with, about how bad Dad was, and how he never loved us, are all made up by you, aren't they Mum?"

"I would never lie to you, Clara. You've just made up those lies yourself, haven't you?" Maude spits, then in a worried tone adds, "Don't you dare tell Sabrina these lies."

"Mum, don't bother phoning me again. As I said earlier, I have other plans for the weekend. And don't try and threaten me either. I've never lied to Sabrina in my life, and she knows it." Clara cuts the call, and a huge weight lifts off her shoulders. She is starting to finally feel free of the endless family drama of her mother's making.

*****

"I'm so proud of you Flat White!" Sven says.

"Thanks Detective Svensson, I couldn't have done it without your help. And I certainly wouldn't have had the courage to confront Mum without your coaching last night," Clara acknowledges.

"It sure was a long night, full of revelations and tears. I couldn't believe the real story unfolding before us," Sven replies shaking her head.

"Rua mōwai, two flat whites," Jasmine announces proudly.

Turning to Jasmine, Sven takes the offered coffee, "Tēnā rawa atu koe, thank you very much Jasmine. Ka mau te pai, that's excellent te reo!"

"Listen to you two!" Clara exclaims, "Jasmine, I'm loving the way you are giving te reo a go. Far better than my little efforts."

"Hey you two, it's not a competition," Sven interjects, "it's about making te reo common everyday usage. It's a language that nearly died out, and would have, if certain people had had their way. But some staunch people started to revive it in the mid-eighties. Do you know we have two official languages in Aotearoa, New Zealand?"

"Too easy Sven, English and te reo," Jasmine answers.

"BUZZ. Sorry Jasmine, you are wrong. The two languages are te reo and sign language," Clara joins in.

"What! So English isn't even an official language?" Jasmine replies shocked.

"No it isn't," Clara laughs.

"Wow, who knew?" Jasmine walks back to the counter to serve the next customer.

"So Sven, have you found out any more on my Dad?" Clara asks.

"Not yet, Flat White, Emily's IT contract finished yesterday, which was why we were able to get all the printouts. But there's a new guy, Chris, who I'll try and talk to this afternoon. Alex the SHIT manager might be on to me, though, so I'll have to be careful."

"Look, Sven, I don't want anyone getting into trouble over this. But I'd really like to track down Dad and talk to him about what we've found."

"Well, we have made a great start Flat White, but you have to remember something," Sven advises.

"What's that?"

"This is probably going to be a long race, not a sprint. So buckle up buddy, we're in for a bumpy ride!" Sven laughs, then asks, "Besides, haven't we got some celebrating to do tonight? Didn't a certain someone score herself a job?"

"Ha! Damn right there, sister! Some serious celebrating, plenty of bubbles on the train tonight. I'm glad you're driving us from Waikanae to Waitarere." Clara teases.

*****

"Hey Flat White, is it your round?" Freya asks as Sven approaches.

"That woman's voice is dreadful," Clara comments. "How do you put up with her at work, Sven?"

"I know, right. Cat is diabolical." Sven takes a seat, "Thanks for getting the first round in. Sorry I was late."

"Drink up. I'm just off for the next round. You've got some catching up to do." Clara staggers slightly when she stands, before winding her way through the passengers towards the buffet car.

"Hey Robert! Can a girl get a drink around here?" Clara asks, leaning between two hulking young men talking rugby.

The barman sees Clara and walks over. "No wonder I

didn't see you miss. Gentlemen, please move away from the bar so the other customers can get a drink."

The rugby boys look surprised and move off towards the front of the train, a flash of purple momentarily catches Clara's eye. Turning to have a closer look, she notices the pinstriped purple jacket. *Margaret again?* Distracted, her attention snaps back as the barman addresses her.

"Now, what can I get you?" Robert asks, "Sorry, I can't remember your name."

"A four pack of bubbles, please, Robert." Clara hands over her card. "It's Clara, and I'm not surprised you can't remember everyone's names, there are a lot of people on the Kiwi Con."

"Here you go, Clara, I normally recognise the face and the drink that goes with it," Robert explains smiling, "Enjoy."

"Thanks Robert, this should keep us going for a while," Clara replies, before weaving her way back to the girls.

*****

Stopping next to the rowdy table in their carriage, Clara takes a deep breath and asks, "Excuse me for interrupting your conversation… ah Claudia, a quick question, does Margaret Johnson normally catch the train, I think I just saw her down by the buffet car?"

Claudia replies quickly, "I think that is highly unlikely… Clara isn't it? I actually saw her drive off to her bach up the coast about two hours ago."

"Sorry, my mistake," Clara apologises and heads back to her friends.

"What was that about?" Freya asks.

"Yeah, fraternising with the enemy," Sven laughs. "Did you tell Cat to keep her voice down?"

Clara drops the four pack onto the table, "Do I look like I don't want to start my new job on Monday, Sven? I thought I saw Margaret and was just asking Claudia about it… I've seen that jacket somewhere and I keep seeing it everywhere… but evidently she left work early today, so my mistake."

"Come on you two, let's chill and plan our weekend," Freya intervenes.

"Sorry if I came off a bit strong. Come on, you propose the next toast," Sven says.

Taking a deep breath, Clara raises her newly topped up glass, "Here's to my two best friends, without whom I'd never have made it through this week."

"*Skål!*" They chorus.

*****

Freya puts the ancient key to the bach into the rusty lock, wiggles it about, and finally gets it open.

"Wow everything looks the same. Just like back in the day. Ooh I can't wait to get inside. When did we come here last, the three of us?" Clara wonders.

"Come on let's get these goodies inside," Sven says as the girls enter the bach.

They start a fire as the temperature has dropped, and Sven and Freya start preparing a pizza for dinner. Clara excuses herself for a walk along the beach to clear her head.

Kicking off her slides as she leaves the bach path, Clara walks barefoot onto the sand, enjoying the still warm sand between her toes. Weaving her way through the wildly strewn driftwood, Clara meanders to the edge of the tide. Softly lapping waves throw the odd piece of driftwood or shell up onto the beach.

Deep in thought she walks and the events of the last few weeks run through her mind, like the conflicting words with Judge Martin Jacobsen over dinners in fancy restaurants. The lies her mother has been telling her all her life. Losing her favourite job and then selling her house on a whim. Then there is Jack, patient and kind-hearted Jack, who up-sticks and left, no doubt due to hearing about her affair.

The life she had so carefully built, now broken like her heart. Tears stream down her face, blurring her vision. She takes a seat on a nearby driftwood log and asks herself, *How could I be such a fool to believe all Martin's sweet talk? Am I a jinx? Am I being punished by god? Is Mum right? Am I just deluding myself? Is this all my fault?* Clara lets the tears flow, sobbing into the westerly wind, wrapping her arms around herself, allowing the hurt and pain to wash over her.

Chapter 7

Friday Night Clara Comes Clean

As Clara enters the bach, wiping sand from her feet, Freya looks up and catches how red Clara's eyes are. Concerned, Freya rushes from the fireside and throws her arms about her friend. "Hey, you've been crying. What's up?"

This sets Clara off sobbing again. "How could I have believed him… bloody Martin… all those lies… damn it, here I go again."

Sven joins her friends in a three-way embrace, "Darl, I so wish we were wrong."

"And, then I get this text," Clara says, pulling out her phone to show her friends.

Clara, where are you? I was expecting you to get take-aways from the restaurant for dinner tonight. You are such a disappointment. Poor Fred was looking forward to seeing you. I expect to see you tomorrow for morning tea. Mother.

"God, she's a bitch!" Sven shakes her head.

"Who's Fred?" Freya asks.

"I'm going to need a drink to tell this story," Clara replies. "My shrink has said sometimes poetry can help my recovery, so I have a poem to share that explains some of this…"

Sven laughs. "No, not another poet? Our crusty old English teacher would be very proud of us, after all."

*****

The girls gather around the fire, a platter of rice crackers, with an assortment of cheeses and sauerkraut toppings, on the coffee table. Freya was on a cushion on the floor beside the faded floral armchair, where Clara is sitting, leaning slightly forward to fish her journal from her bag. Sven sprawls carelessly across the couch, wine glass in hand.

"Ahem," Clara clears her throat, then swallows a mouthful of wine for some Dutch courage and announces, "Okay, these are a bit rough, but from the heart. This one's from early in the week…

OMG, I'm now out of work
All because of that fucking jerk
I can't hold down a job, or a bloke
I'm so anxious I need a smoke
My mother torments me like a cat and mouse
Now I've gone and sold my bloody house
My mates think I belong in a loony bin
Yes both Sven and even FIN
I've lost my radar, my navigation
'But what to do?' I ask myself with hesitation

Do I stay put and drive Sven crazy?
I can't see straight my mind's all hazy.

"OMG Clara! I don't think you're crazy," Freya protests.

"Geez, Miss Burnell would have given that an A+." Sven nods in appreciation. "Oh, and for the record, you aren't driving me crazy and you can couch surf at mine as long as you like."

"Thanks girls, I appreciate it. But I've got a couple more to share," Clara continues, "This one I wrote after Sven rescued me at Frank Kitts park…

My heart's beating out of my chest
I'm overwhelmed and all the rest!
I'm telling you without a word of a lie
I think I'm going to horrifically die
My heart's beating incredibly fast
I feel like my die's just been cast
Feel my heart as it seriously pumps
Listen to it as it ticks and jumps
Please help me, I'm so afraid
I'm serious this is NO CHARADE!

"That was when you phoned me at work on Wednesday. I raced down to help and you got real with me. But I had an inkling as I was walking back to work, that you were holding something back," Sven recalls.

Freya accuses. "You guys didn't tell me about this."

"I haven't told anyone about this, Freya. Not Sven, or even my shrink. Well I tried to tell Mum years ago, but she never believed me," Clara blinks back some tears, then takes a big breath. "Sven this is the main reason I was crying in the park, I'd just seen… well, the poem says it all. Okay, here goes…

> *OMG, it's 'Fred the Ped'*
> *His fat face, shiny and red*
> *Rotund and seriously overweight*
> *Mum loves him, her best mate!*
> *He's slimy and such a creep*
> *Words escape me f… bleep, bleep*
> *Greasy hair and piggy eyes*
> *Everything he says utter lies*
> *I can see through him, through and through*
> *Just watch what he can sneakily do*
> *Don't you ever turn your back!*
> *That's when he's likely to attack*
> *Watch him closely, please be warned*
> *I'm NOT a woman sourly scorned*
> *He's a paedophile so evil, please stay away*
> *Run while you can, now don't delay!*

The fire crackles as both friends stare, open-mouthed at Clara. There is a large elephant in the room and neither of them knows how to address it.

Finally Sven plucks up the courage, asking gently, "So you were running from this Fred guy… OMG, that's the guy your Mum keep's asking you to apologise to!"

"The Fucker! Where is the Bastard? Freya spits vehemently. No one gets away with molesting my friend."

Both Sven and Clara turn and look at their normally

airy-fairy hippy friend, in amazement.

"Ah Freya, what exactly do you intend to do?" Sven asks.

"I'll… I'll… I'll chop his willie off!" Freya declares.

Clara and Sven burst out laughing.

Freya looks at them quizzically, "Why are you laughing, I'm serious dammit.

"Thanks Fin, I needed that," Clara laughs, wiping her eyes.

"So Flat White is there anything else you want to share? When exactly did this happen?" Sven gently enquires.

Clara responds hesitantly, "I would rather not go into too much detail now. My shrink says it's sometimes not the best idea to revisit the incidents until we've worked through more therapy. It started just before boarding school and the first year of boarding school. Mum and Dad would go out and Mum's friend Fred would look after Sabrina and I."

"Incidents, that's plural. You mean this happened more than once?" a shocked Sven asks.

"I was only nine. The first time was right before Dad left and then a few times after."

"I'm definitely chopping his willie off now, fucking ped!" Freya asserts.

"I felt so disgusting, but the bastard threatened to do the same thing to Sabrina. I just felt so dirty, used and frightened that he would do the same thing to little Sabrina." Clara's voice falters, her eyes welling up again.

"I remember that you hated going home, but thought it was your duty to check on your Mum but you were really going home to look after your kid sister, weren't you?" Sven recalls.

"Didn't anyone see anything?" Freya asks.

"No, he was too clever. Everything was his word against mine. When he hinted he was going to 'play' with Sabrina after he said I was getting too old for him, I told Mum in front of her friends," Clara sighs.

"And then he got locked up?" Freya asks.

"If only Fin. He said I had an active imagination and denied everything and bloody Mum backed him up," Clara shakes her head at the memory.

"So what happened then?" Freya queries.

"I remember it as clear as if it was yesterday. Mrs Robinson was looking daggers at Fred and she took him outside to talk to him, while Mum was telling me off. When they came back inside, Fred was as white as a sheet. He left and never babysat for us ever again." Clara recalls.

Sven takes a gulp of wine from her glass. "So who was Mrs Robinson?"

"She was a district nurse, and her husband was the local Police Sergeant. It was years later that I pieced that together and I asked Mum how to contact Mrs Robinson so I could thank her. But Mum said they had both died in a dreadful car accident, so I never got to," Clara retells, breaking down in tears again.

"That's so tragic," Freya cries, jumping up and hugging her friend.

Sven joins them in another group hug, then after some time, and the tears have eased, she breaks the embrace, declaring, "Right, that's enough heavy talking for now. Let's have a break. I have an idea. Let's put the trusty old pizza on, it will soak up some of this alcohol. Then we can toast marshmallows in the fire and plot some justified revenge."

Chapter 8

Waitarere Weekend

Enjoying a day of fun, fossicking amongst the multitude of charity and vintage shops in Foxton and Palmerston North, then spending a couple of hours swimming and boogie boarding at the beach, Clara and Sven are sitting around the fire, waiting for Freya to show off her new wardrobe.

Topping their three glasses up, Sven calls out, "Come on Freya, your bubbles are getting warm!"

"Okay. Are you ready?" Freya calls from the bedroom.

"Yep. We're sitting on the couch, waiting for the fashion show," Sven yells back. "Cheers, Flat White."

"*Skål*!" Clara clinks her glass against Sven's, then she lets out a wolf whistle, "Look at you!"

Freya does her best fashion runway stroll from the bedroom into the lounge. Stopping halfway to put one hand on her hip, pout and look left and right, before continuing on towards the couch and her friends.

"Wow, rocking it babe! I think if Zac were here, you'd be in serious trouble!" Sven laughs.

Joining in Clara continues, "He'd have you back in that bedroom in a flash!"

"That sundress is just so you, Freya, I love the leather jacket over the shoulder look, too."

"Those stiletto boots," Sven adds.

"A hint of intimidation and spice," Clara raises her glass to Freya. "Poor Zac won't know what's hit him!"

Freya grabs a glass of bubbles and joins the girls on the couch. "Okay, okay I get the hint. Zac is the one. I promise I'll talk with him on Monday."

"Sooner rather than later, Freya, I'll expect details hot off the press," Sven demands, "or else you'll have me to contend with."

Taking a sip of her wine, Freya glares at Sven, then asks, "So if I'm sorted on the boyfriend front, where does that leave you two?"

"Well, I'm certainly hopeful, but have you seen my work colleagues at BS? There's no talent there," Sven replies.

"And I'm off the market for a while," Clara says adamantly.

"Now don't bite my head off here, Flat White, but what about Jack?" Sven asks gently.

Clara sighs. "He does put on the action man, I'm-bullet-proof, act really well, but you can see his tender side in the little things he does."

"He's been pretty reliable over the last few years," Freya adds.

"Yeah, but he's in Nepal mountain biking and I've cheated on him. He won't want me anymore," Clara replies.

"You don't know that for sure," Freya says.

"Show me anyone who takes back a cheating partner, and I'll show you a door mat," Clara replies.

"I wouldn't exactly call Hilary Clinton a door mat," Sven replies. "Just hypothesising here, if you did try to get him back, you would have to lay everything on the line and be completely honest with him."

"Geez, Sven, I'm only just starting to get honest with myself! I'm not sure if I could."

"You've been honest with us Flat White, and if there's one thing I know about Clara James, it's that if she puts her mind to something, she will achieve it," Freya says.

"Here's to the Trinity Trio finding love," Sven proposes, raising her glass.

"*Skål!*"

The girls settle into their seats, deep in thought. Clara being the first to break their reverie. "Sven, just an out-there question. What would you actually do if you bumped into Charlie? Maybe if you ran into him, at say a café in town?"

Freya getting into the swing of the game, adds, "He would be single without kids and still good-looking, hypothetically speaking… yeah, what would you do Sven?"

Her eyebrows creasing, Sven takes a sip of her wine, then replies, "Hypothetically, I would finally buck up the courage to ask him who that girl was, and if she was worth breaking off our engagement for?"

"What? You never found out who she was?" Freya asks shaking her head in disbelief.

"No Fin, I was so hurt, I just ran away overseas," Sven replies.

"More knee caps to break, Freya?" Clara jests, "At this rate, we'll have to come up with a mobster nickname for you. Something like, *Baby Face Freya*."

"Oh, Oh, what about *Hammer-hand Fin...* or, *The Steel Stiletto?*" Sven enthuses.

Whipping off her stiletto ankle boot and smacking it into her opposite hand, while putting on her best mobster voice, Freya asks, "Where's da wack-job dat needs a bit of dis..."

The girls all burst into laughter, carrying on into the wee hours.

*****

Cruising down State Highway One from the bach back to Waikanae in Sven's classic Capri, a slightly flushed Freya comments over her shoulder to Clara in the back seat, "Oh, I see what you were talking about yesterday, riding shotgun Flat White."

"Would that be the vibrating bucket seat Freya?" Clara asks laughing, "It certainly stirs you up."

"It's been a while girls since I've seen any action, settle down," Freya replies, her face turning bright red.

"Poor Zac! He doesn't know what's coming," Sven teases, then adding, "Not that I can talk.'"

"So, Sven, if there's no one at work that takes your fancy, which I find hard to believe in a place the size of the BS Ministry, will you try one of those dating apps?" Freya asks, trying to turn the attention away from herself.

"No way," Sven answers vehemently.

"Hmm, that sounds like you may have tried that before," Clara probes.

"Absolutely, sneaky sly Sven on the pull, eh?" Freya taunts.

"Okay, okay, I'll come clean," Sven relents.

"Go on. This I have to hear," Clara adds.

"Well, it was a few months back, just after I settled into the Waikanae flat. One night I was lonely and I decided to try out the website *Find Your Soulmate.Com,*" Sven begins.

"You dark horse! How did it go?" Freya asks.

"Not the best. I was seriously put off after the two dates I ended up going on," Sven recalls.

"Oh no! What happened?" Freya sympathises.

"You hear all those stories, about how a loved-up couple found each other online. I read plenty of glowing testimonials on the website, before I set up a profile. What a have," Sven adds bitterly, "you end up being stalked by crusty old men who are twenty or thirty years older than you."

"What?" "No Way!" The girls shriek.

"Yeah, I should have twigged when the first guy invited me on a date in Petone," Sven continues.

"Well, if you had waited, you could have come to Portobello. But there are some funky places in Petone," Freya concedes.

"Yeah, but the RSA isn't one of them," Sven indignantly replies. "And as for the second date, well, let's just say he used an old photo of himself, so I didn't recognise him when he arrived at my table wearing an eye patch and walking with a cane. My grandfather, Olaf, is in better nick, and younger than this dirty old trickster."

"Well speaking of not finding your dream man in the first round Sven. You were incredibly lucky in those stakes early on. You did find your Prince Charming, but decided to let him go," Freya adds.

Sven looks a little hurt, "Now guys, that's history, he was the right one at the time, but if I'd got tied down with him, I would never have travelled."

"I know it's been a long time and I probably wouldn't recognize Charlie, but I could have sworn I saw his twin brother yesterday while we were shopping in Palmy," Freya adds.

Sven replies, "He doesn't have a twin brother. Can we change the subject now, please? Charlie Rogers is history. He would have well and truly moved on by now—wife, kids the whole rigmarole. I'm not interested. In fact, I've almost resigned myself to the fact that I'll be a spinster for the rest of my life with Edward."

"But, imagine if he was available…" Clara tries.

"Come on girls, that's just a fantasy," Sven shakes her head, then considering for a moment, "But okay, if he was… well let's put it this way, if he's still the same… I don't think I could say no."

"I knew it!" Clara confirms, then grabbing her phone, "I might just do a little Google search and see what I can come up with…"

*****

They drive back up to Sven's and unpack. Edward Sven's aloof but gorgeous cat, is sitting there waiting for them patiently on the doorstep meowing his head off. Sven's friend, Gracie from the beach had kindly been into feed Edward, but it had been all of six hours since he had last been fed, so he was beside himself.

"I can just see you becoming a cat lady, Sven," Freya

comments as she starts making a salad.

"Ouch! Well, I suppose if I had to trade Edward in for a man, it would be no contest. Edward would win every time." Sven replies.

"I've found him!" Clara yells excitedly from the deck. Then she comes running inside with her tablet, "Look, Sven, look! It's Charlie! He's only up in Palmerston North. Freya you did see him outside the charity shop!"

"What?" Sven says, disbelievingly.

"Show me too," Freya calls.

"Look, here's a photo, it says… *Palmerston North Detective Sergeant Rogers, being awarded the New Zealand Bravery Decoration for rescuing a wounded colleague under fire in the line of duty.*" Clara reads.

"OMG! When was this?" Sven asks.

"The article is dated two years ago. Sven, doesn't he look hot in uniform?" Clara adds.

"He's still as handsome as ever, Sven," Freya chips in.

Her heart racing, Sven sits down at the red Formica table, "I think I need a drink AND a cigarette."

"Sorry Sven, it looks like I've upset the apple cart," Clara says, "I was just trying to help, well and be a little nosey."

Sven replies, patting her friend on the arm, "No drama Flat White. I just didn't realise I still had feelings for him."

"Well he's much better than ol' bung eye from the RSA," Freya says lightening the mood.

"I think I'll have to give this some serious thought, girls," Sven smiles.

"I think we all do, don't we?" Freya adds. "Hey, with New Year just around the corner, how about we make another Trinity Trio pact. Let's all this time next year have found true love and be hooked up. What do you reckon, girlies?"

Chapter 9

Monday Morning New Job...

As the girls disembark from their Kiwi Connection carriage, Sven hesitates, waving her besties off, "You girls go on, I've dropped my phone and I'll text you for coffee after the meeting."

Freya and Clara wave and carry on up the platform, with the hordes of black and white clad public servants, lanyards and shoulder bags swinging, "Oh Freya, I've got a funny feeling in my tummy," Clara discloses.

Looking at her friend who has normally got it all together, she asks, "Butterflies over the new job, Flat White? Or something else?"

Dismissing her gut feeling of dread, Clara replies, "Yes, yes, that's it, butterflies."

"Now why doesn't that sound convincing to me?"

"Look out!" Clara shouts as she stops suddenly, throwing her arm across Freya's chest, to prevent her from moving into the path of an oncoming electric unicycle.

"What the..?" a surprised Freya says, "Well, I've never seen that before."

The solo-wheel rider makes a sharp turn doing a complete 360 degree turn, then bowing to the girls, "Apologies ladies, I didn't mean to give you a fright. Important business, I must away." Then with a quick salute, he speeds off, weaving through the crowds, stopping ten metres away outside the door Clara had spotted on Friday.

As the well-groomed man draws the keys from his weather- beaten shoulder bag Clara comments, "Oh, so he's the private eye."

Freya looks baffled. "Private eye?"

"Sorry Freya, I saw the sign on his door on Friday while I was waiting for you guys. Something like *White Rabbit Investigations*. Maybe he's the Wellington equivalent of *Cormoran Strike*."

"He could be, but how has he got an office at the Station? Come on. Plenty of time to solve that mystery later. You don't want to be late for your first day on the job," Freya prompts as they leave the Station and cross Bunny Street on the green light.

At the next crossing, Freya turns and hugs her friend, "Good luck, Flat White! I'll hopefully see you at the café with Sven sometime today. That's if Dimitri doesn't have me on yet another project."

"Thanks Freya. I'm not sure what time I'll be able to get away, being the first day with induction and everything, so I may rain check. But keep me in the loop, especially with how you get on with Zac." Clara winks.

*****

Putting on her best smile, Clara enters her new workplace with her head held high, approaching the Reception desk.

"Hi there, you're the new girl, aren't you?" The dark-haired teenager hands Clara an envelope and says brightly, "I've got your visitor's lanyard in there. Oh, and the keypad code for the toilets is there, too."

Quickly scanning the teenager's name badge, Clara responds, "Thanks Brooklyn, I really appreciate that."

Clara walks over to her new pod, and starts with, "Good Morning Ladies. I am checking in for my first day of work, reporting to …"

Claudia addresses her, "Yes welcome aboard, it's Clara isn't it? I see you have a visitor's lanyard from ditzy Brooklyn, but I have been asked to take your photo for your proper lanyard. Also, if you could fill in these forms please. Standard HR forms. Very important, you know, like bank account details etc. for your pay. I mean after all, that's the only reason we are here isn't it, to get paid?"

Clara smiles sweetly, "Yes, of course. Shall I fill them out over here?" She indicates the spare desk at the pod.

"Of course, you can't stand around all day," Claudia replies. "I'll be back soon with the camera."

Clara takes a seat and notices Taylor rolling her eyes at Claudia's retreating back. Smiling Clara concentrates on completing the paperwork.

Pulling her tablet, purse and phone from her hobo bag, Clara arranges them so she can refer to them for various pieces of information. Thinking to herself, *just as well I brought in my passport, I wonder why they need that number?*

Concentrating on the multitude of questions, such

as listing your social media accounts and trying to work through the endless HR pages, Clara doesn't see Claudia coming back with the camera.

Claudia startles Clara with, "I'll get you to stand over by Megan's desk to get the photo."

"Oh, okay, sure…" Clara complies, turning to smile at the camera.

"Each floor has its own break-out room and coffee bar. Ours is over there." Claudia points towards a garishly painted yellow room behind reception. "We could even walk to the Station together, if you like, so I can tutor you through the ins and outs of working here."

"Yes sure, that sounds wonderful." Clara smiles, thinking *that sounds a bit over the top.*

Before Clara disappears behind the partition, Claudia asks in a worried tone, "Did you see my friend, Cat, this weekend? It was really weird she got off in Paraparaumu without even saying goodbye to us, and she left her box of old shoes behind on the train. I bought them in on the Kiwi Con this morning, thinking she would be jumping on, but we never saw her. Do you know if she's okay?"

Clara on her best behaviour being in unknown territory and her first day at work, politely answers, "Ah no, I don't know Cathryn, she works with my friend Sven. I guess she just got into the hysteria of Christmas shopping and forgot her box of shoes. Could she be working from home?"

Claudia shakes her head, "No she wouldn't miss today, as it's the big day for her big announcement. She was all fired up for that, there was no way she would miss work today for all the money in the world."

Just then the front door slides open and in walks her new bosses, Bianca followed closely by Margaret Johnson. The

DCE herself marching in, carrying her brightly coloured purple pin striped jacket over her arm, her stiletto's clacking loudly on the reception tiles.

Margaret heads straight for her nearby office, pointedly ignoring everyone, while Bianca checks in with Brooklyn at reception, before heading over to Clara's pod.

Bianca flicks her long reddish blonde hair back from her face, and asks, "Clara, let's have a wee catch-up over coffee in the break-out room." Then she turns and walks off, leaving Clara to unceremoniously scramble after her.

"Peppermint tea? Coffee?" Bianca asks, "We have a great selection here".

"Ah, thanks, but I'm okay at the moment," Clara replies, her stomach feeling a bit queasy.

Taking a seat, Bianca starts briefing Clara about her new project. She made it quite clear to Clara that she had been with the Ministry forever, in fact it was only her second job since leaving school. She loved it and was not leaving anytime soon, so if Clara was interested in climbing the ladder it wouldn't be into her job.

Clara got the impression that Bianca didn't exactly warm to her. In fact she seemed a little distracted and every time she saw Margaret leave her nearby office, she looked up nervously. Margaret was the only one who had a real office, four glass walls and a door, the rest of the plebs like most government departments were in open plan.

"Look Clara, I'm super important around here, I even look after Margaret's diary," she adds, pulling the diary from her bag. Bianca continues, "And that reminds me, I have some files on a project I want to talk to you about."

Bianca excused herself for a minute and walked over to Margaret's office to collect the files. While she was gone

Clara couldn't resist looking at the page open in Margaret's diary. It was showing last Friday. In pencil, scribbled was 'ETD 17.10 train, back carriage, ETA Pram 18.00.'

Thinking to herself, *Interesting, Margaret can't catch the Kiwi Con often, so obviously this was a one-off and she needed to remind herself of it so entered it into her diary. But didn't ...*

Bianca returns interrupting her thoughts, "Right, let's get down to business. So, on Friday you told me you had run a number of projects this size and had managed a staff of ten plus."

Noticing the accusatory tone in Bianca's voice, Clara goes on high alert.

"Our projects here are very different, very intense, can change at the drop of a hat and the staff are mainly contractors like Taylor and can't be relied upon."

Clara responds, "What do you mean you can't rely upon contractors? I have used contractors in the past that have been fabulous."

Bianca narrows her eyes, "I don't remember you mentioning that in our interview nor is it in your CV. Are you sure you are not omitting to tell us anything?"

"What I said last Friday was accurate. I would never lie about my past experience," Clara replies defensively.

Bianca scrolls through her papers. "You know I realize the agency was very shoddy and forgot to reference check you in haste. I am not happy with their performance. I'm no longer sure of your credentials."

Exasperated, Clara responds, "Look Bianca to be fair, you interviewed me as well. Surely you are of sound enough judgement that you can make your own mind up and you did, you employed me."

"Well I was forced to really. I needed someone to fill the seat today as Taylor is leaving tomorrow. But now I am having second thoughts. Look I would like you to do this psychometric test for me if you don't mind. It's a very simple in-house one. It's best practise, there's one for personality, and one to see how smart you are in the IT line. You can do it back at your desk. Just use Taylor's login. We haven't got a login or anything for you yet. While you are doing that, I'll need you to fill in another form to say that you have never been dismissed from a job and that you don't have a criminal record. I'll go and get that form from HR and will see you soon." Bianca stands.

"Are you serious?" a bewildered Clara asks. "You know I come with glowing references. I have been working as a public servant in this town, off and on, and abroad for decades. I have an impeccable and unblemished reputation."

"Well," replies Bianca. "It depends what you mean by impeccable. A little bird told me otherwise over the weekend…"

"Excuse me Bianca, I don't know what you are implying. Perhaps you need to be a bit clearer about what you are trying to say," Clara suggests, with a terrible sinking feeling in the pit of her stomach.

"I'm not trying to say anything, I think you are now twisting my words. Look I can't waste my time over this. I am happy to overlook what I have heard by giving you a second chance and getting you to do these psychometric tests. These tests cost the organization a lot of money. If you are as amazing as you say you are, and the tests come through glowing, then we don't need to have a conversation like this again. I need to see Margaret, and clear my emails, especially from my friend, Agnes who I believed you worked with? I suggest you go back to your pod over there and complete the tests and I will come and get you in an hour's time."

Clara was aghast. She felt like someone had just knocked the stuffing out of her. Never had she been talked to like this before. Then she twigged, *Not Agnes the secretary from JAB, OMG!*

Walking slowly back to her pod, Clara recalls the last time she had seen Agnes, leaving JAB with her bag to go on holiday. Agnes had smiled a wicked smile as Clara was heading into Yvonne's office. A wave of humiliation washes over her as she struggles with her dirty little secret becoming public. Thinking to herself, *Was nothing secret and sacred in the public service? Clearly not, I can't stay here!* Her anxiety was rising by the minute.

After Taylor has set Clara up with the now shared laptop, Clara logs on and starts the first test, a spatial one about which figure was out of place? *Really how is this relevant to what I have been asked to do? Actually, what have I been asked to do? It's still not clear?*

She looks at her watch, *Fuck it's ten o'clock! I've only been in the office for an hour and a half!*

Clara feels exhausted and harassed. She realises she has been bullied and gaslighted and feels things aren't about to get any better. She didn't even have a hot contract in her hands as with all the rush on Friday a contract had not been written up. Her gut feeling is telling her to bail, but her head is saying, *No you can't. You will never get a job again. But then do you want a job again like this?*

She thinks of her friends. Sven seems to have landed on her feet as usual with a great car, flat, her dream coaching role at the BS Ministry to buy the property of her dreams. Even fey Freya with her inheritance, her new enterprise, with all of the difficulties she is overcoming each one with a little help from Zac. Turning her thoughts to herself, *what is it I want? Does my future lie here? Where is my heart? I need to follow my heart, surely it is not this?*

Clara had never walked out of a job, a relationship or anything before. Ever! She had always stuck to anything she did with 100% commitment and look where it had got her - *homeless, and man-less, so why not make it THREE and jobless*. After all she was jobless last week, so why not continue.

With the settlement of her house due at the end of the week, she still had the deposit sitting in her current account. *I've got enough money to get by for now. Should I walk out and say nothing or should I confront the cow? I think I will feel more empowered if I talk to her face-to-face instead of by text. Besides I want to make it perfectly clear.* She waits another ten minutes and Bianca still does not show. Clara walks passed Margaret's office and sees she is alone with the door open.

Taking a deep breath, Clara knocks on the door and walks in without waiting to be asked. Clara notices Margaret is rubbing something out of her diary and looks up nervously. Clara looks down and sees it is open on Friday and observes the train entry in pencil has now been removed.

"Hi Margaret, look I know you are busy so I will make it quick. I am very thankful for the opportunity to work here on this project to help you and your team out at this busy time, but unfortunately due to unforeseen circumstances I need to be elsewhere. Let Bianca know I haven't started the psychometric testing she required, so that may save some money. I'll be in touch. My regards to Bernard." She feels so empowered, she walks out of the office then thinking of her manners, turns back, "Have a great day."

Margaret is sitting there in her Iron lady suit looking shocked and calls out, "I assume that means you are not coming back?"

Pausing Clara smiles, "Yes Margaret. You are pretty astute, I would say that is an affirmative."

She grabs her hobo bag and heads out passed her pod. Claudia asks, "Are you off for smoko Clara? How did your first part of the morning go?"

Clara stops and turns back, "Brilliantly, thanks. A lot of revelations, everything is so much clearer now. Isn't it amazing what an hour or so can do on a Monday morning in the office?"

Megan replies, "Yes, aren't Monday mornings just great!"

"E noho rā," Clara farewells.

Bianca comes flying out to reception and forgetting she has an audience, yells at Clara, "Where are you going? I haven't finished with you? Come back here! I'm your Manager!"

"Bianca, you aren't my manager. In fact, I doubt you could manage your way out of a paper bag. You never even gave me a contract to sign, so you've got nothing to keep me here… besides, I'm well and truly finished with your bullying tactics! Bye, bye B-arch!" Clara turns and walks proudly through the Ministry door out into the street.

Feeling invigorated and relieved, like someone who just avoided a bomb explosion. *That was one lucky escape. Right. No time for coffees with the besties, I am off to find*

Leo. Monday mornings he is always at that café in Petone.
So this is what it feels like to be in charge of your destiny.

Chapter 10

Monday Morning Leo…

Catching her second train for the day from Platform Three, Clara notices on Platform Nine that the Kiwi Con is now surrounded by police tape completely cordoned off and there are people in white suits going in and out of Carriage four, her carriage. *WTF is going on?*

Then she sees the private eye whizzing by the carriage on his electric unicycle, stopping to talk with one of the white suited forensic officers.

Normally she would be dead excited and would text her besties, but now her mind and heart are in different places.

As the train accelerates, she pulls her journal from her bag, and jots down a quick poem:

Fuck this I'm man-less and out of work
That HR Bianca was such a jerk
Asking dumb questions I could have snored

So irrelevant but she touched a chord
She's helped me ask myself, 'What am I doing?
I'm so angry and anxious I am stewing
Do I want a job in an office again?
Pushing paper and a boring pen?
Or do I want to do something I've never done before
Something my heart and soul cannot ignore
I don't know what it is, but it's not here
I'm out of a job, and I just don't care.

Looking up from her journal, as she feels the train slow down for the Petone Railway Station, she thinks, *I need some direction, I think I know what I'm about to do, but I know Leo can help. I'll be interested to see if he can see anything startling in my palms.*

Walking down Jackson Street to Cheekos café, Clara spots Leo outside at his favourite table on the footpath, where he can watch all the passer-by's. He senses her coming and looks up even before she has crossed the road. He waves.

"Hello my dear, long time no see. Your timing is impeccable."

Clara hugs him and says, "I'm glad something about me is impeccable as clearly my reputation isn't."

"I beg your pardon?" Leo raises an eyebrow.

"Nothing that's worth air-time, just ignore that last comment. Now shall I order your favourite?"

He nods and she signals to Leo's biggest fan behind the coffee machine with her fingers, "Two of the usual please."

"Now what brings you out to Petone at 10:30 on a Monday morning? All good government girls should be tucked away in their little pods, beavering away, shouldn't they? I feel flattered that you have chosen me over the Public Service." Leo laughs.

Clara laughs, too. "Leo, I'm putting my cards on the table. I'm at a turning point. I think I know what my internal GPS is telling me to do, but I've never really trusted my gut feelings before. I'm in foreign territory here. I just need some clarification."

"This seems a tad rash for you, young Clara James," Leo remarks.

"You are right. It's not like me, as I'm always the responsible, boring grown-up one. But you know all those qualities are far too over-rated. I feel very empowered today and that… well… I need to make a decision… I've got nothing to lose."

The coffees arrive and they both take a couple of serious sips, "A phrase from Jiddu Krishnamurti comes to mind my dear, *Choiceless Awareness*, have you heard of it?" Leo asks.

"No, I haven't. What does it mean?"

"Shall we find out? Clara dear. Your left hand please. Time is an asset, so let's begin straight away."

He studies both her left and right hands very hard and is quiet for several minutes. She is in absolute suspense. He takes a drink of his coffee, then looks up and begins, "I remember telling you about a big trip last time we talked, somewhere that will change your life completely. Why haven't you done this yet? No don't answer. Your love line is looking a bit shattered. I feel the big trip is connected with your love line. Now love can mean something or someone you love or all of the above. So don't take it as always meaning a man, it could mean following your love in other ways. I hear bells, a reunion, I see children…"

That's all Clara has to hear. She asks a couple more questions to do with property, homes, New Zealand, and family. And he confirms yet again what she already knows deep in her heart.

"Leo you are a star," and she gives him the biggest kiss on his cheek, leaving a smudged lipstick mark. "Thank you, thank you. Next time you see me, you won't have to ask me about not taking the long trip. I am off. I'm heading for the airport right now."

Leo laughs, "You don't look like someone who is about to board an aeroplane. Where's your passport and luggage?"

"Oh, but I am, I have my passport with me from my new job this morning. And don't be misled by my hobo bag. It carries many things and there are only two other important things, a wallet full of credit cards and a phone, so I can contact who I need to. Look Leo, I'm a woman on a mission. If you see the girls tell them not to worry. I am following my heart this time, not my head and I know what I'm doing. I'll send you a good old-fashioned postcard. Thanks a million, Leo!"

What a whirlwind. She is halfway down the street by the time Leo has got his papers and tobacco out to roll himself a much needed cigarette. Taking a look at Portobello, she thinks, *Good luck Freya.* Something is telling her to get to the airport and get out of Wellington sooner rather than later. It would make sense to go back to Sven's and pick up her case and gear and it would be polite to pop in and see Freya and Sven. But there is an intense urgency running through her, impelling her to keep moving forward with as much speed as possible.

She looks up and just then she sees the orange airporter bus flying down the road. She runs to the bus stop ahead and hails it down.

Airport bound, she pulls her tablet out goes online and books a domestic flight to Auckland for 1.10pm. It's only $49 a last- minute cheapie and then starts looking at the different flight options from there. *Ms Clara James you are off on an adventure of a life time!*

*****

Sitting in the Wellington Airport waiting lounge outside the departure gate, Clara turns her phone off to conserve the low battery. *I must get a new set of chargers when I land. Hmm what to do…*

Looking through her bag, she finds at the bottom the little notebook that Sven had given her where they recorded all the information on her father. *Now I've got some time to review this…*

She flicks through the pages, and stops at a random point, noticing the information about an engineering business in Marton. *He wouldn't still be there, would he..?*

Firing her tablet up, Clara starts an internet search, typing in: *Frank James, Engineer, Marton.*

It comes up blank, so she widens the search by replacing Marton with New Zealand.

Ahh! Still nothing!

In frustration she starts back spacing, then gets an idea and tries: *F James, Engineer, New Zealand.*

Bingo! There're a few hits! Clara smiles, as she starts to review each one.

Oh, Oh, what's this? She reads a news headline from

eight years ago:

Popular Engineer Forced to Close Up.
Francis James, the popular local identity, has been forced to close up his fledgling engineering business due to a downturn in the local economy.

Working closely with other local businesses, Francis had been instrumental in raising money for the local school, to repair the school swimming pool which was damaged in the previous year's earthquake. The Education Ministry had shut the pool down due to a lack of funding thanks to the conservative government's infamous 'Black Budget' cuts...

Clara sits up with a start, *Francis? But I thought Dad's name was Frank? Not another lie of Mum's...*

Restarting her search, for Francis James, she finds more hits. Then cross referencing with the BS Ministry's 'Company' search engine Sven had showed her last Thursday night, she discovers "F J Engineering" in Whitianga.

Pulling up the White Pages website, she searches and finds a phone number. *Oh, fuck, what do I do? I haven't seen Dad since I graduated. Does he want to be in touch? Mum said he never wanted to see us again.*

Her muddled thoughts are interrupted by the intercom announcing, *Flight NZ 4319 to Auckland is now boarding, will seats in rows 1 to 32 please board now.*

Stashing her belongings into her hobo bag, Clara presents her boarding pass to the flight attendant and starts the short walk towards the plane, her mind doing overtime.

*****

Knowing she only has limited time to get prepared for her adventure, Clara rushes from the Domestic Terminal to the International Terminal, only just managing to check in for her flight in the required time frame.

Thank goodness for that! Now, duty free shops here I come! Her old shopaholic behaviour rears its head, as she pops into the different Duty Free shops and buys herself a spanking new designer carry-on case and then sets out to buy clothes and accessories to fill it.

After losing track of time in a whirlwind of manic activity, Clara checks her boarding pass, *OMG! I've got less than ten minutes to get to the gate!* She races off down the concourse, pausing momentarily to confirm the departure time on the Flight Information Board. Clara makes a snap decision, running onto the travellator, her lengthening stride eats up the distance. Calling ahead to the unmoving passengers, "Excuse me, Sorry, in a hurry." They move to one side, allowing her to pass.

Her new carry-on case trails behind her, with her new stainless steel water bottle banging as she rounds the corner of the concourse. Passengers are already in a queue at the boarding gates. Her heart pounding Clara slows to look at the Flight Information Board, only to see that her flight has been delayed by 30 minutes.

Getting her breath back under control, Clara finds a seat next to a power point. She plugs her phone and tablet in to charge. Then taking her journal from her bag she reflects on everything she has been recording over the last week, then seeing her note about hunting down her Dad with Sven, she looks at her Fitbit to check the time.

It's not quite 5pm, Sven should be knocking off and heading for the Kiwi Con soon.

She then recalls how the Kiwi Con is cordoned off. *Wow I don't think I want to be in Wellington right now. Ok I will wait until after five and then I will contact her. I wonder how she got on with the Big announcement at work, and what other startling stuff will be happening down in Public Serviceville land.*

Deciding to be cryptic, Clara texts Sven, *Hey bud you will never guess where I am and what I am up to? I know you love guessing, oh psychic one, you have three guesses.* She pushes the send button.

She checks her phone and sees there are several missed calls from the recruiting agency and a couple of other 04 numbers which she suspects is Bianca. *Who cares, I am not beholden to anyone.*

Then, she pulls out the notebook, and before she knows what she is doing, finds herself dialling a phone number in Whitianga.

Waiting for the phone to connect, Clara wonders what she is going to say.

"Hello, FJ Engineering, Frank speaking…"

"Hi… Ah… Dad, it's me… Clara," she falters.

"Clara? Is that really you Gigi?" Frank asks, using her childhood pet name.

Tears welling in her eyes, "Yes it is Dad oh it's so good to hear your voice."

"Wow! It's so good to hear from you, too, Clara. I never thought this day would ever come," Frank enthuses.

"Did you want this to happen Dad? Mum said you never wanted to see us kids again."

"Clara, don't believe everything that comes out of

your mother's mouth. She stopped… Look, I don't want to waste time going over that, where are you? Can we meet?" Frank queries.

"Ah, not unless you can get to the Auckland airport in ten minutes Dad, I'm about to board a plane."

"Oh," Clara can hear the disappointment in his voice, "then can I ask why you phoned me now?"

"Dad, my friend, Sven, did some digging at her work and I've only just managed to piece it together. You are one hard man to track down. I didn't know your name was Francis?"

"Yeah, Francis is the name on my birth certificate, but I've always gone by Frank," her Dad explains. "I'm glad you and Samantha are still friends, what about young Freya? You were so tight at boarding school."

"Oh, there's not enough time to tell you everything Dad. I guess I'm phoning to ask some advice, I could do with good counsel right now."

"Well, if you're pressed for time Gigi…" Frank begins, "and I don't know the context or the details. Then the only advice I can give you as a father, is to ALWAYS follow your heart. It might get broken in the process, but it's better to have really loved someone and lost them, than to never have loved at all."

Sobbing into the phone, her heart bursting, Clara replies, "Thanks Dad, you're the best!"

"Gigi, I hate to be the one to break this call, but how much longer have you got before you board?" Frank asks.

"About two minutes, the business class passengers have just gone on," Clara answers.

"Look, please stay in touch. Have you got a pen? Here's my mobile number…" Frank waits.

"Yep, go ahead Dad," Clara replies, jotting down the number, "Good, I'll text you my email soon, Love you Dad. Always have."

"To Pluto and back, Gigi," Frank chokes, as he replies with the old bedtime phrase he used when tucking her in as a child.

Will passengers in Rows 24 to 48 please come forward, the flight attendant announces.

That's me, Clara thinks, wiping her eyes and double checking her ticket, and repacking her things into her carry-on.

As she makes her way forward in line, she knows she has made the right decision. Sending a text, *Darl I have a surprise, I know you are not happy with me right now, but I am happy with you. In fact I know for the first time in a long time what makes me happy. Can you meet me at the airport? I will let you know the ETA when I get to the transit point in Melbourne. See you soon Tiger, xx.*

Just then the TV screen above her catches her eye, flashing across the screen is up-to-date news footage of a crumbling high rise building somewhere in New Zealand.

"Oh those poor Cantabrians, that must be Christchurch again. Shit haven't they had enough catastrophe and upheaval in their life?" Clara overhears the older woman behind her in the queue say.

"Oh my God! That's not Christchurch, that's Wellington!" Her partner cries.

The passengers all start talking and gesturing at the screen, as the line snakes forward. "Can we get some volume on that screen?" a passenger yells to the flight attendants.

"If we can all please remain calm and keep moving

forward please. We need to all be seated in time or we will lose our departure slot, I'll see what I can do about the volume, but please keep boarding," the Team Leader announces.

Clara can see the Wellington traffic helicopter circling above Wellington city and is zooming in on the damage caused around the Lambton Quay and wharf areas, then moves on up Willis Street and out across to Courtenay Place and back again, down the motorways and over to the Railway Station and Interislander ferry. It all looks pretty grim.

More coverage from a ground unit this time, what looks like the heritage glass windows from the BS Building are seen flying out of their window frames from the floors above. Clara is beside herself, *Shit that's Sven's building. Oh my god, would that be her floor?!* Checking her Fitbit, *Oh Sven will be okay it's 5.15 she will be on the Kiwi Con and heading home.*

Then she remembers what she saw with the Kiwi Con that morning all cordoned off.

Clara shakes her head, checking her phone and still no word from Sven. *What's she playing at?* She tries phoning but gets the same message that 'the system is overloaded at this time', so texts through again, *Sven this is not funny, where the fuck are you?*

Trying Freya's phone, *Freya, are you okay, please answer?* But gets the same system overloaded message.

Shit I shouldn't have been so selfish I should have popped into Freya's when on Jackson. Damn, damn.

Hearing her phone peep, Clara frantically checks for word from her friends. A sinking feeling washing over her, as she reads Jack's reply, *hey you, look it's not a good idea,*

I need time out. Please don't come over.

Chaotic thoughts run rampantly through her mind as she nears the boarding desk, with her boarding pass in her sweating hand, *oh my god, Jack doesn't want me, that I now know. But an earthquake and two of my best friends are missing. What is the world coming to? I think this is all a sign, I need to get the hell out of here. My god that could've been me, but should I be going? Should I stay and help? How can I leave my friends at a time like this?*

Noticing that her breathing has got shallow and fast, Clara remembers what her shrink Maggie told her. Taking a series of long deep breaths then a big gulp of water from her new stainless-steel water bottle. Her mind calming, she thinks long and hard on whether she should just walk on out of the airport and get a taxi and stay the night in a hotel while thinking more about what she's up to and remembers both Maggie and her father's words.

Clara this is one of those many things that are not in your control. You cannot do anything about it, you have to let Mother Nature do what it has to do. What you are in control of is how you respond and what you do next. Follow your heart girl, follow your heart!

Thinking quickly, she sends another text to Jack, *Not sure if you've heard the news. There's been a serious earthquake in Wellington. Clearly I missed it as I'm in Auckland. I'm stranded and can't get back into Wellington now even if I wanted to. I have nowhere to go right now so I am coming over. My flight is ... please be there.*

Handing her boarding pass to the cute-looking flight attendant, she does a double-take thinking *He's far too well groomed, he must be gay.*

"Welcome aboard Ms James, I see you have been

upgraded to business class. Here's your new seat number. Lucky you, gets fabulous me to look after you all the way to Melbourne, I'll be with you once we've finished boarding. See you soon," his perfect teeth, gleam as he smiles.

Noting his name badge, Clara smiles back, "Wow, things are starting to look up! Thanks Sean!"

As she walks along the air-bridge between the terminal and the plane, her phone peeps. Noting Jack's reply, *Okay I will be there.*

Having second thoughts, Clara stops halfway down the air-bridge, *What am I doing? I should be back home helping!* Other passengers walk passed her. Tears, flowing, Clara turns and starts heading back out to the terminal. *Oh, Sven, Freya, Zac, Sabrina what can I do?*

"Excuse me Miss, but you can't leave now," Sean the flight attendant, seeing the distress in her face, he asks gently, "What's the matter?"

"It's my friends and family in Wellington, I can't be flying overseas now! I should be there helping!" A distraught Clara replies.

Catching her name from the boarding pass, Sean counsels, "Clara, please listen to me. If you leave now, what will you achieve? One more person stranded in Auckland, unable to get to a disaster zone. It will be days before you could get back there. Besides, if you disembark now, we can't fly until we have off loaded your baggage."

"That sounds ridiculous, besides I only have one carry-on bag, why unload?" Clara asks shocked.

"FAA rules Clara, a checked bag without a passenger could be a bomb, and the airline has to double check," Sean explains, then brightens, "remember, you've been upgraded, I'll look after you and if you want to return, do it from Melbourne. It's a classier city than Auckland, come on Clara, let's find your seat."

Turning, Clara continues down the air-bridge into a mostly empty Business Class.

Stowing her carry-on bag in the overhead locker, she sets herself up with her hobo bag close to hand. Putting her tablet on flight mode, then with her phone she sends her dad a text with her email address, asking him to keep her in the loop with the earthquake and that she will call him from Melbourne.

Reclining in her comfortable chair, Clara picks up her phone to try her besties again, being interrupted by Sean the flight attendant.

"Now, now Ms James, that's rather naughty, time to put that phone on flight mode. Good girl, I'll reward you with your favourite tipple in a moment, and what would madam enjoy?" Sean asks beaming that winning smile at her.

"One of your finest bubbles, thank you kind sir," she replies, thinking, *things are definitely looking up! Time enough for maybe even a good movie, and glossy magazine to pass the time, and of course my journal. Patting her faithful journal, you know what? I think you are now my new best friend. You and I are going to share a lot of secrets and a hell of a lot more adventures in the next few days!*

Chapter 11

Melbourne Revelations

In no time at all Clara's fears have disappeared and she is sipping on her favourite bubbles and flicking through a glossy magazine. Noticing an Oscar Wilde quote used by a fallen celebrity's road to recovery, *'To live is the rarest thing in the world. Most people exist, that is all. Be yourself; everyone else is already taken.'*

After take-off Sean comes back with another glass of bubbles. He leans over her shoulder, spotting the highlighted quote and comments, "You know Clara, he is such an inspiration to me. I mean, who has the courage to live their true life, being their authentic self?"

"You've got a point there, Sean. I've just escaped a soul destroying position in a government department. I'm only just starting on this journey to find myself, I got kinda lost along the way," Clara admits.

"Oh we ALL do that, darling!" Sean camps it up with a laugh, "Besides, we must have fun along the way or life would be just so BORING. Now, tell me how many friends and family are you trying to contact in Wellywood?"

"Three, my sister Sabrina and my two besties, why?"

"I have a couple of ideas Clara, here let me show you," Sean indicates as he leans across and activates the inflight entertainment screen, pointing out, "See here, you can buy some browsing time to log into your email account and social media to see if there is any word from them."

"Wow, this must be new," Clara exclaims.

"Just installed last year. The other idea is that if you change your mind on that Melbourne shopping spree, you can always get another ticket back to Auckland from the airline help desk. So, is it retail therapy in Melbourne or visiting friends?"

"No. Just the first transit stopover before heading onto Kathmandu. It's been ten years since I was there last."

"Kathmandu! What a coincidence! I'm rostered on for the whole flight plan!" Sean exclaims, "Well, a fit wee thing like you would have no trouble scaling Mt Everest, I could never do that!"

"Oh no, I'm not a climber!" Clara laughs, then getting serious, clarifies. "My life is at a crossroads and my boyfriend… well ex-boyfriend since I cheated on him, is there. I made a huge mistake. I'm just hoping he will take me back. That sounds so last century doesn't it? No, more like I need to see if we still have feelings for each other and if it's worth trying to make it work."

"That's the attitude Clara. I'll be back soon. We're just about to get ready for the meal service," Sean waves as he heads forward to the galley.

Clara's fingers speedily log into the inflight web browser, as she rapidly scans her email and social media.

Seeing nothing new, she drifts off in thought on her last few exchanges with Jack, trying to remember just when was it that Jack left? *I know he moved out about three weeks ago.*

Picking up her tethered phone, the charging cord trailing across her lap, she looks back through her calendar. *OMG! It was six weeks ago! I must have been so smitten with Martin, I just didn't notice! No wonder he didn't want me to come over…*

Sean comes back down the aisle with a book in his hand, "Special delivery for one special Clara James!"

Breaking out of her gloom, Clara shakes her head, "What's this?"

"After seeing you interested in that Oscar Wilde quote, I thought you might like to have a read of this…" Sean passes her a copy of Susan Jeffers 'Feel the Fear and Do it Anyway'. "I know it's an oldie, but it's a goodie." Sean beams pleased with himself.

"Thanks Sean, I've heard of it, but never read it. Best top up these bubbles and I'll see if I can knock it off before Melbourne." Clara's eyes twinkle.

"Your wish is my command, Madam," Sean replies formally, doing an elaborate bow, before turning back towards the galley.

How thoughtful, well this looks like a sign I had best take notice of, Clara smiles to herself, then opening the book, she starts to read, getting lost amongst the pages.

*****

After finally getting the airport's free Wi-Fi she logs into both her tablet and phone. Then proceeding to battle with her phone's settings to get the local carrier to pick up her roaming package, Clara settles back in the transit lounge to get news from home.

Still nothing from the girls! She sees an email from her Dad, and starts reading:

Dear Gigi,

I'm on cloud nine at the moment! I'm so pleased – what an inadequate phrase – that you found me. You will have to tell me more about how you and Samantha managed that one day.

Speaking of whom, I'm not sure how to get a hold of either Samantha or Freya. However I did find Zita's old phone number in Lowry Bay. Unfortunately no answer, but I'll keep trying.

How is Sabrina? Does she know you've contacted me?

Wellington is a mess. Surprisingly few casualties so far, but the hospitals are overrun and the transport system has completely broken down. That turd of a Prime Minister looks like a startled possum in headlights trying to run for cover after gutting the emergency services in the last two budgets, a steady hand on the economy, what a joke!

Fortunately, cooler heads have taken control. The armed forces have mobilised, our last remaining frigate and cargo ship, are being packed with supplies and are due to leave Devonport later tonight. While the Army has mobilised with the Engineers from Linton and other support units from Waiouru already on their way.

I'm at home with Angus and Peg Robinson, who have come around to celebrate our reunion over a BBQ. You may remember them from before. Angus has retired from the Police and is now a beekeeper. I'm helping him get his truck back together after he smashed the chassis crossing a creek to retrieve some of his hives. Peg is still nursing, in the hospice up here, but only part time these days.

If you can email me the contact details for your friends, I'll keep trying to get in touch with them for you.

Now, please remember to phone me and let me know what your plans are.

With Much Love

Dad xo

Clara dries her eyes, after finding a small packet of tissues in her bag. With her phone now fully charged, she makes a call.

"Hi Dad, it's me."

"Hi Gigi, great to hear from you. How was the flight?" Frank asks.

"Great Dad, I got upgraded to Business Class so flew in style," Clara replies. "I've just finished reading your email. No, Sabrina doesn't know we've made contact. Hopefully her and Mum have left for their holiday up north and aren't caught up in chaos. Thanks for trying to contact my friends. I hope Zita and Harry, her dog, are okay."

"Zita has a dog? Wonders will never cease," Frank says surprised.

"Why is that?" Clara asks.

"As I recall Zita was afraid of dogs. When I first met her at your Boarding School summer sports day, all those years ago, it was when I rescued her in the car park. Poor Zita had been bailed up against the fence by this huge Huntaway, who was barking its head off at her," Frank retells.

"Poor Zita indeed! What happened?"

"Yours truly, grabbed this dog by its ear, which took the dog by surprise and then walked it back to the farm ute it had slipped it's collar from and tied it back up," Frank replied. "By the time I had done that, her son, Zac, and young Freya had come back to look for Zita as she was missing the next event."

"Oh, I do remember that day. It was a scorcher and Freya won all three of her running races. Sven and I gave her a hard time about winning in front of Zac, teasing her about him being her boyfriend."

"I didn't notice that, but I helped Zita to calm down and made her sit with your mother and I under our beach umbrella. I'm sure I remember her saying she would never have a dog in her life after that experience," Frank recalls. "Listen to me go on about the old days, that's what pensioners do in retirement homes!"

"That's where Mum is, at the Meadowbrook Lakes Retirement Lifestyle Village, and you're right. That's all the conversations are ever about, the past and their ailments."

"So that's where Madam Maude ended up. No doubt she is lording it up over everyone there," Frank remarks.

"Like you wouldn't believe, Dad," Clara shakes her head. "Unless, of course, she's finding fault in anything I do."

"I'm sorry Clara, but your mother is such a bitch," Frank apologises.

"No need to apologise Dad, I'm well aware of that. But if you don't mind me asking, tell me something, what did you ever see in her?"

"Clara, do we have time to go into this? And do you really want me to dredge up the past? How long before you catch your next flight?" Frank asks.

"I've got about half an hour and I'm in the transit lounge already, so not too long and I want to hear about your life too Dad. Like are you happy? When and why are you in Whitianga? Did you ever re-marry? But first I want to try and understand how you two got together and had a family?" Clara rapidly fires her questions.

"Okay, and I want to know more about your life too Gigi, and especially where you are off to and the real reason why." Frank starts, "I met your mother dancing at the Empress Ballroom back in the early seventies. There was something about her that just caught my eye, so I asked her to dance and she said yes and we danced until three in the morning. You have to remember that back then, New Zealand had only recently changed from the bad old six o'clock swill to a more reasonable closing hour of 10pm for bars. With Nightclubs staying open until a previously unheard time of 3am, it was exciting. We were young, I'd finished my apprenticeship so was earning a bit more money and splashed it around, living the dance club night life."

"So, it started off well then?" Clara asks.

"Well, yes, from then on it was a bit of a whirlwind. Dancing and boozing most nights of the week. I'll say this much for Maude, she sure knows how to move on the dance floor. And then she suckered me," Frank explains.

"I can't imagine Mum being a dancer, but what do you mean 'suckered' you?" Clara queries.

"That's when she said she was pregnant. Being the romantic fool that I was, I said 'well let's get married then'. So we did," Frank pauses.

"And then I came along and ruined everything," Clara

interrupts.

"Believe me Gigi, you were never the reason we weren't getting on."

"What? Oh, I get it, she told you she was pregnant so you had to marry her. Isn't that a shotgun wedding? That makes sense because Mum showed me your marriage certificate years ago and it was nine months before I was born." Clara puts two and two together.

"No, Gigi, you didn't come along for another two years. I should know when I got married, and I can scan you my copy of the marriage certificate if you want proof," Frank replies. "But I wouldn't put it past old Maude, the fraud, to doctor her certificate, just so she could win an argument or prove her point. She's pulled that one on me a few times."

"Forging her own marriage certificate, just to prove something that isn't true? I'm glad I'm sitting down! I mean, Sabrina and I use to call her Mad Maude, behind her back, but that's beyond… that's just insane," Clara shakes her head slowly from side to side.

"Sadly, I agree. But she is very clever with it. It wasn't until after Sabrina came along, that she got particularly nasty. She would phone me at work, expecting me to rush home at the drop of a hat because she had caught you trying to harm your sister," Frank divulges.

"What! I'd never hurt Sabrina! I love her!" Clara exclaims.

"I know Gigi, I know," Frank replies soothingly.

"Did I really hurt her, Dad?" Clara starts questioning herself, trying to recall old memories.

"Never Gigi. I never found any real evidence, despite what your mother said," Frank answered. "It gradually became clear to me, that I had to get you away from your mother. This is why I looked into boarding schools for you."

"But Mum said it was because she was an old girl of the school and it was family tradition for mothers and daughters to go to the same private schools."

"Yes, she always made it sound like it was her idea all along, but I knew that if I hinted at Nga Tawa, Maude would take the bait," Frank clarified.

"But why did I have to get away from Mum?" Clara asks.

"This is going to sound daft, but I was afraid Maude might do something to Sabrina and make it look like it was your fault," Frank explains.

"You're right Dad, it does sound daft… it's just crazy, this is way too much to take on at the moment. But I have a fifteen hour flight coming up so plenty of time to process this and then come back for more questions when I land. Okay, as mad as this question is going to sound, why was Mum trying to set me up to harm Sabrina?"

"I'm still trying to work through that myself, Gigi. But I always thought she was jealous."

"Jealous! Jealous of what?" Clara cries.

"I'm no psychologist, but I've had plenty of time to think it through and I believe she was jealous of our relationship. We had such a strong bond. Our humour is the same and we even look a little alike," Frank reveals.

"Oh Dad, that is crazy. I was just 'Daddy's little girl', you made things fun…" Clara stops mid-sentence, thinking back to the past.

"Are you there Clara?"

"Yeah, sorry, Dad, I was just remembering how you used to take me to the park to fly my kite," Clara apologises.

"Gigi, we must nearly be out of time. Promise me you will phone me when you land?"

"Will do Dad. They're starting to queue now. But, to answer your earlier question, I'm going to Kathmandu to see if I can patch up my relationship with my ex, Jack," Clara explains.

"Well, he must mean the world to you if you are travelling halfway around the world to talk to him. That's one hell of a gesture!" Frank remarks.

"I can't go into details now, but you are right Dad, he does mean the world to me. I just got carried away and wrecked everything." Noticing Sean gesturing frantically to her to board, Clara breaks off the conversation, "Oh, that's me, Dad I've got to board now. Thanks for filling me in, I've loads more questions, talk soon, Love you!"

"To Pluto and back Gigi," Frank replies.

Her eyes well up as she grabs her things and walks forward to where Sean is waiting.

"Come on Clara quickly," Sean whispers urgently, thrusting a new boarding pass into her hand, "I've managed to upgrade you again, quick get to your seat before the Team Leader gets back!"

"Oh, thanks Sean," Clara replies and races onto the plane.

*****

Sitting quietly reading Sean's book in the empty first class section, Clara sees one of the flight crew approaching her. Looking up, she notices the crew member do a double take and then walks over to Clara.

"Excuse me Miss, are you sure you are in the correct

seat? She asks.

"Why yes," Clara feigns mock surprise, as she hands her boarding pass over.

Checking the ticket thoroughly, the attendant shaking her head dumbfounded, "I was sure we had no one in first class, oh well, I'll allocate a crew member to look after you Miss James."

"Why, thank you, ah Courtney is it?" Clara enquires rhetorically impersonating a Louisiana accent, after quickly scanning her name badge.

Courtney walks off to the galley and Clara can hear some heated whispers exchanged.

Geez, where did that Louisiana accent and manners come from?! Clara asks herself, wondering what Sean was playing at.

Sean walks towards her from the galley with a glass of bubbles in his hand. "Your favourite tipple I believe Miss James?" He asks with a grin a mile wide.

"What are you playing at Sean? Am I about to get kicked off this plane?" Clara asks in a low tone.

Sean remains standing after delivering her drink, announcing in a raised voice. "Now I don't quite understand what has happened Miss James, must have been some mix up with the booking clerks. But the upside for you is that as you are the only first class passenger, you must have your very own first class flight attendant."

"But…" Clara starts but is interrupted.

"Hush now, what it means is little ol' you, gets little ol' me all to yourself! For the entire flight!" Sean beams.

"Well I never! God I'm sounding more and more like a Southern Belle!" Clara wonders.

"I do declare!" Sean mocks, then taking a seat beside

Clara, he confides, "Thanks Clara for being a sport. That bitch Courtney didn't like the way I was being generous in Business Class on the trip over. She was going to put me in economy as we had no First Class passengers and she had rostered others onto the Business service. So I managed to reissue your boarding pass while I was on the desk."

"Oh you little trickster," Clara winks, "Thanks, I could get use to this up market lifestyle."

"Oh darling, the pleasure is all mine. Now, I can leave you alone or if you want to talk, I can hold a half decent conversation," Sean advertises, then laughs, "Well at least I can provide drinks and light entertainment."

"Now THAT I can use, shall we be daring and get the bottle?" Clara asks.

"Oh I like your style girlfriend! I'll be back with bubbles and nibbles and an OJ for me. Well, I am on duty after all," Sean smiles, camping it up, "Back soon sweetie!"

Chapter 12

Trepid Encounters

The plane taxis to the terminal, while Clara suddenly gets nervous again, "Oh Sean, we are nearly there. I don't know what to do, do I get a ticket and head back to NZ? Or try my luck here and keep going?"

"Come on Clara, we talked about this. Jack is the right man for you and if it doesn't work out, then we have Plan B you can put into action. I hope it all goes according to Plan A. I tell you for what it's worth Jack is one very lucky guy." Sean replies, dramatically putting his hands on his hips to make his point, then wagging his fore finger at her. "Now pull up those big girls' panties, little lady, and go and get your man!"

Smiling at Sean's antics, she packs her things into her bag. "Thanks Sean, you are a star. Now stay in touch."

"Oh you won't get rid of me that easily Clara James! And you can message me anytime," Sean waves.

Recalling her palm reading, she hears Leo's words

echo in her mind, *it's your time now, you need to do this big travel first, then everything else will fall into place. You are not being selfish it is what you are destined to do. You can't put it off anymore!*

With those words echoing in her mind, she digs deep and finds the confidence and courage to get off the plane and follow her destiny.

*****

Walking through the airport Clara suddenly feels another twinge of nerves. *I'm really here, just outside there is the love of my life. I have been such a prat, why did it take a married man and a few other not-so-flash things to understand that?*

She waits patiently in line to get through Customs and Immigration. Everything seems to be in slow motion, and she can't stand the suspense. She knows it's some cheek just suddenly appearing over here. With Jack now living in the hills above Pokhara, west of Kathmandu and nowhere near the capital city, she realises just what she has asked him to do.

Collecting her thoughts Clara goes through the efficient Customs and Immigration section. She can see the eagerly waiting people in the arrivals' hall through the glass windows.

There in the distance is a tall man, with a white face, in a sea of brown faces. As she gets closer she can see he has a different demeanour and how relaxed he looks, compared with when he was back in Wellington. He's wearing blue faded jeans, a rolled-up sleeved shirt and boots. His hair is longer and he is growing a beard. *Hmm very handsome, very handsome indeed. My god I have never seen him look so chilled. Something or someone is agreeing with him up here. Just as well I am here, it better not be SOMEONE, that's made him look that so god damn hot and relaxed.*

Clearing Immigration, after receiving a stamp in her passport Clara walks through the automatic glass doors to the other side.

Gingerly, she walks up to Jack and drops the handle of her case to give him a hug.

He responds, but a little hesitantly. Seeing her again, his heart leaps, but he is still questioning himself *Why am I really here? She could have caught a taxi or shuttle to her hotel.*

"Hey Jack, how goes it? Fancy meeting you here of all places," a nervous Clara tries to be funny, playing it down as she suddenly is confronted with the surreal reality of the situation she has just created.

Her thoughts racing, *What happens if he doesn't want to be with me? I have only booked accommodation for a few nights. OMG, what have I done?*

Jack takes her carry-on case from her, being all business-like, he announces in a flat tone "Follow me Clara. How was your flight? Any dramas?"

Oh, I love a guy who takes charge, one who knows his way around she says to herself.

"Ah yes, I met a lovely flight attendant, good-looking, charming and funny, but he was gay, which is just as well as we don't want any complications do we?" Instantly regretting she has said something wrong already. *Oh my god you idiot, that's why Jack left! You were having an affair, don't make up another one or you will show him that you haven't changed!*

Jack stops in his tracks and stares at her, thinking *Where is she going with this?*

"Just joking!" Clara tries to recover, "What about you? This place obviously agrees with you. You look absolutely fabulous! What are you doing? Is the food as wonderful as I remember? How long are you in town? And where are you staying?"

Jack laughs, remembering Clara's inquisitive mind as one of the things he really admired about her, and answering truthfully, "Well I think I have found my special place. I am in the mountains away from everyone. I should say away from the hectic tourists. How do you say it in Swedish… small-tron-something?

"*Smultronställe*," Clara clarifies, adding, "You look really fit. Are you working out at the gym?"

"Well thanks, I guess I have filled out a bit since being here. The taxi rank is just over there," he points. "Anyhow, no, I am not working out at the gym, I am building and repairing, maintaining some little old wooden buildings. Soon we'll be starting to build something bigger and better, a proper school room and hall."

"What? You have gone back to building?" Clara is having to walk fast to keep up with him. "You said you would never do that back in Wellywood. What's changed?" Her mind jumping to the conclusion, *OMG! He's met a woman and is loved up! That's the only possible reason he would go back to building!*

"You're right, I did say that, didn't I?" Jack recalls, then explains, "it's for a good cause. Look let's get a cab first and we can talk later. This place is a little too crazy at this time of day, well Kathmandu is crazy at any time. So let's get you to your accommodation. Where are you staying?"

Looking at her phone, she replies, "It's the Śānti Viśrāma Hotel, do you know it?"

"No, but keep your maps app open," Jack advises, "so I can make sure we aren't taking the scenic route, if you know what I mean."

"Thanks Jack, I really appreciate your help," Clara replies gratefully.

*****

The trip to the hotel is rather quiet, with Jack occasionally pointing out some of the tourist sites. This gives her time to reflect that there was a lot she needed to tell him and explain why her behaviour had been so out-of-order. She may not have been in therapy that long, but long enough to understand some of her motivations. Like, when she was starting to get so defensive, or flighty and so unreliable, changing her mind and moods every five seconds. Such a contrast from her normally conservative behaviour.

As the taxi pulls up outside the hotel, Jack whistles, "Wow, no expense spared as usual Clara." He calls Clara by her real name. He actually finds Flat White an offensive name as he believes her girlfriends are taking the mickey out of her flat chest, when in fact they are referring to her favourite coffee.

She checked into the hotel, and Jack goes up to her room with her. Jack, while being friendly, is also distant and a little standoffish. Protecting himself, Jack asks, "So, how long are you thinking of staying? You didn't really explain. Are you on a stopover for a shopping spree in London? It does seem a weird place for you to stopover. I would have thought Milan or Paris would have been more your scene?"

Feeling jetlagged, a little hung over and dehydrated, she avoids the question. "Look I have a lot to say, but do you mind if I have a quick shower to wake up? I think I need a strong cup of coffee too. But first can you tell me what your plans are? Where are you going and what sort of time-frame are you on?"

"Well as I may have mentioned and I don't know how flash your geography is with Nepal, but I am living over in Pokhara which is miles away. It's a day's bus ride away from the capital here. Your timing is quite good in some ways and not so good in other ways. Let me explain briefly. I was coming over to Kathmandu anyhow as I needed to get my visa stuff sorted. I am on a travelling visa, can only stay 30 days, but my new employer has filled in an application form so I can go onto a working visa to stay longer. So I am in town to get my visa sorted and buy some more clothes. However, it is a fleeting visit and I need to get back in Pokhara at the latest the day after tomorrow. So your timing was good. And you?"

Clara takes a deep breath. "Well Jack, I'm not on a stopover, I've come here especially to see you. There's a lot I need to say to you. An apology is the top of my list. I am really sorry the way I treated you and I hope someday you can forgive me."

She stops, sits on the bed next to him and looks into his grey eyes, "I am serious Jack. That was cruel, and you of all people, did not deserve it. Can you find it in your heart to try and understand?"

There is an awkward pause and a hush envelopes the room. Jack stands up from the bed, his brow furrowed, obviously deep in thought.

Waiting for what seems an eternity, Clara breaks the awkward silence, nervously talking rapidly to mask her pain, "It's okay Jack, I understand. It's all a bit too soon and sudden. So I will let you percolate on that one. Look how about ordering some room service and coffee if you want and I'll be real quick, I just need to wake up. I kinda feel like I am only half awake and in fact this is all a dream. I never thought yesterday I would be here instead of on the Terrace in Wellington and that I am in a hotel room in downtown Kathmandu. Do you get what I mean?"

Having broken the spell he was under, Jack replies, "Yes I do. I can't believe you are here, either. Okay, look you know I'm not into wasting money on room service. I am sure even you are a little peckish. Let me go off and get some takeaways and drinks and I will be back in half an hour. That should give you plenty of time to freshen up."

"Yeah, great idea! You go and I can unpack and nest, you know how I love nesting."

Looking shocked, Jack queries, "Clara you are not thinking of nesting here, are you? Can I ask just how long are you staying?"

Plucking up all her courage, Clara responds, "Well my darling that depends entirely on you. I am not on a stopover I am not on some rampant shopping spree. I am here purely to see you." Seeing the look of disbelief in his eyes, Clara adds, "Well that's not entirely true, it's for you, but it's for other reasons. I have a couple of things on my bucket list which I would like to tick off."

"Oh okay so it's a bit of a tick-box exercise is it?" Jack starts sarcastically, then as his hurt wells up inside, he lashes out. "That sounds more like you, like the judge, just another trophy or accessory to acquire, tick off and then carry on to the next item on your list, once you or they discard you."

"Ouch! That's a bit harsh," Clara answers, then pleads, "Sorry, I am trying to play it down by saying bucket list, it's much, much more than that. Please Jack and I am not using this word lightly, you have to TRUST me, on this. I am being real for the first time in a very long time. I'm here with the right intentions and you're part of this. So please don't give up on me yet?"

Jack noticing her eyes welling up and realising he was being cruel, nods half-heartedly, adding as he leaves the room, "Okay Clara, I'll see you back here in half an hour and if you haven't already changed your watch, change it to the local time, or otherwise we will fall out over getting the times mixed up."

As the door closes, Clara with tears streaming down her face, whispers, "Thanks Jack."

Chapter 13

Getting Real…

L eft to her own devices for the next thirty minutes, Clara unpacks, jumps in the shower and rehearses what she is going to say to Jack a thousand times over in her head, then in front of the bathroom mirror. In her mind it sounds so cheesy, but it's true.

Clara turns the TV on and opens the old-fashioned windows to let some fresh air in. The room has that stale hotel smell of too many cans of air freshener. Clearly the windows haven't been used for ages. Opening the sliding door she walks out onto the balcony. From below comes the sound of noisy traffic. People crowd the footpaths outside with a view of the hotel entrance. Obviously, there is a lot of action happening down at the *porte cochère* as a number of cars come and go and she can imagine the bellboys greeting guests and taking their suitcases, just like they did with her less than an hour ago.

Suddenly feeling homesick, Clara realises what she has

just done. Within 12 hours she has jacked in her job, fled an earthquake, and caught a plane to Kathmandu.

Clara had visited Nepal many years before and had fond memories. She enjoyed the people, the sights and everything had seemed so exciting and colourful. But she never believed she would return nor for the reasons she had.

Jack comes back and knocks on the door. Clara is dressed and was looking and feeling much better.

Doing a double-take, Jack comments, "Wow what a transformation. You look as fresh as a daisy. I suggest we eat first. We have plenty of time to talk later. I see you have made yourself at home." He indicates the open windows and doors. "You know the place has air-conditioning. That is such a Clara thing, needing as much fresh air as possible. "You would love where I live. There is 24/7 fresh air. However, for you the down side is there are no shops, just lots of gorgeous school kids."

"Well I hate to shock you, Mr Fenton, but I love kids. In fact, I have been doing some serious thinking or should I say reflecting over the last wee while. And like I said I haven't been the easiest person to be with recently. But I know why, I've been unnecessarily far too hard on myself. Look what I have to say is going to take a while. I need to know what you are up to and where are you staying, because once I start, I won't be able to stop. And I get the impression you are on a tight schedule or you would rather be elsewhere. Can you just give me a rundown of what's happening and where are you staying?"

Jack looks a bit bemused, "Since when do you care about what schedule I'm on. It's usually all about Planet Clara isn't it? Okay, I am staying with some people I've met, a lovely family down the road for the next few nights. I met their daughter where I am staying…"

He doesn't have a chance to finish his sentence as Clara jumps in at the word *daughter*. "I knew you had met someone else, I could tell. You just seem so happy and relaxed. Okay so spill who is she? Who is my competition?"

Jack jumps in defensively, "Look Clara there is no competition. I am happily single. I am not with anyone, not you, not her, not anyone. You seem to be forgetting one important thing. YOU cheated on ME. Did you think I was stupid or something? Did you think I would be your little lap dog and always be at your beck and call?"

Clara starts getting tearful, "I know I was a jerk. I wasn't thinking straight. I'm so sorry." Blinking back her tears, determined to keep the conversation going, she asks, "But whose parents are you staying with?"

Recognising that he was reacting and that he is wanting answers himself, Jack responds a touch more gently, "There is this wonderful woman doctor at the compound I am living on. She is one of the leaders there and very good with the kids."

With a sinking feeling Clara thinks *A doctor! I've got no chance!* But replies with, "Please go on, I am interested in your new life…"

With some initial scepticism, Jack soon gets in the swing, continuing, "I haven't really got to the bottom of it, but what I have gleaned is this. She is an ex-pat like us and came over on a hiking tour, you know to do the usual thing and climb Mt Everest or at least do some of the treks. One of the treks she did is out by Pokhara, where she ran across this little village on the outskirts and just fell in love with the place. She had just broken up with some bloke back in

New York and was over the city life, so three years later and she is helping run a not-for-profit mission and building up this school. The mission desperately needs teachers, doctors, builders and such like, architects, planners, horticulturalists anyone that can donate their skills and time to help build the community."

"Really? That sounds a wonderful idea," Clara adds encouraging Jack, thinking *I haven't seen Jack this fired up ever!*

"Oh it is, Clara, I tell you there is something for everyone over here. I think even you would love it. It's a different world to downtown Wellington and Public Servicesville. You know what? It's my turn to talk out-of-turn now, but god knows what lights your fire, with all this 'strategy, words on a page, blue sky-thinking crap' you used to bring home and talk about. It all seems so senseless. This school, for example is real blue-sky thinking, and it is making a huge difference to all these kids and their families."

"Yes I can see it has made a huge difference. You are such a different person. You seem to have a spring in your step. Much more engaged. It's like you have a purpose now. I am so jealous. Can your lady doctor friend prescribe me some of whatever you and her are on?" *So I wonder why is she so amazing?*

Clara is beginning to get the picture that Jack wants to talk and what she has to say is far too heavy right now, and besides she still feels tired. So, what she wants to say can wait. Besides, it's taken her most of her life to come out and be real, what difference will another hour or so make? However, she does feel nervous as he has made it clear that he is off in two night's time so she has limited time to say what she needs to.

"Ok Jack for a change you have the floor, take it away, I want to hear more about this school and this amazing magical doctor."

"In a nutshell, I wanted to return to Pokhara. I had been there a couple of decades ago and even though it was a bit of a tourist mecca, it was my favourite out of all the other parts of Nepal. I just loved how it was small enough so you could meet people in a café or bar, but what I loved was its easy accessibility to the treks. You know I'm not into doing those high-altitude treks well not at our age, I value the oxygen my lungs get, so why go higher? Far too much of a strain. I like the Annapurna Base Camp trek, not too high and not too low. Lots of great tea houses to stop at along the way, and the people you meet in these houses and on the treks are just amazing. Everyone stops and talks to you and the sherpas now, their English compared with back in the day has got so much better. Anyhow I can see why Sir Edmund Hillary fell in love with the place and did his school over here."

"That sounds great and I want to hear more. Hey I'm parched, do you want a cuppa?" Clara asks lightly as she checks the electric jug for water and prepares two cups. "So what makes this school of yours so different to other normal ones?"

"Well it's a bit like those Montessori or Rudolf Steiner schools back home. They have real values and principles they live by and they get right into things like self-directed learning and covering all subjects, especially the creative ones like art and music, rather than the three R's."

"Wow, go on." Clara is enthusiastic.

"So well-rounded, but with a local twist. It's also a bit of a Hindi-Buddhist cross with the kids starting each day off with mindfulness classes. How cool is that? I was never really into this mindfulness craze, but man I'm hooked now. I go along each morning and join in. It really sets me up for the day. I feel the difference, how calmer I feel as a result of doing it, but also seeing the kids. You know some of them have come from some really hard backgrounds. Just seeing them meditating, sitting there for half an hour each morning, then later on in the day they do walking mindfulness so they walk around in the gardens that are being built. It's just very heart-warming. None of them go around with cell phones attached to their ears and fingers like the kids do back home. It's very, very refreshing."

The jug clicks off automatically, alerting Clara to continue making the tea. "Wow you are so lucky. So how did you land such a number?"

"Well I was doing my usual staying in a hostel routine just down the road from here, and I got talking with some guys who were heading back to Australia. They had been working at the school, doing up buildings, and one was an architect and they were designing a hall and music room and a little meditation room. They had been there for a couple of months but were running low on cash and felt it was time to go home."

"So you saw an opportunity?" Clara passes the cup to Jack.

"Thanks, Clara, yeah they were so fired-up about the place and it just sounded so worthwhile. I got the details from them and went to the school to see for myself what it was like. And I wasn't disappointed. I tell you, Clara, you broke my heart and this place was exactly what the doctor ordered. It was so uplifting to actually feel needed, useful instead of some hand-me-down. That's how you made me feel when you took off with that judge. Did you think I was so stupid I wouldn't notice, or hear any of the rumours that were starting to spread around town? You know Wellington is a small place."

Clara steps in, "Jack I really do care for you, you don't know how much I do. In fact I …"

He puts his hand up for her to stop, "No Clara you sucked me in for far too long. If you cared about me you would never have treated me the way you did. You wouldn't treat your worst enemy that way. Sometimes I just don't know where your head is. You make out you are such a career woman and climbing the ladder is all that matters and then you go and shag a married man, a judge because you think that's going to fill your void or whatever your sad pathetic life is missing right now."

Jack's harsh truth is all that is needed to set Clara off. She breaks down and cries. Sobbing through the tears, she answers, "Jack you have no idea, I had never told anyone the truth. When you have finished, I want to tell you why I do have a void, why I have been filling it with booze, unavailable men, work, work and more work."

"That I'd like to hear," Jack replies.

"Ten out of ten for guessing that I had a void, what you have seen isn't the real me. And if you let me, I'll show you that hidden part, but first I have to explain some things." Taking a breath, trying to buy some time, Clara asks, "Look I think now is a good time for a pre-dinner drink, what do you think?"

"No, we are not centring everything around alcohol, Clara. You don't need alcohol to talk. You don't need alcohol to get over how your mother doesn't love you. You don't need alcohol to have sex…" Jack is angry.

"Sex!" she exclaims. "Who said sex was on the menu? I was only talking about alcohol. Don't hold back now, Jack Fenton."

"Look Clara I know you think you are god's gift to men, but I am not throwing it out there, sex is the last thing on my mind," Jack fires back.

"Great," Clara heatedly replies, "Well that's a relief, because I haven't flown thousands of miles just for a shag…" She stops herself because she realises she is falling into old patterns and putting her defences up, "Let's just calm down a bit, shall we?" She says to herself, *Now remember Sven's words Clara, be real, be truthful and authentic!*

"Maybe this was a mistake, trying to get some answers, look it's getting late. Shall we adjourn until tomorrow. Whoops sorry bad taste in words, didn't mean to do the legal judge thing on you again," Jack apologises.

"It's okay Jack, but I would like to say a few things tonight, so you can sleep on it. Okay?"

He looks at his watch, "Look I don't want to be back late as it is an elderly couple I'm staying with and I don't want them to worry."

"Okay, I'll try and be quick. I wasn't honest with you," Clara begins.

"Ah yep, no shit Sherlock, I know that, you cheated on me." The sarcasm is dripping in his voice.

"I know, but before then, I had started going to a therapist, a clinical psychologist in Wellington. She does this cognitive behavioural therapy stuff, CBT, and the reason I am going is to treat myself for a diagnosis that I am just trying to come to terms with - PTSD. It's something I thought happened to other people, like war vets, but I didn't know I had it. I didn't really know what was the matter with me …" Clara pauses.

Jack stares open-mouthed, clearly shocked, "I had no idea… Okay… go on, you have my attention."

"Well when I was younger…" Clara begins and relates her childhood abuse from Fred, his threats against Sabrina and how her mother dismissed her truth and still supports Fred. Finally, she breaks down in tears as she finishes.

Seeing the woman he used to love being so real and hurting, Jack gently asks, "Oh my god, Clara why didn't you ever tell me?"

"Because I thought you would think I was dirty. I didn't tell anyone, I kept it to myself. I thought it was my fault. I thought I had asked for it. You know, I thought it was my fault that Dad left home. I thought it was my fault that both he and my mother didn't love me and never wanted me around. I just thought it was normal to jump from one relationship to another, drink hard, party hard, work hard. It was always extremes. I never seemed to be able to find the right man. That is, not until I met you. I did a really stupid thing with the judge but I realised that when it was too late and you had already gone…"

Softly, Jack comforts, "Clara, I never knew. But I can see how this plays out. You trying to cover everything up with booze and hard work…"

"Maggie, my shrink reckons that my erratic behaviour can be a so-called normal reaction to rape and abuse. I am up and down, pushing back the booze to numb the pain, running from one drama to another. Jack, I've been running, from myself for most of my life thinking that if I just worked my butt off and dressed up to the nines, everyone would think I was amazing and they would believe I was this great success, which clearly I am not..." She breaks down again, sobbing into her hands.

Jack his arms around her, in his first real sign of affection. "Oh Clara," he soothes, "that's it, let it out, I've got you. Just cry, that's the best medicine for you right now. Better than any bottle of Bollie. Just cry. You're safe now, I've got you."

Clara cries her heart out, like she has never done before feeling completely safe and at one in his big, strong arms.

Chapter 14

Night One Conversations and Revelations

Taking pleasure in the old familiar feeling of Jack's arms around her, Clara's sobs ease.

"Oh Jack, I must look a right mess. Excuse me while I find a tissue," Clara snuffles.

As he releases her from his embrace, Jack notices his protective feelings stirring inside his chest.

Clara grabs the tissue packet from her bag, turns away to clean herself up. Then taking a big breath, she states, "Okay, I'm almost there. Now are you sure you don't want any alcohol, because it kind of gets worse?"

"Thanks for the offer, but I'm okay. Come on, babe it can't get worse."

"Some time ago I wanted to start a family. There was only one small problem I thought. I didn't have anyone I wanted to have children with. Then I met you. I knew it was different, you were different."

"Hey, before you go on, you know I didn't want to have children and I still don't. I am past that stage now. It's hard enough managing and motivating myself, let alone some kids. Plus, I don't want to sound too insensitive, but they are a costly exercise and from what I see with my brother, kids today are so ungrateful. Mum and Dad thought my brother and I were a handful, but today! Have you not seen how spoilt and demanding kids are? Then they grow up and turn into teenagers, so bloody selfish and so unaware. Not at all like the kids over here. Anyhow, sorry, I interrupted…"

"Well, apart from my biological clock ticking, I really want children. It's not because I'm running out of time. I just realised I have been chasing the wrong rainbows, I thought money and prestige and status was really important. The Merc, the architecturally designed house, the high-paying career, but they mean nothing when you're not happy, or when you're not with the right person. Jack, I want children and I want YOUR children."

Whoops it was out.

"I'm really flattered, but look I'm so confused by what happened to us. I thought we were really solid and then something happened and you got all funny on me, you just detached. You got into your boozy parties and acted like a mad woman, so aloof. And now you come all this way saying you want my babies. Does love come into it at all?"

"Of course, I love you. That goes without saying," Clara replies earnestly.

"It doesn't really. Love is a good foundation to base a relationship on, some faithfulness, trust, time, shared values, goals, and then maybe a child. Look I don't know if you're on the rebound, or what it is. I feel flattered you have told me everything. I had an idea something fucked up might have happened to you, because often you were hot, then cold and sometimes I wasn't sure what was happening."

"I'm so sorry, Jack…" Clara begins.

Jack cuts her off and continues, "Look, I'm really sorry for your pain. And believe me when I say I am… what's the right word, it's not this but, happy it is all coming out because I think it's better facing these things than covering them up. But, there's a big 'But' here. Look, I've had a glimpse of happiness here and I am not going anywhere. I am not racing back to New Zealand to have babies, or get a so-called 'real job'! I have a real job here, and plenty of kids around me. I don't need babies," Jack finishes adamantly.

"Jack I didn't mean now. Look I know that this sounds like it's coming out of nowhere. But I'm really trying to be straight up and honest with you… I can't have children," Clara states.

A look of confusion comes over Jack's face, "What do you mean, you can't have children? You've just been telling me how much you want them."

"This is really hard to say. Hang on a minute, please," Clara reaches for her glass of water to take a drink.

"I'm all ears Clara," Jack looks on, pondering just where the conversation will go.

Finishing her glass, she walks over to the fridge and refills it, asking, "Do you want one Jack?"

Jack nods, accepting the offered glass.

Clara sat down again. "Well when this repeated assault happened as a kid, the wanker had this fucking disease and he left me with it! I got chlamydia, and as I was so young, I didn't know… so it went undiagnosed, and that led to PID, which… well, the short story is I can't get pregnant. I am as barren as the Sahara Desert. I will never be able to have children. So there you go Jack, that's me in a nutshell."

Jack shakes his head, wondering just how well he really knew Clara, and marvelling at how she has coped, "That is so fucked up!" Then realising, says, "That's why you always insisted on protection. I thought it was because you were a career girl and weren't taking any chances."

"It might seem like an excuse, but you can see why I kept myself medicated with alcohol." Clara searches Jack's eyes seeing some understanding, then continues, "But I am slowly coming to terms with it, thanks to therapy. Naturally, I'm still angry about all this. I've been in denial. I have been one angry fucked-up gal for ages. It's a bit of a rollercoaster some days… look Jack, I'm really sorry for the hurt I've caused you. I felt I just had to tell you the whole story. You deserve the truth after what I've put you through."

Jack walks back over to her, hugs her, then sits across from her to explain, "Look Clara, I am sincerely sorry to hear about everything you've told me. And I will be there for you, if you need to talk to someone. But I really don't want to be with you after what you did to me."

With those words, Clara flinches, feeling like she has just been slapped across the face and her heart is breaking all over again.

A determined Jack continues, "Like I said earlier, I don't want to be with anyone. I am done with relationships. My first relationship was a disaster, then I tried again with you and that was a disaster and now I am just ticking along quite nicely on my own. I don't need a partner to feel complete and I certainly don't need any toe-rags to complete the so-called happy nuclear family. Look you need your house, your career, your pay packet, your car, I simply don't want that sort of life anymore. I just want the simple things in life. Like I have here."

"Jack, you're not getting it. I don't need any of that shit anymore. I've sold my house, I lost my job, I…" Clara begins.

"You what! You sold YOUR house! What planet are you on?" Jack asks incredulously. "You LOVED that house!"

"YOUR planet Jack! Don't you get it? Material things don't interest me anymore. I want a completely different life."

"I don't want to lead you down the garden path, Clara. It's late and I don't want you getting over-tired. I need to get going. I am not being a cold-hearted bastard. I just need to get to my digs. It's been a long day for me as well, travelling on that bus. I'm so sorry I can't give you what you want. I don't know what your future looks like, but it's not with me. We want completely different things. You can't convince me that in such a short time your life has changed so much. That's not the Clara James I know. Get a good night's sleep, babe. I'll pop by tomorrow. I really appreciate you being honest with me. I know how hard that must've been for you. You are very brave."

"Jack, you are not getting me," Clara pleads.

"Yes I am, Clara," Jack begins assertively, "We had our time… in fact a great time. Look I seriously have taken on board everything you said. Let me sleep on it. I probably won't change my mind, but how about I meet you here tomorrow for lunch? Then maybe we can go out and see some of the sights?"

Jack kisses her on the cheek and without looking back, heads out the door.

Clara feels absolutely devastated, then agitated *Why was Jack being so distant? I said some real heavy things and he didn't seem to hear anything. I don't want his pity, but most of all I don't want him to see me as this heartless materialistic spoilt little bitch, because I am NOT!*

*****

Jack descends in the elevator and walks out into the chilly Kathmandu evening air, shaking his head thinking *Man that was heavy. Poor thing, what she has been through. I suspected something pretty big had happened in her life. But it does explain all the dramatic mood swings, but god I didn't expect something that graphic and PTSD.*

That brought back a memory of a couple of his school friends who had joined the army. Remembering going out to a few bars when they had come back from their overseas peacekeeping assignments, reacting to the backfiring of cars, mistaking them for guns going off. It seemed a bit funny at the time, but as he saw how much they drank and then got into fights going off at the drop of a hat, he recognized some of the same symptoms in them, as Clara had sometimes displayed in their relationship. The sudden mood swings, being hypervigilant, excessive drinking, denial. It starts to make sense in his head.

*****

It hasn't gone according to plan. Clara had found Jack at times quite cold and standoffish and wasn't sure what to do. *Did Leo get it all wrong? Is my big love not over here? Was he referring to something and someone else?*

Trying her besties again, but getting the same overloaded message by phone, she decides to try email. She starts her tablet and logs into her email. There are no emails from home. Her message begins:

Dear F and S

You will never guess what I ended up doing? I walked out of my new job and was gone by 10am after that middle manager bitch tried bullying me. I was on the train to Petone and had seen Leo for a reading. Before I knew it I was heading to the airport and on a plane to Auckland. You know I usually carry my trusty passport, and I treated myself to a new carry-on case and clothes at the airport. I just got the basics, nothing flash, and I am now sitting in my hotel room in Kathmandu, my first night. I met this amazing steward on the plane – charming, good looking, but GAY. Isn't that always the way? Anyhow, he upgraded me from Premium Economy to First Class. Long story short. I have many questions and I'm not even sure you'll get this.

1.   What's the story with the earthquake? Are you guys okay? Are you alive? If so, where are you and who are you with?

2.   The Kiwi Con – I saw her parked up at the Railway Station on Monday morning then on the news last night, or whatever day it was (I'm confused with the time difference). I heard there was a murder. Cathryn Tennyson? Is this true? Who murdered her?

3.   I've met up with Jack. It hasn't gone at all well.

As the saying goes, 'I'm in Kathmandu, what to do?' He's building and doing repairs and maintenance over in the mountains near Pokhara. Remember that place, Sven? Didn't it rock? Anyhow, he doesn't want me.

4.   Please write, I am lonely, I am homesick, and I think I have made a complete fool of myself. I've just revealed to him I want children but can't, and I have PTSD, and I did it all without alcohol! Not a single drop! I nearly drank the plane dry, but not the hotel's mini bar.

OK babes, I am sooo jetlagged, so I am crashing. Please, please write or text ASAP. I MISS YOU GUYS. Love your high maintenance homesick Trinity gal on the other side of the world, xoxo

Then she sends a quick email to her father:

Hi Dad,
It didn't go as well as I had hoped with Jack. I know you don't know him, but Jack Fenton is an absolute gentleman – you would really like him. Kind, honest, intelligent, fit and he's a builder. We might be sightseeing tomorrow, but I'm fading fast with jetlag, so I'll try and phone tomorrow.
Love Gigi xoxo

One more and I'm done, Clara thinks as she quickly texts her sister:

Sis, hope you are OK! I'm in Kathmandu trying to make up with Jack, don't tell Mum! I'll call soon, C xo

Forgetting to shut the balcony doors and windows,

Clara collapses onto the bed, and falls asleep, listening to the night city noises of Kathmandu way below.

Her last thoughts: *What is Jack thinking? Will he come back or have I really done it this time? I am not going home yet, I am staying, but where to now? I have another night's accommodation and then I'm on my own. No job, no man, no home, just a dream…*

Chapter 15

Day Two Touring and Turmoil

The knocking at the door slowly awakens Clara from her slumber. Her heart leaps, *It's Jack! He HAS come back!*

Feeling a bit embarrassed as she hasn't showered or anything, she lets him in. "Morning, sorry I've just woken up. This is a bit déjà vu, but do you mind if I have a quick shower to wake up?"

"Sure Clara. I have a great programme planned," Jack replies, "so don't take too long."

Turning the tap right down, she feels the sting of the cold water on her head, instantly her brain clears from the jet-lagged sleep. She washes quickly, thinking *Hmm he seems to be a in a better mood today. Maybe things will be different, maybe...*

She dresses in her sports leggings and trainer shoes, singlet and quarter-zip merino top, and pulls her hair back into a ponytail. Giving herself the once-over in the mirror, she nods at herself, this is the new you, let's go!

As she emerges from the bathroom, Jack does an admiring double-take, *How does she do that? Look a million dollars in five minutes?*

Grabbing her phone Clara quickly scans her email notifications for a message from home. Seeing nothing, she packs her bag, "Right, where are we off to Tour Guide?"

"Did you ever go to the Monkey Temple when you were here last?"

"Not that I recall." She frowns, thinking. "I did the Palace of course and a couple of temples, but then I headed out to Pokhara with Sven. That's such a coincidence that you are there now."

"I know right. Okay, I've got a couple of cool places to take you, then. But let's have some breakfast first shall we? We both always work better on a full stomach."

*****

Enjoying herself over a large breakfast of coffee, juice and eggs, Clara starts, "Hey Jack, I was serious yesterday. Don't know if you know, but I loved that teaching English job I had in Stockholm and working as an au pair for that French couple that time in *Le Lavandou,* in the South of France at the beach. I would really love to get back into teaching English and to children. I just don't know where yet."

"Really?"

"Yes, and I'm not going back home. Not yet. Besides I have nothing to go back to."

Jack thinks hard for a moment, then offers, "Look Clara, if you are serious, I could take you to the village school where I work. They are always on the lookout for volunteer teachers. They won't pay you, but you get accommodation and food in exchange, but only if you are serious…" Jack eyes Clara intensely, "You would feel such a sense of achievement, a sense of real purpose."

Clara looks at him, disbelief written all over her face. "Are you serious? I would love to look into this."

"Yes I am serious," Jack replies, then enthusiastically he continues talking rapidly, "I could get another seat on the bus, I'm booked on for tomorrow. What do you think? Even if you don't like it then you could just do some of the treks and then fly onto your favourite Europe."

"Jack I would love to check that out. That would make me very happy. Do I need to get a work visa or anything?" Clara is excited at the thought.

Realising that he could be leading Clara on, Jack sits back in his chair, raising his hands up, "Hey slow down Ms Speedy Pants. Nothing is guaranteed. Just come over and see what you think? But look as for us, can we just take it one step at a time. You've got to understand that the Clara I'm seeing in Kathmandu is not the Clara I left behind in Wellington, so I am still coming to terms with this new you."

"That makes two of us, Jack. I'm still uncovering the real Clara James. The fun-time, party girl is still in here along with the hurt, damaged little girl," Clara thinks a moment, sipping her coffee. "Being authentic and true to yourself isn't easy with my past conditioning. But I'm a stubborn Taurus with Leo rising, so watch out!"

Jack laughs, "Now that's the Clara I know. Hear me roar!"

"Thanks Jack," Clara smiles, "that's all I can really ask,

let's see where this goes?"

They spent the rest of the day touring around Kathmandu, enjoying the variety of gold coloured deities adorning the *Swayambhunath* Monkey Temple after climbing what seemed endless steps. Laughing together as the monkeys slid, screaming down the banisters they were using to climb up. The rainbow of coloured prayer flags, strung from trees and buildings, fluttering above them.

They spent a number of hours strolling through the beautiful Garden of Dreams, admiring the exquisitely manicured landscapes and fountains, pergolas, and pavilions which had been restored to their former glory of earlier years. Pointing out to each other some of the plants they recognised, stopping occasionally to enjoy the fragrance from some of the exotic flowers.

To get around town, they caught crazily painted taxis that drove equally as crazy, dodging other buses, cars and cyclists along their route, always accompanied by the ever-present shrill of motorcycle horns.

The constant sensory overload of colour, noise and smells assaulting her senses almost overwhelming her at times, but slowly becoming more at ease, she relaxed in the comfort of Jack's companionship.

Before Clara knew it, Jack had dropped her off at her hotel, leaving early to spend time with the host family.

*****

Taking advantage of having the evening to herself, after still hearing nothing from home, Clara spends a couple of hours writing furiously in her journal, recording how she is feeling, her hopes and dreams, and how she feels her relationship is rekindling with Jack.

She makes a cup of tea, and sits down to check her tablet and phone for any news from home. Worrying as there is nothing from the girls, Clara reads an email from her Dad:

Dear Gigi,

I hope your sightseeing went well with Jack. A builder eh? Then I'll definitely get on with him. Tell him if he's not careful, I'll have a couple of projects for him to work on when you come to visit. I hope you'll come and visit someday and make an old man very happy.

Still no word from your friends, and Zita isn't answering her phone. I've been checking the casualty list on the BS Ministry website for their names, fortunately they aren't listed so I think that's a good thing. But with phone and internet being down, it could be a few more days until we know for sure. Sorry I couldn't be of more help.

On the home front, Wellington is still a mess. The politicians are calling for calm and saying it's not the time for finger pointing, bloody crooks the pack of them! All I can say is that the emergency services are all doing a splendid job, every last one of them deserve a medal.

Gigi, the only advice I've got is be yourself, if a man can't see how special you are, then he's not the right one for you.

If you get a chance, please remember to phone me.
With Much Love
Dad xo

Blinking back the tears, Clara decides that there is no

way she's going back to Wellington in the aftermath of the earthquake. It just sounds so terrible so she tries texting both Freya and Sven again.

Deciding the only thing she can do especially if she is off to a school that prides themselves on the principles of mindfulness and meditation, that she should start her meditation practice. She throws the bed cushions onto the floor, positions herself on them and starts breathing deeply and slowly.

Maggie had taught her coherent breathing, slowly in on four and out on six, she then scanned her body and started meditating.

Managing ten minutes before the peaceful silence is interrupted by her phone pinging.

Clara jumps up far too quickly, the blood drains from her face, her head spins while her legs give out under her, she crashes back down hitting her head against the chest of drawers by the bed.

Stunned she lays there for a few minutes so overwhelmed and feeling out of sorts, more tears streaming down her cheeks. *My god all I seem to do at the moment is cry, cry and cry some more.*

She gingerly touches the dampness on her forehead and when she pulls her hand away blood is dripping from her finger. She lets out a short scream.

Standing more slowly this time she hesitantly enters the bathroom, checking the mirror to see the damage. Her temple is pulsing, and she can see the bruise starting to darken and swell. Just a small cut with blood oozing out of it. She grabs a face flannel and bathes it in cold water. *That will do. I hate the sight of blood!*

Back to the bedside, Clara reaches for her phone to see

who had messaged her. *It's an email from Sven and Freya! Thank God for that!* Clara reads on:

Dear Flat White, you dark horse!

The Himalayas, how exotic! What about our New Year's Eve plans? We were going to have them over here. How can we do that now with you gone? You deserter, you piker...

No, just joking, this is fabulous news that you have followed your heart. We are both writing this.

We are all okay over here, Sven took a bump to her head in the quake, but Charlie got her help and she is recovering here. Yes, Charlie is back on the scene! Wellington is starting to calm down a little since the big shake up. Everyone we know is okay – well, relatively okay. I think some people are quite traumatised by it all. You were so lucky to miss this one. A little bit of damage here, nothing serious. Everyone is either working from home or just taking their holidays early. A lot of people have got as far away from Wellington as possible and headed up north to warmer climes and less shaky ground.

Yes, it was Cat who was found dead on the Kiwi Con on Monday morning, a suspected overdose, but now not so sure. Charlie has reopened Cat's investigation, hence why Charlie is back on the scene...

Sven and Charlie after all these years apart are finally working things out and it looks pretty solid from my perspective. (Freya commenting) and Sven agrees, Pokhara rocks – see if you can find that little bar we danced in.

And Freya finally kissed Zac, it's great to see young love (Sven commenting).

Anyhow, what are you doing for New Year's Eve? Let us know! Wish we could be with you. Remember that New Year's Eve we had once up in Sweden, out in the archipelago – wasn't it great? Zooming around in the snow on those cute little sleighs.

OK, well we are signing off now. Charlie and Sven are staying here at Portobello with Zac and me, and business has taken off big-time since the quake, but it will quieten once everyone goes away as planned on holiday. You know how Wellington and the CBD dies over Christmas and New Year's with all the public servants away.

Now kia kaha girl, stay strong and be straight with Jack, you know honesty is the only way to his heart.

Take care and keep us posted on where you are going for Christmas and New Year's and we will have some bubbles and a Wellington Pilsner for you down here.

Take care, Love F and S xxx

Relief washes over her. She gulps back a glass of water and then lies down on her bed to process this latest news. Falling asleep with mixed up images racing through her head of Sven, Freya, Jack, Bianca, Bernard, Cat and Margaret on the Kiwi Con all dancing the locomotion through the carriages.

*****

Waking in an awkward position, Clara rolls over to glance at the bedside clock, seeing it is just after seven. Lying in bed, she stares up at the ceiling, her mind doing over-time about what was happening back home and here, sorting out how she is feeling about Jack.

After a great deal of thought, Clara realises, *maybe one day we can be more than friends again? But for now what's most important is regaining his trust and friendship, I didn't realise how good he makes me feel. I like the sound of giving back to the community, sharing some of my skills with people who really need it. I can't wait to see the compound set up, besides that, I am dying to meet Mary.*

Clara attempts to get up remembering she needs to check out in a few hours and catch the bus with Jack, but still feeling tired, she falls back to sleep.

*****

The urgent knocking at her door, wakes Clara from her slumber.

Rising unsteadily to her feet, she opens the door to see Jack, her heart jumps, smiling, still half asleep she invites him in, "Come on in good looking…"

"Oh my god Clara, what's happened?!" Jack answers shocked at her appearance. "Get back into bed!"

Clara mockingly says, "Wow Jack, now there's an invitation. What took you so long?"

"It's not funny, Clara. You look a mess. You have blood running down your face! Tell me how… my god did you sleep like that? Have you seen a doctor, has anyone seen to this?" Jack urgently asks.

Clara laughs, "You're joking. You think I am going to find a doctor that speaks English in this city in the middle of the night? I'm not having some half-trained medic putting dirty needles into me! Besides it was a small accident. I just got up too fast. Fell over and banged my head."

"You really should have this seen to." Jack pauses to

think a moment, then makes a snap decision, "Look Mary is in town, she came over last night to see her parents before they leave for the States, I'm calling her now."

"Do you think that's necessary?"

"Yeah… Hi Mary, look Clara's had an accident, can you come take a look?" Jack turns to Clara, demanding, "Did you take all the necessary vaccinations before you came over?" Getting a nod from Clara, he continues, "Yes she has… Ah huh… yep… thanks Mary, we will see you soon."

Disconnecting the call to Mary, Jack walks over to the bedside, "Look, you know you have low blood pressure and you are skin and bone. You need to look after yourself better." He looks around the room. "Did you get onto the booze when I left?"

"No I DID NOT! Look I'm fine, okay? I got my vaccination shots when I went to Thailand last year, remember." Clara states, "Come on I need to check out and we need to get to the bus."

"You're not going anywhere young lady," Jack replies assertively, "Not until Mary has given you the once over. Now tell me what happened."

Clara deciding that she likes this caring side of Jack, proceeds to tell him about the phone, fall and the email from the girls.

"It's great to hear some positive news from home, Clara."

Their conversation is interrupted by a knock at the door. Jack answers it and lets the visitor in, "Mary this is Clara, Clara this is Mary."

The two women briefly look each other up and down, checking each other out in a nanosecond. "Hi Clara it's lovely to meet you. I'm a doctor, ah… that bruising doesn't look too good. Do you mind if I have a look?"

Nodding her assent, Clara thinks, *I guess if I want to work at this school, I need to make a good impression.*

Clara pays attention and does what she is asked. Mary looks her over while Jack stands back looking troubled. *He looks so cute when he has that big concerned look on his face. I wish it wasn't pity though he had for me and it was something else. I really know how to fuck up anything good that happens in my life.*

After completing a couple of tests, Mary turns to Jack as if Clara wasn't in the room. "I'm a little concerned about this swelling, it doesn't look like concussion, but I don't think she is safe to travel right now. I think rest and another couple of nights in Kathmandu would be good for her."

Piqued at being told what to do, Clara responds, "Look I'm perfectly fine, I'll show you." Trying to stand up too quickly, she falls back onto the bed.

"Right that settles it, you are going nowhere!" Jack says as he picks her up in his arms and places her gently back between the bedcovers and tucks her in. In an assertive tone he says, "Stay there and don't go anywhere."

He has a quiet chat with Mary in the hall, before returning to Clara's side.

Jack takes one of her hands in his. "You know you look so vulnerable. I love it when you just drop all those airs and graces and are just the real you. You look like a little girl who has lost her teddy." Smiling he continues, "I am cancelling the tickets, and then ordering some room service. Then we are going to have a serious talk and you are going to listen, just LISTEN FOR A CHANGE, young lady, Okay?"

"Yes Sir, whatever you say," Clara nods with a twinkle in her eye.

Just then her cell phone pinged again. Jack reaches over to grab it and insists, "And that phone is going off for now. We can check it out later."

She resists, "But I need to know what is happening Jack! I haven't heard from Sabrina yet!"

"Clara, you can hardly keep your eyes open, just settle and I'll contact her. I've still got her cell phone in my contacts. Now close your eyes and rest my sweet one." Jack replies in a soothing voice.

Suddenly tired from her body telling her it wants to heal, she drifts off to sleep, thinking, *did he really just call me his sweet one?*

Chapter 16

Rest and Reset

Sleeping most of the next day, Clara was in recovery mode. Jack didn't let on, but he hadn't left the hotel, alternating between sitting at the small dinette table and chair, and the room next door, where he slept.

After fare welling her parents at the airport, Mary came back to check on Clara's progress before returning to Pokhara.

She took Jack to one side and they talked in the corridor, "Look Jack I don't want to interfere, as it's none of my business what your relationship is with Clara, but you clearly care about her, probably more than you are letting on?" Mary looked at Jack for answers.

Jack hesitantly responded, "I don't quite know myself. This is the girl whose actions sent me over here. She is the one that hurt me and I don't want to risk getting hurt again. I have found myself a new job at the school and this is where I belong now."

"I realise that, and from what she says she sounds pretty legit about wanting to come over as well and help out. She genuinely loves children and we don't exactly have a whole lot of English-speaking teachers knocking down our doors wanting to come to the remotest parts of Asia to teach English. Besides if she is a friend of yours that is reference enough for me. I would be happy to take her on. But I have two things that I feel need to be said."

"Go on, Mary."

"Well Jack, first as you know she needs to rest, at least another day or two. And second, how do you really feel about the woman you loved, who broke your heart, living and working so close together?"

"Between you and me, Mary, I'm conflicted. There are emotions stirring again that I never thought would come back. I think I need the next few days to work through them," Jack confides.

"I thought as much. Well, here's my advice, whether you want it or not. Just make sure you are both honest and real with each other. God knows my ex wasn't, and that trebled the hurt when I finally cut him out of my life."

"Thanks for being straight with me, Mary and thanks so much for everything you have done. I don't know what I would have done without you."

"Yes, you do, Jack. You are a survivor, and so is she. I think   something has triggered your friend which has led to some erratic behaviour. I believe she is trying to come to terms with it and how to deal with it appropriately instead of suppressing it or acting out. So be gentle on her. She needs support and especially to feel safe."

"That I can do," Jack replies sincerely.

"And one last thing. She must really love you to have

come all the way over here to apologise and be real with you," Mary shares her insight.

"Thanks a million Mary, you are a star," Jack replies.

"I have to go. I'll see you back at the school in a few days. Don't rush, just keep in contact."

*****

Jack opens the curtains to let the daylight in and the doors onto the balcony for fresh air. He hears a murmur. It's Clara waking up. He walks over and sits by her, "Good morning or should I say good afternoon, Sleepyhead. How are you?"

"Jack? You're still here. Why?" A puzzled look crosses her face.

Jack says nothing at first, as his emotions stir. He looks into her eyes, searching for the right words to express himself. "Of course I am still here, Clara. Where did you think I would be? Do you think I am that heartless that I would be long gone? Leaving you in a foreign hotel in a foreign land with no one to call on?" Jack shakes his head.

"Thanks Jack," She smiles and tries to move, but her head still hurts and she feels a little dizzy.

"I'm going to order some food. What do you fancy? Anything special?" Jack asks.

"I can't decide, but I do feel like something savoury. Do you think they can whip up some eggs?"

"I'm sure they can. Look, just so you don't worry needlessly, Doctor Mary has been checking on you and says you will be fine with a little more rest, so if you are up for it, we'll head off, maybe tomorrow or the day after for Pokhara. At this time of year, there aren't a lot of tourists around so we don't have to book the bus. And if you're not up to the long bus trip we can always catch a plane, it's only an hour and fifteen minutes by air. So, your call, but no decisions need to be made yet."

"I will leave it in your capable hands. Look Jack I am really worried about the girls. Have you heard anything?" Clara asks.

"No, let's check while we wait for breakfast."

Jack orders in the eggs, OJ, toast and coffee and then they turn on Clara's phone and tablet. After a flurry of notifications vying for their attention, there is only one text from Sabrina worth looking at. Jack reads aloud, *"We are all okay Sis, but watch out, Mum's on the warpath! Love S kiss, hug...* At least I think that's what the x and o means. So Clara, what's this warpath your psycho mother is on?"

"It could be anything knowing her, she's probably about to blame me for the earthquake," Clara replies, adding, "I'm so glad Sabrina is okay. She might be the favourite daughter, but I know that comes at a cost."

"I never could work out your mother. From the first time we met, she got my back up," Jack divulges.

"Really? What happened? I mean, I know I was there, but Sabrina had me in a bear hug if I remember rightly," Clara recalls.

"You probably missed it then, but her first words to me in that highfalutin way of hers, *was Jack Fenton, now what sort of name is Fenton? Sounds awfully common. Where is your family from?"* Jack shakes his head at the memory, "I was so offended I nearly walked out right there and then, but I was there for you, so I stayed."

"Oh Jack! That's appalling!"

"Well, I didn't give her the satisfaction of driving me

away, I figured that was what she was trying to do. Besides, all I told her was that I came from a long line of builders."

"You have me intrigued, now. Can I ask where the Fenton's are from?" Clara asks curiously.

"My Uncle Alan was the genealogy buff, and he reckons he can trace us in a direct line back to the 1300s. The Fenton's had a family seat in West Yorkshire, which is where the Earl of Hebden, one Archibald Fenton, built his fortune. He was a sheep baron and after winning an Earldom, built Hebden Hall. I'd like to visit it one day. It's not too shabby, either. Uncle Alan took a few photos when he was over there in the 'eighties."

"Wow, that's so cool," Clara exclaims, "To set your mind at ease Jack, there's no blue blood in our family lines. I'm not sure why Mum carries on like she does."

"I'll let you in on a little secret," Jack teases.

"What's that?"

Looking a little sheepish, he says, "Well, I've always likened your mother to Hyacinth Bucket from that old tele show."

"Ha, Ha! Good one." Clara laughs as there is a knock at the door.

Jack goes to investigate and returns carrying a large tray laden with their room service, "Shall we eat on the verandah?"

Basking in the sunshine, they sit outside enjoying their meal. Clara is clearly feeling much better as she scoffs everything on her plate. The colour slowly returns to her porcelain white face.

"I think I will be up for travelling tomorrow. Now don't die of shock, but I would like to try the bus. I think the magic bus would be a great way of seeing the country."

"That's great Clara. You are certainly looking more perky."

"Have you told the school I am coming? Do they know I'm a qualified TESOL English Teacher?" Clara asks.

"Mary knows, and she is one of the directors there." Jack pauses. "I don't want you getting your hopes up. The school is not exactly the Ritz and it's cold at night this time of the year—the heating's not flash. We're also very remote. No fashion stores and beauty salons close by. In fact, if you want a taste of all that sort of stuff and you're up for it, Kathmandu is probably the best I can do for you in that area. So maybe today you have a small fix in the shops."

"Jack I haven't come all this way to go shopping."

"You would usually. So excuse me if I am not quite buying the fact that you are not here on a shopping spree. Look, how about you take a shower and we will go out in half an hour?"

"Okay…" Clara looks at him sideways.

"And remember to take everything slow though. No dizzy fits in the shower… I just want to finish this sketch and make a few phone calls."

"What are you up to?" Clara asks quizzically.

"I'm building a school hall and I think today I'll go and source some supplies." Jack smiles at her.

"That's the pot calling the kettle black, isn't it? You are off on a shopping spree clearly, and it's ME who's tagging along?" She laughs and leaves to have a shower.

They spend all day out and about, looking at shops, eating, walking and taxiing around town to see the sights. They pop into temples and buy a few goodies for the school. Clara buys a few clothes but of a practical nature, for warmth, hiking and casual wear.

Feeling almost back to normal, Clara decides that she is up for travel on the magic bus leaving early next morning. She pays her hotel bill the night before and orders an early room service breakfast. Then, she and Jack retire early, each to their own room.

Leaning up against the headboard of the bed, Clara puts her tablet on her lap and starts typing. Sending off three emails, one to Freya, one to Sven and one to her mother.

It's been four days since the earthquake and it's the end of another working week in Wellington. A lot would have happened, and Christmas is fast approaching.

She sends an email to Sven first.

Hey babe, how are you? I'm still at the hotel in Kathmandu, but off to Pokhara tomorrow with Jack. Not sure where we stand, but we are communicating and being straight with each other – fuck it's hard!

How's things going with Charlie, now is that a coincidence or what?

We are off on a bus early tomorrow but have good reception here, so please email me back before we go, and tell me everything? Love me x

Right one down, two to go, Freya's next!

Dear Freya, I feel so bad I walked right passed your Portobello on Monday and could have called in, but was so selfish, all I could think of was myself. I saw Leo for a reading after I walked out of my job at morning tea time on Monday. A case of bullying and I just couldn't be bothered, life is far too short. So I took myself to Kathmandu via Auckland. I've been here three nights and I'm on my last night here at my hotel. I'm with Jack, and to be honest not sure where things stand, but I am hanging in there. I have hope. It can't all be bad, he is letting me come to Pokhara, to the SCHOOL he is working at. I might try my luck at teaching English again. Time to follow my heart and see where that takes me. Sorry I left without saying goodbye. What are you doing? How are Zac and Portobello? Please email back ASAP. Love me x

Thinking to herself, *Last one. Typical though, I could have been in the earthquake and Mum didn't even think to contact me to see if I was okay, so why am I bothering? Right might as well get this email over and done with even though it will be pointless.*

Dear Mum and Sabrina, how are you both? I am really glad that you are going up north for Christmas. I know how much you two love the Bay of Islands and the weather should be great as usual at this time of the year. Sorry I won't be there with you but say hi to all the family for me. Did you get much news about the earthquake in Wellington? I am assuming you were nowhere near Wellington at the time, having left for your holiday, so you will probably be fine. I was in Wellington on the day of the earthquake. Anyhow I flew out a few hours before the earthquake and I am now in Nepal. You know how much I love the place so finally all these years later I have managed to get myself back over here. I know it is a weird time of the year to come but there are actually less tourists and Jack is here with me so all good. Ok love to you both, take care and Merry Christmas. I will try and write again before Christmas. Love Clara xx

She pushes the send button, then gets up to brush her teeth. A ping comes from her tablet, and she races back to open up the email, saying out loud, "Yay! It's from Sven!"

Hey girlfriend, you are full of surprises! I heard you had walked out of your job. I heard through Bernard actually. Margaret was not at all impressed. In fact I had to hear a whole running commentary about how unprofessional your conduct was and she would make sure you were never employed in Wellington again. Anyhow, why would you care? Look there's too much to say so I will just write a bit now and more later. Ok where to begin?

Well in a nutshell Charlie, yes my old Charlie, Charlie Rogers is the head of the investigation for Cat. That's why the carriage had gone quiet on Friday night. She was found dead in the WC on the train on Monday morning.

Clara says to herself, *there's something nagging in the back of my brain about last Friday...*
She reads on...

With Charlie investigating at the BS Ministry on Monday, well you know me, I couldn't resist putting my old copper training into practice. I know I never finished the training, but you know me once curious always curious. So I helped out the best I could. I found loads of prescription bottles in Cat's desk drawer and we worked out she wasn't murdered! She died of natural causes. But now there is some new information that she could have been murdered. Look there's too much to say. You know our lives - too much happens in a week let alone a year!

Freya is okay she's out at Petone and I'm staying with her at the moment. In fact her grand-dad's building is mint, whereas the others are munted and as a result her place is doing a roaring trade, on the accommodation, food and entertainment side. But I will let her explain more.

Oh and one more thing in this SHORT email, I promised to write. I am actually writing this from Portobello. Charlie was giving me a ride home when the earthquake struck and we got trapped downstairs in the BS car park. I was knocked unconscious, dodgy head pains but I'm okay now. Just taking it easy and Charlie is looking after me here. Look I'll write more later. Oh and Gracie is looking after Edward. Take care you, love me xx

Walking back to the bathroom to finish cleaning her teeth, Clara is deep in thought. Recalling the argument outside Margaret's office, with the lady in the red suit. *Dammit! The lady in red was Cat! I'm sure of it!*

Sitting down at the dinette she thinks back to the Friday evening train journey. *That woman in the purple jacket was Margaret on the train! Oh, and the entry in her diary proves it!*

Beside herself, she quickly sends a reply back to her friend:

Hey Sven, Look I know this may sound weird and I have no solid evidence, but I don't think that Margaret Johnson is as holy as she makes out. Can you get Charlie to contact me please, as I may have some information for him?

I've seen Margaret and her Stockholm purple jacket, all over town and on the Kiwi Con on Friday! Then there's her diary entry I saw on Monday about catching the train. Things just aren't stacking up.

It may be nothing but there are too many coincidences.

Maybe your new lover boy may want to look into that. Okay don't know how good the coverage is over in Pokhara so just wanted to send you this before I leave. Take care xx

Putting her electronic devices, her battered Lonely Planet guide and a few other essentials into her hobo bag. Thinking she has done everything she can for the moment, Clara packs most of her things into her carry-on case, just leaving the essentials out for a quick getaway in the morning.

Chapter 17

Magic Bus

Waking to the sound of her hotel room phone ringing, a bleary eyed Clara fumbles for the receiver, mumbling, "Hello?"

"Good morning Ms James, this is your wake up call, breakfast will be delivered in twenty minutes," a perky front desk receptionist announces in an immaculate British accent.

"Thanks." Clara gets out of bed and drifts off to the bathroom. She hears the shower start next door. *Jack must be up too… I wonder what adventures today will bring?*

*****

With a towel wrapped around her head, Clara races from the bathroom to answer her cell phone. Not recognising the number, she hesitantly answers. "Clara speaking."

"Kia Ora, Clara, it's Detective Sergeant Charlie Rogers. I got your message via Sven," a deep voice booms over the line.

"Oh, hi Charlie, it's been a while."

"It sure has. Look I know it's early there, but we are in the middle of an operation and I just need to confirm what you've seen before we initiate our next search warrant," Charlie explains.

"Okay, I'll be quick. I saw…" Clara divulges everything she can remember about Margaret Johnson, the Friday Kiwi Con sighting, the argument between Cat and Margaret in the street, the diary entry being erased and adding the meeting with the Police Commissioner and Margaret in the café.

"E hika! The Commissioner again! We're finding that he's got his fingers in a few pies. Tēnā rawa atu koe, thanks so much Clara, I'll need to set up a formal interview over the phone at some stage, but you've been invaluable in helping this case and probably others we are just starting to uncover!"

"Look Charlie, there is one other thing, I have a few photos on my phone of Margaret and the Police Commissioner, I'll email them through to you if you can text me your email address?" Clara adds, "Hey take real good care of my friend, okay?"

"I'm doing my best for Sven. She's a feisty one, as you well know. We're taking it slow and steady, but it's damn good to have her back in my life," Charlie confides. "Excuse me Clara, my partner Rex is trying to say something… Yeah Rex, it's a go… sorry Clara, I have to go, thanks again, ka kite āno."

As she disconnects the call, there is a loud knocking at her door. Opening it, she is greeted by a pumped-up Jack.

"Ok up you get sleepyhead." Jack walks in with their

breakfast. "Oh, you are up. You must be keen. Eat up. We have thirty minutes before the bus leaves. The bus stops right outside, so not too far to go."

"Good, plenty of time to eat and enjoy a coffee while I check my emails," Clara finishes drying her hair.

"That's a great idea, not much coverage in the compound. I normally head into Pokhara to an internet café a couple of times a week," Jack advises.

"Oh, so the school is out of Pokhara then?" Clara asks.

"Yeah, it's near the village of Khapaudi. Still on the lake and lots of rice farms. It's very beautiful," Jack replies. "Do you want these eggs?"

Slapping his hand away from her plate, "Hands off, you cheeky bugger! No, nothing new from the girls or the family, apart from a quick email from Sven last night. But I just got off the phone with Sven's Charlie."

"Oh? What did he want?" Jack enquires, slowly reaching for her eggs again.

She gently pokes the back of his hand with her fork. "That'll teach you. I'll fill you in on the bus, or you will just sneak my eggs again," Clara tucks into her breakfast.

*****

The magic bus ride is enchanting in places and hysterically scary in others. Fortunately, Clara sleeps through most of it but each time they take a corner too fast and the brakes are applied abruptly she wakes. Jack reassures her constantly that it is just normal driving and nothing to worry about. One hour out of Pokhara she refers to her old Lonely Planet book to find out a bit more about the second largest city in Nepal. *Pokhara with a population of 265,000 lies 200k west of Kathmandu. The Annapurna range has three of the ten highest mountains. The city's nickname is 'the city of eight lakes' and is proudly the tourism capital of Nepal being very popular as the base for trekkers.*

Looking up schools, she discovers there are over 100. *Yes and I am going to one of them.* Clara admires the photos of Pokhara portraying its beauty, from gorgeous sunsets over the lake, to Buddhist monasteries and temples, mountains, treks, you name it they had it. Pinching herself she realises she is only miles away from Pokhara on Phewa Lake in central Nepal, gateway to the Annapurna Base Circuit, the popular trail in the Himalayas.

They arrive in Pokhara in the late afternoon. Clara notes the modern changes, but is relieved to see that it is mostly how she remembered it, a place of beauty, a real wonderland. They take a taxi to get some supplies of bottled water and fresh vegetables from a local supermarket.

"I'm sure this wasn't here when I was here last Jack," Clara exclaims, as she takes in the shelves loaded with colourful packets and tins of foreign looking groceries.

"Probably a few changes since then, hey…" Holding up a familiar green can of potato chips, Jack shakes his head as he replies, "Check out the price of these!"

"What people will pay for a taste of home eh?"

"I know right! Come on, let's get going, don't want to keep the taxi waiting.

*****

As the taxi climbs the windy road, Clara looks back out over the gorgeous views. "This is amazing, Jack and I get to share it with you. I can't believe I'm here. Less than a week after leaving New Zealand, I'm here back in the mountains."

They arrive at the school gate. It looks pretty sparse and run-down, just a few buildings and what resembles the beginning of a small garden and a large playing field. Jack gets out first, pays the fare and takes the bags, "Ok, madam follow me. Now remember this is not the Ritz. No expectations."

A little startled about the isolation, the bareness of the place and the tumble-down nature of the buildings, Clara nevertheless gets herself together and allows Jack to lead the way. It is Saturday afternoon and the place is empty. The wind is blowing and all you can hear is the wind rustling through a tall teak tree and the rattling of tin, obviously coming from a roof or something that is not tied down.

Jack leads her into a tiny room, "Say hello to your accommodation. I have talked with Mary and you can stay in here for now. It's part of the old staff quarters." Looking at the disappointment on her face he explains, "This is one of the original buildings. One of my jobs is to upgrade the staff quarters to make them more appealing for expats who are no doubt used to a slightly higher standard."

Clara looks around the room. There is one single bed, a rundown chest of drawers and material hanging over the window to create some privacy. A little desk in the corner and a heater and a couple of glasses along with a wash basin tucked in amongst the furniture.

"Next on the tour itinerary is the ablution block. You don't get your own loo and shower, but no one is around, so you don't need to share it yet." Jack drops her bag in the room and leads her back outside.

They walk over to a slightly larger building and there are the showers and toilets and at the end of the building a small kitchen and dining room. Jack explains, "This is for the staff. Hopefully we can attract a few more maintenance guys or builders after Christmas and a couple more teachers. Pretty much everyone has gone home for Christmas, or finished here waiting for the new crew coming in the New Year. I am dying to hear what you think? But first I will show you where I am and then let's go and unpack the food and gear and then go onto the deck, the views are to die for."

Jack shows Clara his room which is a tiny house across from the kitchen with a verandah, next to a garage with an old van parked outside. They unpack and Jack starts cooking dinner. He pops open a bottle of local wine. "I shouldn't really, as this is an alcohol-free place, when the kids are here, but I guess it's okay over the holidays. There is only us here tonight. Mary and Simon are due in the next day or two. Mary texted me earlier to say that they are visiting another school over in Bhalam. Simon is an interesting Brit, but you'll find that out for yourself later."

Clara tries her phone with no luck.

"Sorry the coverage is not flash down here, but if we go up to where the lookout is, we can try a bit later." Jack serves up dinner with wine and they sit out on a small makeshift verandah.

"Cheers Clara," Jack clinks glasses with her, "It's great to have you here."

Sipping her wine tentatively, Clara's eyes go wide as the aromatic sweetness assaults her taste buds. "It's ah… wine, but not like back home!"

"True that, you get used to the honey and herb combo

though," Jack replies smiling.

It is pretty cold and they wrap up warmly and sit next to each other so Jack can share his manly body heat with Clara.

"You get skinnier each time I see you. Have you lost more weight? You may want to get some warmer clothes from town as the huts aren't insulated yet either. That's another must do on my list. We will go into the town over the next few days so we can do that, but first your thoughts. Be honest Clara. Only the truth…"

Still a little shocked and wondering what she is getting herself into, Clara pauses for a moment. She is mindful of how to respond, knowing how much the school means to Jack. She does not want to offend him. "Well again, I hate to disappoint, but I actually really dig the place. Yes, it's pretty basic in places, but what would you expect? The school is in its early stages and it's only had you for a few weeks. Even you, Superman, can't come up with too much in that time. I think it is quaint, fully functional and the views are to die for. Just look at that, you can't get much better." She gestures towards the Annapurnas.

Jack sips at his wine and looks out over the mountains taking in the fresh crisp air. "This is the perfect time of the year too, no one is around. Clara, I am a bit concerned as I don't know how you are going to survive up here? You've seen the digs. They're pretty basic. How are you going to get on walking across the dirt to the loo in the middle of the night?"

"I'll be fine. How about you stop worrying about me and let me work it out. Like you said, no one is back for a few more weeks yet, so I have plenty of time to acclimatise. There's obviously plenty to do. I don't speak the language.

I have no idea what you teach kids. And I am not exactly fit, so I will need to get back into exercise to handle the altitude and who knows, maybe one of these treks."

"Did you not do a trek when you were here last time?" Jack asks.

Sipping her wine, Clara replies in a mock British accent, "Let me tell you a story. Are we settled children?"

Jack laughs, "Go on then."

"When I was here last time, I came at the end of the season, so all the organised treks were over. I had to hire myself a Sherpa and trust him to take me on the Annapurna circuit. He was a real sleaze and it was a very bad idea."

"Really? You have my attention."

"I wasn't looking forward to the first night in the hut, and we still had some way to go, when we ran into two lovely English girls who were doing the same as me. So I told them about the sleaze and they let me join them and their Sherpa. Mr Sleaze took off and we all had a great time trying out all the different Tea Houses."

"Sounds like a lucky escape alright!" Jack exclaims, then pointing, asks, "Shall we go up to the little lookout and see if you can get any coverage. It's all a bit intermittent, but again that's half the beauty. Who wants to be in touch with the other side of the world when you have your own private world here?"

They climb to the summit leisurely and take in the view from the lookout.

"Amazing, Jack, I can see why you haven't got sick of the view yet."

Jack checks his phone. "Sorry Clara, I can't get any signal."

"No drama. I'm okay Jack, I've caught up with the

girls. I know they're safe and they know I'm safe and with you." She winks at him. "That can be another thing to do when we go into town. Besides I just want to chill and enjoy the view before it gets too dark and cold."

They stay up there for a while, half in silence and half talking. Jack can see that Clara has started to change and wonders if it is permanent.

"Tell me about the kids, here, like their ages and who are some of your favourites?" Clara turns away from the view and looks at him.

"Like I said, it's a newish school and they are slowly building up the roll. But the ages range from five upwards, girls and boys, all from Khapaudi. They have never travelled further than Pokhara, so they have led pretty sheltered lives. Most of them are good kids, but some have behavioural problems, disabilities. They come in all shapes and sizes. I don't know the kids personally, yet. But they all know that learning English will open many doors for them. So you won't find it hard to persuade them to come to class. Mary is back tomorrow so you can ask her more then."

"So what does Mary do? Besides checking in on jetlagged patients who bang their heads," Clara jests.

Jack smiles. "She does a bit of everything which is what you end up doing over here. She's the doctor, teacher, counsellor, landscaper… She can turn her hand to most things in the short time I've known her."

"Sounds like it. Do you fancy her, Jack? I think you might,"

"Mary? Hell no. She's just a really nice lady. Very kind, knowledgeable and entertaining. You should get her to tell you a few stories about her life and travels. Once she starts, she can't stop."

"So, what's Mary's story. How does a bright, vivacious good- looking woman end up here in the mountains?" asks Clara.

"I could ask you the same thing. Seriously, Clara, were things that bad back home? You know it would be good if we could talk, before the others come back. I feel we need to iron out a few things. No more surprises or secrets. What do you reckon?"

"Fair enough. Shall we start back down? It's getting a bit cold. Ok where do you want me to start, with the judge no doubt?" Clara asks.

Standing, Jack agrees, "Yes you read my mind. That would be good. Let's address the big white elephant in the room first."

"Well you know how I have been going away a lot with the Court and staying a night or two here and there around NZ. The man in question, just happened to be the one I ended up working for mostly and because there is a shortage of judges and ones who are prepared to travel. It ended up being me and him."

"And does this judge have a name, Clara?"

"Yes he does, but I don't really want to tarnish his reputation."

"But he didn't mind tarnishing yours? I mean why did you lose your job and he didn't. It takes two to tango doesn't it? Or were you portrayed as the wicked witch and he was helpless and cornered into having an affair?" Jack says with a trace of bitterness.

"He wasn't such a bad guy. I tell you it all happened over 24 hours. One minute, I have a job, my house and him, and the next I have nothing. You had left a few weeks before. All four I lost. Life is so fragile."

"Well you did deserve it, Clara. I mean, was I not enough for you? I thought we had trust, history and a future, but clearly we didn't. That's what rocked me the most. I thought we were tight and forever. We had discussed all sorts. Clearly, we hadn't talked about everything. There were the small matters of children, the judge, PTSD." Jack looks down at the ground, then realises, "Shit Clara, I feel so bad. I wasn't really there for you, was I? I mean, how could I not have known about all those things?"

"To be honest Jack, you did get a bit distant yourself. I used to tell you about my job and I would ask you a question about it later, and you had no idea, what I had been talking about. It was disheartening," Clara replies softly.

"To be fair, your job was pretty boring for the likes of me. Remember, I'm just a simple builder. I don't understand synergies, and all that government department acronym crap. You were obsessed with your job and climbing the ladder. I sometimes felt surplus to requirements, almost a fashion accessory. If I'm honest with myself, I knew you were having an affair. The signs were there, but I chose to ignore them. You know Wellington is very small and word did get around."

Feeling incredibly guilty Clara couldn't believe she had gone ahead with the affair. *What was I thinking, but evidently after what I have been through, it is kind of normal. We find it hard to trust people and commit and like to get in first and reject the other person before they reject us. But I can't tell Jack that. It makes me sound like even more of a head case and it's just a cop-out. What do I say to that?*

Slowly the words come to her. "I know Jack, I was

completely out-of-order. I have no excuses. All I can say is I am really sorry. I guess I didn't know what I had until it was too late. I hope not too late. I wouldn't jump on a plane lightly and come halfway around the world unless I was serious about us. I know it looks like I am running away from a great big mess at home, and really who could blame me after all the shite that has happened back there? However, it was all of my own making and I only have myself to blame. I'm sorry for what I did to you Jack, and I am sorry for what I did to myself."

Jack cuts in, "Clara I know you're sorry. You don't have to keep telling me. Let's play it by ear, eh? Let's just see how you get on when everyone comes back to school. I am really happy here, and don't want to up-sticks the second I get here because you have a change of heart and realise this is not for you and rush off back to New Zealand. I have to be sure you're committed in more ways than one. Clara, I've found something really special and meaningful to me here."

"I'll let you into a secret. For all those years I reckon I had got so used to conforming and being a clone and part of the system, I thought it was the norm. You know, commute to work, stay inside four walls for over eight hours, sit inside sterile meeting rooms, or take on extra work and travel with more stress, talk crap, dish out crap and then go home, get pissed, shop, eat, sleep and then do it all again the next day. Then spend the weekend catching up on sleep, partying hard, being seen in the best places, shopping and for what? Just to do it all over again the following week. And why? Just to pay off the mortgage on some poxy house on a hillside, next to a whole lot of others where everyone is doing the same thing."

His admiration is growing for her, "You're serious, aren't you? You're over that way of life now. You've seen the light."

"I have Jack. That's not who I really am, buying into other people's agendas and worldviews." Clara touches her heart. "That was just the persona I chose to show to the world. You see, I know you don't have much time for my mates, Sven and Freya, but they are like me. We have all been through heaps together and on our own. They are my only real best friends. We have always been there for each other. Quite a bit happened to us when we were overseas in the UK and Sweden. Don't get me wrong it was mostly good, but there was some real shit that went down. Especially in the Baltic States! Also for me when I was not even a teenager."

"Yes Clara, I don't want to pry but are you up to telling me everything that happened to you? Maybe one day? Not now." Jack tries to be gentle.

"I will, Jack, all I can tell you right now is what we talked about in Kathmandu, it was a family friend who everyone trusted and worshipped. They even do to this day. He used to babysit me and that's when it happened."

"Bastard!" Jack spits.

She breaks down and cries, "I'm in therapy and I'm working through this, but I've buried it for so long, and now it's like I can't stop it. Whether I want it to or not, it just keeps coming back, even stuff I had clearly forgotten." She brushes the tears away. "I still have work to do on myself. I get triggered. I hear some music, I smell something, and the events and emotions just come pouring out. Trigger, trigger, trigger. But yep, it was all those trips with the High Court, those nights away in certain towns when it first started and the triggering began."

"Oh, babe, that is so awful. I wish you'd told me?" Jack puts his arm around her shoulders.

"Because I felt dirty and cheap, like a real scrubber. I couldn't tell you and risk losing you." She realised how ironic that was.

Jack got it as well. "But guess what, babe? You did lose me anyhow. What were you thinking, jumping into bed with a judge, of all people?"

"I've always felt empty, and I thought if I raced around with some rich, prestigious judge then it would look good. I would look clever enough to attract an intelligent man. I mean, you never thought I believed that working in a glorified secretarial role was anything special. You were right. I used to love hiding behind all those terms and jargon, so my job sounded more high-flying than it actually was."

"So you slept with a judge just to massage your bruised ego?"

Clara takes a big breath. "I'm not proud of it. And you know he's not the bad one, here. I led him on I persuaded him to jump into bed with me. Yeah, of course he gave the usual lines of 'my wife doesn't understand me' first. And it no doubt felt good for his ego, playing with someone half his age. Anyhow he helped Freya with her court cases. She had a lot of red tape to get through to get Portobello and then when she got it they served an injunction on her to stop her having the keys, to stop her running a business… Oh honestly I'll tell you the whole story one day. It was really bad. If it wasn't for Martin she would now not be the proud owner and business entrepreneur of Portobello. So he served a purpose. Whoops I think I just let the cat out of the bag. His name is Martin, Martin Jacobsen."

"I did know actually. I was told who it was, but thanks for coming clean with me." He sighs, "Clara you can't use people to serve a purpose."

"I don't mean that. I am trying to justify, why I had a fling with a married man. I admit it. I was shallow and instead of facing up to stuff and going to therapy much sooner. I'm now dealing with this shit and really it's like Courtenay Place buses, they have all come at the same time and I am finding it hard to cope."

"Okay, I get that. So Clara your therapy, what are you doing about that? Should you be jet-setting halfway around the world while you're in therapy? Does your therapist know you have bolted? Who do you think you're going to see here in the Himalayas? They don't exactly have western clinics and psychology services here. It's a very poor country."

"I did think of that. But I never planned to go away forever. I just wanted to see the lay of the land with you first. I do have some medication, if I need it, and I have my journal and some CBT—Cognitive Behaviour Therapy—exercises which I do every day. I've also taken up mindfulness meditation which I'm still learning. I have my Fitbit here and Sven and I check in with each other to see who has done the most exercise each day, well when I get a Wi-Fi connection. I have my mates I can check in with, even if it is via email, but no doubt we can get Skype in town. Speaking of which, I guess I could always do a Skype call with my shrink. So, without really planning too much, I'm sure I'll be okay." Clara explains.

Jack nods. "I feel flattered that you've come all this way and I'm impressed with what I have seen and heard so far.

You have changed a lot since I last saw you. I guess I fell in love with you originally because you were so goddamn independent and so calm, cool and collected, not to mention classy. But I actually prefer this more vulnerable, real side. It's getting late and I can feel that cold mountain air, the temperature has dropped. Let's get you to your room. The gang are back tomorrow and there's a few more things I want to discuss with you before then. Besides, Doctor Mary said to keep a good eye on you and make sure you rest. You have obviously made an impression with her. Let's see if you can continue to do that, especially tomorrow when you have your interview, or should I say informal chat."

Jack uses a torch to guide them as they walk across the school compound in silence. Clara thinks, *I can't believe it I am living in the Himalayas and with Jack. I am homeless, jobless ... and I don't care. For once all that stuff means nothing.*

He opens the door to her room. "Are you going to be okay with getting to and from the bathroom? How about you use this torch for the first few nights until you get used to it? Do you mind if I come in?"

"Jack you know you don't have to ask. Of course, you can."

"I've been thinking and I really want to give us a go. I'm not saying no outright, like I wanted to at the airport. I just feel a bit responsible for your wellbeing and I don't want you staying way up here, isolated in a foreign country, unless it's where you want to be. I am just the icing on the cake, so let's see how the next few days pan out, eh?"

"Sure Jack. That's all I can ask. Believe me, I'm not in a rush. Can we go into town tomorrow? I really want to check my emails and see how the crowd are back home."

"Of course. The guys arrive late afternoon, I think, so that gives us another whole day. There are a few more things I need to do before I crash. I'll see you in the morning." He leans over quickly and kisses her on the lips, smiling, "Night, sweet one."

Her whole heart melts. "Night Jack," and she gives him a big seductive smile.

Oh my god, I'm in heaven. Man, have I missed those big lips.

As Jack walks away, thoughts race through his head, *God I wish she wouldn't look at me that way. I could so easily slip in beside her, but I'm not going to. I respect her too much. What she's told me is huge, and I am not going to take advantage of her vulnerability right now. I can wait and hold off until I am completely sure. Damn, is this too good to be true?*

While Clara lies back on her bed thinking the same, *God, is this too good to be true?*

Chapter 18

A Piece of the Puzzle

Jack walks over to Clara's room mid-morning worried as he hasn't seen her stir and is afraid something may have happened. *It's just not like her, usually she would be banging on about how the bargains in the shops are waiting.*

He breathes a sigh of relief as he sees she is awake and writing in a journal. "Good morning sleepyhead, how was your night? Were you kept awake by the wind and any strange night noises?"

Clara's face lights up seeing the concern in his eyes, "No not at all Jack. In fact, I have only just woken up about an hour ago. I felt really warm and safe. I've even done my morning meditation."

"Wow, that's great Clara!" Jack replies in amazement, and then asks, "So what's that you are writing in?"

"This is my new best friend. It's a reflective journal, it's part of the therapy I was telling you about last night. I write down all my emotions, any triggers and how I react to them all. It's this CBT thing, where I have a thought, which leads to a feeling and that leads to some action or behaviour."

"Interesting, go on," Jack prompts.

"Well, if I can see a pattern that I don't like, I can try and change it. Like the old days when I used to automatically react to something I didn't like, or suppress the feeling I was having, by downing a drink or going off on a shopping spree. By recording it, those patterns become clearer."

"Clara that is seriously impressive," Jack enthuses, "Let me see if I've got this, ah… say you are driving on the motorway and someone cuts you off, or is tailgating you, then instead of getting road rage and giving them the finger you think about it first, pause and then try a different response, like maybe putting some music on and waving at them."

"Exactly Jack, you've got it."

A look of understanding comes over his face, "Wow, imagine if everyone did that, wouldn't the world be a better place to live in?"

"It's pretty hard to change a lifetime of habitual thinking and behaviour. So it may take me a long time," Clara replies honestly.

"From where I'm standing, I've already seen a change."

Clara blushes slightly, not used to hearing positive praise, "Thanks for noticing."

Jack looks at his watch. "Have you had anything to eat? I need to get into town soon to get some more building materials."

"Yeah, sure have. I tucked into some fruit in the kitchen before my shower. I'll be ready in five." Clara closes her journal.

*****

Jack left Clara at his favourite internet café, and heads off with the school van to collect his supplies.

The friendly café owner, shows Clara around his place, pointing at a pod of computers, each in their own little cubicles. In his *pidgin* English he says, "We have lots of web available Miss, over there or you can buy the code for your laptop."

"Thanks, I'll have a code and a coffee please. Can I sit at the table by the window?"

"Yes miss, I'll be right over." The enthusiastic man beams.

Clara sits and places her tablet on the white tablecloth and looks out the window into the street. She notices the shanty-like buildings opposite, all with their brightly coloured, eclectic signage in at least two languages, all vying for the passer-by's attention.

"Here you are, Miss." The café owner places the piping hot coffee and Wi-Fi code in front of her.

"Thanks so much," Clara smiles.

She logs in and see's she has several messages in her inbox. Immediately deleting three from Bianca, she reads a couple from her friends and one from her Dad.

She decides to write a quick reply to both the girls, to keep them up-to-date:

Dear Freya and Sven

Thanks a lot for your newsy emails as usual. I am so happy that everything has worked out so well for you both.

I can't report much on the love stakes as Jack and I are still up in the air. I think he is interested, he kind of gives me that impression. It's like he looks like he is going to go in for the kill and give me a big kiss or hug and then it turns out all matey and he just wants to take one day at a time.

I think he is protecting himself after what I did to him. And fair enough.

I am trying to convince him I have changed, but to be honest sometimes it's even a bit hard for me to believe I have. I mean I have had three opportunities to go shopping, like serious shopping and I haven't really gone too mad. Once at the Auckland International Airport, and I just bought a few basic items of clothing. Then in Kathmandu the other day, just a few again, mainly practical for trekking over here and then again today as I am in Pokhara, and haven't even gone to the shops yet!

I'm just sitting here sipping on a coffee, taking it easy, is that changed behaviour, or what? I guess I am changing faster than I thought!

Anyhow I have an interview this afternoon as a volunteer English teacher. I am finally going to put my TESOL qual back into practice.

Keep me in the loop with both your relationships, I wish you guys the best!

And just to tease you. Jack kissed me last night, just the once and very quickly, so I don't know what that means yet. He seems to pretend it never happened, so far today.

I am signing off now. No internet at the school, so don't be surprised if you don't hear from me for a while.

Love me x

She feels guilty about not contacting her Dad and takes a big gulp of coffee before typing:

Hey Dad!

Sorry I haven't phoned, it's been a bit manic and the phone calls from Pokhara are a bit pricey, so it will be emails until I get back to Kathmandu.

I've heard from the girls and they are all okay, even Zita and Harry. Sabrina got a hold of me to say that Mum was on the warpath, whatever that means. When isn't she?

Jack and I are getting on okay and I've got a job interview this afternoon, English teaching at the school Jack is working at.

I'm planning on staying here to see if we can rekindle our relationship, if not, then I'm not sure. Maybe a holiday in the Coromandel to visit my Dad, if that's alright with you?

Hear from you soon
Love Gigi xo

Sitting back in her chair, she stares out the window at nothing, thinking about what visiting her Dad would be like. Getting one of his big bear hugs, well they seemed so big when she was little.

Her reverie is broken by the sound of her phone ringing, she quickly answers.

"Kia Ora Clara, you sure are hard to get a hold of, it's Charlie here," the booming voice identifies himself.

"Hey Charlie, how can I help?"

"That's what I'm phoning about. I understand you are in Pokhara?"

"That's right. No coverage where I'm staying. I'm in town today at an internet café."

"That's great, can you please go to the Tourist Police

Station in Pokhara and ask for Officer Girvesh Thapa. I've arranged for him to take an official statement from you, so we can add this to our prosecution."

"Sure Charlie. Girvesh is expecting me? I won't get locked up, due to things getting lost in translation?" Clara jests.

"Sorry if I'm not laughing Clara, this is serious. We're talking about taking down the Police Commissioner who was covering up Margaret's homicide. There are some big shots involved in this…well…this conspiracy, and everyone is running for cover and burying evidence. As soon as I get your statement, we can connect some more dots. So please don't leave out any detail, no matter if you think it's irrelevant or not. Let me decide that, okay?"

Suddenly realising the stakes, Clara gets serious, "I've got my pen and paper ready, can you please spell Girvesh's name and do you have the address…"

*****

Clara and Jack walk back to the school van, after leaving the Tourist Police station.

"Thanks for the text, Clara. I would have panicked if you hadn't been at the café when I returned," Jack admits.

"Thanks for picking me up Jack, I'm not sure how turning up to the job interview in a police car would have looked," Clara jests.

"True that! Now mind your head. You will have to get in the van from the driver's side," Jack advises.

The school van is loaded to the gunnels with building material. Lengths of timber stick out the passenger's window. Clara asks, "Is that even legal?"

"Ha-ha, it is over here. Come on get in and let's get back to the compound for your interview." Seeing Clara eyeing him sideways, Jack assures her, "Don't worry, I'm driving slowly, okay?"

Clara looks at him dubiously, "Okay then."

Changing the subject, he asks, "Now, what's the crack about this detective Charlie and a homicide?"

"You'll have to drive slowly, if I'm going to tell the whole story before we get back," Clara warns, as she climbs into the van. "Wow it was only last week, Wednesday morning when I found this little café called *Munamuna* in Wellington…" Clara begins.

*****

They drive through the school gates, and Jack shakes his head yet again. "I guess that just shows how much of a village Wellington is. What with you being around all those places and seeing what you saw. You know what, Clara James? I'm dead impressed! Oh, sorry about the bad turn of phrase there, a bit callous for Cat was it? Woops god rest her soul?" Jack apologises.

"Yeah, I guess with Sven being so close to the investigation, we'll probably find out all the in's and out's eventually."

There were two cars parked beside the school office. Clara's nervousness returns. "Oh damn, Mary's here already. I was hoping to have a quick shower and get changed!"

Sensing the change in Clara's state of mind, Jack soothes. "Don't worry Clara, you go and get ready. I'll go and stall Mary. I've got a few things to straighten out with her about the renovations she wants completed before school starts."

Clara breathed a sigh of relief. "Thanks."

"Come on, give me a quick hand with the timber then get in the shower. I can manage the rest." Jack then reassures her, "Don't be nervous you will be fine."

Clara helps Jack take in the timber which they store in the garage. She races back to her room and freshens up, thinking, *Okay here we go, Clara. You will be fine. Don't look back, it's the present that's all that matters. Breathe...*

Putting on some bright red lipstick and her new top from Kathmandu, Clara then shakes out the suit she was wearing on Monday for her last job. Thinking to herself, *I hope I'm not overdressed.*

Jack knocks at the door. "Okay are you ready? You're on. Let's go and meet everyone. It's really informal, so don't sweat. Honestly, it's just a casual chat."

They walk off across the school grounds towards the office, the sky overhead looking dark and ominous. The wind has risen and Clara absentmindedly runs her fingers through her hair noticing her stomach full of raging butterflies.

"By the way Clara, did I tell you how hot you look? That top really works with your suit, and I like what you've done with your hair, as well. It makes you look at least five years younger," Jack observes.

"Flattery like that will get you EVERYWHERE, young man," Clara laughs, "but please no more. I have to concentrate." Taking a deep breath, she thinks, *Best foot forward Clara, don't blow this one!*

Chapter 19

Stormy School Interview

Clara walks nervously into the makeshift office in a small temporary portable building. The place is packed with two desks facing each other where the occupants are seated, a filing cabinet in the corner and a small table with two plastic chairs around it. Space is at a premium, Clara thinks *nothing like getting up close and personal with your potential bosses in advance.*

Jack follows her, but stays behind outside the sliding door, "Morning Mary, and Simon welcome back to the Ritz. Simon, I would like to introduce you to Clara. Clara James, she comes with great recommendations, I'm sure you won't be disappointed. Would anyone like a cuppa to soften the serious talk that lies ahead?"

"That would be very nice, thank you, Jack. What's up with the weather?" Mary asks.

"Looks like a storm brewing." Jack ambles off to the kitchen, dodging raindrops.

"Thank you, Clara for coming all this way." Simon begins formally shaking Clara's hand, waiting for Clara to sit again before retaking his seat. Pushing his spectacles up on the bridge of his nose, he continues, "I believe you have only been in the country a few days and you have already met my colleague Mary in Kathmandu, after a nasty bump? I trust everything is okay now?"

"Yes, all good, thank you, Simon. I think it was just a combination of jet lag and a lack of sleep. But I'm all good and rearing to go." Clara replies enthusiastically, noting the elbow patches on Simons' tweed sports jacket.

"Wonderful, wonderful," Simon repeats, looking at Mary.

Mary takes over, "I see your forehead looks in much better shape. Shall we get started then? Simon, do you mind if I kick this off?"

"Wonderful, wonderful, yes please go ahead," Simon defers.

"Well Clara, I want to make it quite clear upfront that this is an unpaid job." Mary pauses, "But in return you do get accommodation and food. And a huge sense of achievement."

"Thanks Mary, Jack has warned me and explained that this is a charity. That's one of the reasons that this role attracted me," Clara explains.

"Excellent, excellent,' Simon says.

Mary looks at Simon a frown creasing her brow. Hissing through her clenched teeth, "Simon, you're doing that repeat thing again."

"Sorry, sorry. Oh, there I go again," Simon apologises.

Shaking her head, Mary turns back to Clara, "I'm glad you're aware of that. Now, what can you tell us about yourself and your skill set for this role?"

Clara nods. "Firstly, I am a qualified TESOL teacher and I have been teaching off and on for some time abroad such as in Sweden with a few businesses initially before working at the Swedish Prime Minister's Office and then part-time in Wellington at the university there." She pauses to take a breath. "For the last seven years I've had a role in the Justice sector. But I've always had a huge sense of achievement, satisfaction, purpose and enjoyment from teaching and I would like to return to it. I have come to a stage in my life, where, how I can put this delicately, where climbing the career ladder has no part in my calling any longer. I would prefer to put my time, energy and passion into something where everyone benefits, a win-win for the community."

Just then Jack walks back in with the round of coffees. He smiles to himself listening to Clara's formality. It is like listening to some old-fashioned English gentry speaking. He winks at Mary.

Mary smiles back at Jack, "Right those are very good answers Clara. Thank you." She takes a sip from the cup Jack has offered her. "Simon would you like to continue? I think I have just burnt my tongue on the coffee. Very nice, but I forgot how hot the water is here."

"Yes, yes, of course. Ok Clara, it's my turn. Now I would just like to say we are very informal here. Please talk with us freely. I understand you have worked in HR previously? Can you tell me a little about the work you have been doing and how that may compare to this role?" Simon enquires.

"Sure, yes I have worked in HR, mainly OD and Change Management, although I did start off in L & D,"

Clara replies.

Raising his hand, Simon interrupts, "Forgive me Clara you will have to translate the acronyms and jargon for me. I haven't worked in the corporate world for some time. I don't know if Jack has said anything about me, but I came to Nepal twenty years ago and I have been setting up schools and not-for-profit organisations since then. I haven't been back to Blighty for some time."

Warming to Simon, Clara could see he was trying hard to make her feel at home and relaxed. She knew she was probably appearing uptight and far too formal, but she didn't know how else to act in an interview being used to set questions of the *'tell me a time'* variety.

"Apologies, about the jargon, I guess teaching English I should know better. That's what people struggle with the most don't they? Right, so I started my career off in training, learning and development, which I got into from my teaching English qualification. Back home Learning and Development usually falls under Human Resources. I was then shoulder tapped into Organisational Development and training the senior managers. Then we outsourced most of the training to outside providers and I then moved into strategy work around what our senior leaders needed. I would do a needs analysis and then find the right people to come in and do the training themselves. I hope I have made it a bit clearer and practiced what I normally preach, and translated into Plain English, to cater for all audiences, no matter what their backgrounds are." Clara finishes on a roll.

"Yes, yes, quite. Clara, with all that knowledge and skill set, what do you suppose you could offer to our little school here?" Simon enquires.

"I believe I have a great empathy and insight into what children are thinking and, due to my creative streak and life experience, I can make the classes fun and informative. I know how to utilise lesson plans with learning objectives, but also, I can think on my feet and quickly change the activities, duration and content to suit the audience and time of the day. For example most people, especially children, feel a bit lethargic after lunch, trying to study on a full stomach, so I plan more game-based learning." Clara is confident that she's saying the right thing.

The rain gets louder as the wind picks up, Mary looks outside rhetorically asking, "What is with this weather? It's nowhere near monsoon season."

"That's in summer, isn't it?" Jack asks from behind Clara.

Clara looks around to see Jack standing right behind her, staring out the sliding door. She finds it a little off-putting as she is trying to make a good impression and can't with him standing so close to her. Clara's breath quickens its pace.

Mary senses Clara's nerves and irritation, thinking quickly she asks, "Hey Jack, maybe you might like to go and check the buildings are all closed up and leave us three to it for a little while."

Jack disappears into the worsening weather, and Clara smiles thankfully at Mary.

"Any questions for us, Clara?" Mary asks.

"Yes, I have a few. Just the usual—how big is the roll, when will the kids be back, what is the age range? Any other teachers, and how the charity is set up, but I can leave some of that until later?"

"Great questions. I'm sure most of those answers

will come out naturally as we progress. But are you still interested in the role?" Mary counters.

There is an almighty crash outside.

"Ah, if I may interrupt, ladies," Simon interjects as he stands, "I believe we should investigate that."

All eyes turn in the direction of the noise.

"Oh my god! The school house!" Mary exclaims.

"Where's Jack?" Clara frantically asks as she tears open the sliding door.

"Come on ladies, let's find out," Simon calls. Clara races outside towards the school house block. It is partially crushed under the weight of an old teak tree, blown over in the wind.

The rain soaks through her suit immediately, as Clara crosses the muddy schoolyard, yelling, "Jack! Jack! Where are you?"

With Mary close on her heels, they run as fast as they can towards the scene of devastation. Simon follows. The wind and rain lashes at them.

"Simon, check his room," Mary calls.

Clara flings open the door to the accommodation wing. "Jack, where are you?" she shouts.

"I'll try the kitchen, Clara. Don't worry, we'll find him." Mary runs off.

Clara's mind is a tangled jumble of incoherent thoughts. She looks into each room. Not finding him, she races back outside. Simon jogs with a limp towards her. He is carrying a first-aid bag. "He's not in his room."

"That leaves the class room," Clara replies, tears mixing with the pouring rain, running down her face.

Mary appears from the kitchen end of the block, "Only one place left."

As the three of them approach the crushed classroom, the door bursts open. Jack, shoulder first, falls through the opened door. He staggers to retain his balance, and looks at his friends, "What a welcoming party."

Clara throws herself into his arms, burying her face into his chest, "Oh Jack, are you okay?"

"I am now, sweet one." Jack softly murmurs, as he returns her embrace with a fierce hug.

"Thank god you're in one piece," Mary says relieved.

"Looks like we won't be needing this then," Simon comments as he hefts the first aid satchel.

"Geez, I was lucky." Jack turns to look at the damaged class room, gently patting Clara on the back. "Everything happened so fast. One minute I was closing the windows in the class room, and then I heard that sound and saw the tree falling towards me. Luckily the tree fell at the front of the class and I was near the door. Then the damn door was jammed and I couldn't get it open."

"Jack, I thought…" Clara begins, but Jack puts his finger on her lips to silence her.

"Hush now, babe. Nothing happened to me," Jack interrupts.

"May I propose that we reconvene in the kitchen, and get out of this beastly weather for a jolly good cup of tea," Simon suggests.

"Bugger the tea Simon," Mary cuts in, "we need something a bit stronger after that scare." She notices Simon's frown. "Purely for medicinal purposes, of course."

"Yes, yes, quite," Simon adds, as they hurry towards the kitchen.

*****

They gather together around the kitchen table, each with either a glass or a cup in hand, Mary is the first one to restart the stalled conversation. Waving her bottle of bourbon, she asks, "Anyone for a top up?"

"Yes please Mary, you know I think I could get use to a wee dram in my tea. It would make a splendid nightcap," Simon observes.

Clara shakes her head and Jack offers his glass, "Just a tad more thanks, Mary."

"Can I ask a question?" Clara enquires, "How will this affect the school?"

"Well, without a classroom in winter, we can't hold any classes," Mary comments.

"Jack, would you have any idea how long it would take to rebuild the classroom?" Simon asks.

"Sorry guys. That's a bit of a 'How long is a piece of string' type of question." Then thinking about it, replies, "Once this storm eases and I have a closer look, I'll have a better idea. There is the wall, a few windows and the roof which are the obvious starters. But it's the structural support that I'll need to look into further and that could take time."

"I hope we don't have to put off the start of the new term," Mary remarks, then turns to look at Clara, "Or we won't be able to hang onto our new English teacher."

"Are you serious?" Clara asks.

Picking up the cue from his colleague, Simon carries on, "Quite, quite serious Clara. We would be delighted to offer you the position. But the question remains…" Simon pauses for dramatic effect, "will you take the job?"

"Of course!" Clara leaps excitedly from her seat and spontaneously hugs Simon and Mary, "Thank you. Thank you."

"You may be waiting for some time before the class is ready," Simon advises.

"With all due respect, Simon, you can't have met many Kiwis," Clara replies.

"Why is that?" he asks.

"Because when the chips are down, that's when you know who your friends are." With a determined look in her eye, she recalls, "When Jack and I first got together, I didn't know anything about building. So he enrolled us in a night class at the local polytechnic and we completed a multi-skills course together."

"Is that a Kiwi romantic thing?" Mary asks in disbelief.

Laughing, Jack replies, "No Mary, it was because Clara didn't understand what I was doing at work and I thought it would give us a new shared experience. It came in handy when she started renovating her house, as we could do most things together. It was a great course that covered the basics of painting, electrical wiring, plumbing and building."

"You didn't mention this skill set in our interview, Clara," Simon jests.

"I'm not an expert, but I know I can help Jack," Clara beams.

"Excellent, excellent! I may be a bit slow with my gammy leg, but I can help, too."

"Well then, Jack, I'm in too, so it looks like you have yourself a building crew," Mary adds.

Looking around the room with a big grin on his face, Jack thoughtfully replies, "Thanks guys, I'm sure we'll make a great team. Can I make a suggestion?"

"What's that?" Mary asks.

"That we get out of these wet clothes and get warm. I don't want anyone pulling a sick note tomorrow," Jack laughs.

Chapter 20

Storm Aftermath and Message from Home

With the storm easing overnight, Jack was up early to inspect the damage. To his surprise, Clara was already up and in the kitchen setting out a hearty breakfast.

"Morning Jack, one egg or two?"

"Two please. You know, I could get use to this," Jack teases as he takes a seat at the table.

"Steady on, Tiger. I've set up a roster. You're on kitchen duty tomorrow," Clara fires back, pointing at the newly drawn up spreadsheet, pinned to the notice board, "That way, we can all get on the job early, fed and watered rearing to go."

Mary staggers into the kitchen wearing a brightly coloured silken kimono, her hair in complete disarray, croaking, "Coffee... I smell coffeeeee."

"Perfect timing, Mary. The percolator finished a few

minutes ago," Clara informs her brightly.

Pouring herself a cup and taking a quick mouthful, Mary sighs, "Ahhh, that's better." Turning to Jack, she asks, "Can we clone her?"

Laughing Jack replies, "Nope. They broke the mould after she came out."

Clara grins at the compliment and serves Jack his eggs and toast.

Joining in the laughter, Mary comments, "You Kiwis, I don't know how we will cope with two of you."

Simon knocks on the door as he enters, "Can anyone join this party? Or do I need an invitation?"

"Great we're all here, I'll take your order for eggs and toast in a minute. Sorry that's all I could find at short notice." Clara waves at Simon to sit at the table. "Now, if I can draw your attention to the notice board, I've rearranged it all so we have a duty roster here, and then if we have a quick toolbox meeting over breakfast, Jack can assign us the various tasks so we can get the classroom rebuilt as soon as possible."

"Did you put her up to this, Jack?" Mary asks.

Nope, I told you guys Clara is a one of a kind," Jack answers proudly.

"Nice, nice organisational skills, Clara," Simon nods admiringly, "Is this part of the management strategy skill set you mentioned yesterday?"

"Thanks, yes. Although I didn't think I'd be needing them here," Clara smiles.

"Thanks for the eggs, Clara." Jack stands, "Well team, I'll get started assessing the damage and then we had best get into town and see what's available to get the repairs underway."

"Sing out if you need a hand," Clara calls after him. "Okay Simon, Mary, would you like some eggs and toast?"

"Indeed! Indeed!" Simon replies enthusiastically.

*****

Jack drops Clara off at the internet café and heads in the school van to the building supply depot around the corner.

The friendly café owner smiles as Clara enters, "Ah, you a friend of Jack's from Khapaudi school? Welcome, I Nugah Devkota. You like coffee and web? Get special price."

"Why thank you, Nugah Did I say that right?" Clara clarifies.

"Yes, yes, here's de web, I bring coffee soon," Nugah says kindly in his pidgin English, passing her the Wi-Fi code.

Her table by the window from a couple of days ago is free. Clara takes a seat and sets herself up. She decides to write in her journal first, before checking her emails and reading the news from home.

Her writing is interrupted by Nugan, "Coffee, Miss."

"Thanks, Nugan. My name is Clara and I hope to be one of your regulars."

"Yes, good Miss Cla-ara," Nugan answers struggling with her name.

Sipping on her hot coffee, Clara thinks, *I can see myself down here a couple of times a week. Maybe with Jack sometimes. That was a close call yesterday, best email the girls.*

Firing up her tablet, she sees an email from Sven and her Mum. Opening her friend's one first, she reads:

Hey Flat White!
Both Freya and I have some exciting news to share, but we are working on a plan and dates.
So this message is a real tease for you.
Three guesses where we, including Zac and Charlie, will be for New Year's Eve?
Your one hint - Skål!
Now what are your guesses?
Love Sven xx

Sitting back in her chair, Clara thinks staring into space while sipping her coffee. *Skål could mean anything. Geez we always end up over indulging when we all get together. The last plans were to go to Waitarere. What else has changed? They wouldn't be going overseas, not with Freya's business taking off. So must be somewhere different to our old plan...*

Hitting the reply arrow on Sven's email, Clara types:

Hey Sven,
Here's my guesses:
Waitarere – the old plan
The Swedish High Commission – you have somehow managed an invitation, you Jammy Spoon or
Portobello – Freya is hosting a Scandi themed New Year's Eve party?
Have fun!
News from here, Jack and I are taking it one day at a time, but I'm hopeful.
We had a storm yesterday and a tree fell on the

classroom nearly crushing Jack, a very close call. Only damage was the classroom, not Jack! While I was having my job interview, which I got! So I'm the new TESOL teacher here.

School won't start back until we get the classroom fixed which could be some time, Jack's working out the details today.

Catch up soon!
Love Flat White xo

Taking a deep breath, Clara opens the email from her Mother:

Dear Clara
I am very busy with Christmas approaching fast but wanted to take the time to write to you.

I have some very sad news and I think you should be sad as well. I know you made those awful unspeakable accusations about him which really are unforgiveable, but I think you will be sorry for such words.

You really do have a vivid imagination. That has always brought our family into disrepute.

But Fred, my dear Fred Elliot has died.

I only heard about it yesterday and I am absolutely devastated.

I am trying to get hold of your father to let him know but he is as unreliable as you and I can't get hold of him. He is obviously having another senior moment and has run off with yet another floozy to the Islands or somewhere equally as crazy. Wherever it is that middle-age men escape to instead of facing up to their responsibilities back here?

Speaking of which what on earth are you doing on the other side of the world at this time of year! It is freezing cold over there and here it is lovely and warm. Why would you want to escape the New Zealand summer?

You should be here working to support your poor aging mother and trying to settle down with a reputable man like a lawyer or accountant, none of the Blue Collar riff-raff you seem to be attracted to.

Anyhow, I thought you should know about Fred's death. The funeral directors are awfully busy at this time of year. You know a lot of elderly drop off due to the summer heat, but they have been kind enough to squeeze in the cremation before Christmas.

I want you to come home and represent the family at his funeral.

Obviously we can't make it back from the Bay of Islands in time, so you will have to fly home.

I'm sure it would mean a lot to his family and may make up for those nasty accusations you made.

Kind regards,
Mother

Clara sits in a state of shock, her mouth ajar and her mind a whirl. She re-reads the email to make sure she understood her mother's toxic words. *Fred Elliot, the wanker is dead. The big family man, the big business man, the loving husband, the adorable father, the big man around town is dead. The pig who raped me is dead.*

Needing to find out how he died Clara types his name into the search engine to find his obituary:

Frederick Olsen Elliot (FOE), died at his home surrounded by his loving wife and family... he had only suffered for a short time. Please all donations and flowers to the Cancer Society...

Suddenly the intense hatred she felt for the man melted and she felt sorry for him, *Oh does that mean he died of cancer? Did he suffer? I wonder what sort of cancer?*

Thinking back to her last encounter with him, *Oh, was he leaving the specialist when I saw him? Was he wanting to apologise to me? Am I bad for running away?*

Breathing faster and shallower, Clara feels an anxiety attack brewing. She can't sit any longer. She unexpectedly starts to cry and can't stop, as all the memories pour through her, the past triggering. *Oh my god I am going to have a panic attack, I need to get out of here.*

Before she has time to log off, or gather her things, she runs blindly out into the street. Looking frantically left then right she starts towards the Building Supply yard, but stops to lean against the side of the building, her mind racing.

Oh my god he's dead. What does that mean? He wasn't really that bad was he? Did I make him do what he did to me? Could I have stopped it? Did I lead him on? Was it all my fault as usual?

All these questions go through her mind. Clara feels an intense sadness and doubts herself.

Am I really that bad person my mother portrays? Shit, did me coming out with what he did all those years ago, did it create the cancer? Am I the reason he died? Shit, everything I do is bad everything I do turns to custard. What the fuck am I doing here?

Going into an absolute meltdown, Clara starts hyperventilating. She can't breathe. She can't see, oblivious to everything around her.

As the school van pulls up outside the café, Jack sees Clara bent over, hyperventilating. Suspecting a panic attack, he leaps from the van, calling her name, "Clara, Clara, it's me. It's okay, babe. Hang in there."

Clara looks around wildly, not seeing Jack approaching.

Walking in front of her so she can see it's him, Jack calls gently, "Clara, Clara it's okay. Listen to me. Breathe, just breathe, take a deep breath. Nothing else matters, explain later, just breathe."

He sits her down against the shop wall and waves the gathering spectators away. "It's okay, it's okay, I've got this. It's all okay."

Burying her face into his chest, Clara can't see who he is talking to and assumes he is talking to her. Just listening to his gentle voice makes her feel less stressed. But she is in self-blame mode and can't help the intense raw emotions she is feeling.

Jack says softly, "Tell me when you're ready, but just breathe deeply for now. It's all okay, I've got you and I'm not letting go of you. We are not going anywhere. Just breathe."

She gasps, struggling to find her voice, "He's dead. The wanker is dead," Clara sobs, "and it's all my fault."

"What wanker? Who's dead? Okay that's enough no need to talk. We can talk later. Where's your tablet and bag?"

Just then he looks up and sees Nugan, the smiley Internet Café owner outside with Clara's gear under his arm. Jack yells out, "Over here Nugan, mate. I'll be there in a minute to settle the bill."

Walking over to them, Nugan replies, "No need Mr Jack, Miss Cla-ara good customer. She okay?"

"Thanks Nugan, I think she will be soon." Jack takes Clara's bag from Nugan. He picks Clara up in his arms and carries her to the van thinking, *Shit she's been through enough, hasn't she been through enough? Why is there something always coming up to bite her on the bum. Getting sucked in by the agent to sell her house overnight, losing her job because of an affair, then getting bullied at her new job, having a fall the other night in the hotel room, me walking out on her weeks ago and not understanding why she behaves the way she does. Then the wanker I suspect who causes all this goes and dies. How the hell did she find this out?*

While he soothes her in the van, driving back to the compound, Jack slowly realises that he does love her, not only that, but he is in love with her and wants to spend the rest of his life with her.

He has been putting his own raw emotions of rejection in the way, and not wanting to risk getting shat on again. But now he realises that life is far too short to be putting his love on hold anymore. He has to tell her. Now is not the time, though. Why should she have to jump through hoops and prove to him that she is the real deal, that she is staying on at Pokhara. *Hasn't she had to prove herself all her life to her mother? To the father who abandoned her, to every employer, that she's good enough? I am going to tell her what I truly feel later, but for now, I need to get her home. Shit, why wasn't I here for her sooner, why couldn't she have opened up to me back in Wellington. I just hope she is okay enough to stay over here while she is going through all this PTSD stuff.*

Clara's cries turn into sobs and her breathing starts to sound regular. Looking vulnerable, she looks up. "Jack thanks so much for being here for me. I don't know what I would do without you."

"It's okay, Clara, really it's okay."

"I am so sorry for this little performance," Clara pauses, takes a deep breath and continues, "My bloody mother just sent me an email to tell me that Fred Fucking Elliot has died and I should come home for the funeral and I should feel bad about what I had said about him …"

"With all due respect to your mother, Clara, she needs to feel bad about her words, her actions. But don't stop me there. I'm not going to waste my time and energy on that woman. That's for another time, but she has a lot to answer for. Right now the most important thing is for you to rate yourself enough, to look after yourself first and foremost."

"Thanks Jack," Clara replies, "That's a tall order after my upbringing."

On a roll, Jack continues, "Look Clara, I would suggest that any further correspondence from your mother, you forward to me to deal with before you open up and read any more manipulative, controlling emails from her."

"I'll think about that one. I feel I need to be able to deal with her by myself, but maybe for a little while."

Halfway around the lake on their way home, Jack stops the school van. "Clara can I have a few words with you, if you don't mind?"

She looks at him worriedly. He sounds very formal. *Where is this going, oh god, is he going to send me packing back home?*

Seeing the panic returning to her face, Jack reassures

her, "No, sweet one. Don't be alarmed, it's all good. Look this is one of my favourite places. I have been coming to this look-out for the last few weeks and always wanted to share it with someone special and now I get to. So jump out and let's stretch our legs."

The two of them stand side-by-side, arms around each other's waists as they admire the view. "I'm so sorry I don't think I knew the extent of what you have been through until today. To be honest I don't know much about PTSD. But whatever happens, Clara, I want you to know that you are not alone. I think that that's half the problem, you have felt so alone that you had to combat everything by yourself. Well no longer, babe. I'm here. You have a new home, a new job, a new life. Clara, you have a true friend in me and while I'm around you will never be alone again? Do you understand? I will never let you down again?"

Speechless for the second time today Clara clarifies, "Are you really here for me? Do I not have to prove to you that I am here for the right reasons?"

"No, sweet one, you don't and I'm sorry being yet another person you had to prove yourself to. I know who you are, as you keep showing me time after time, and I know this one thing too…"

Blinking back tears, Clara asks, "And what's that, Jack Fenton?"

Jack places his hand on her heart, answers her question, "I know that you love me, and I love you."

Grabbing a fist full of his shirt, Clara pulls him in for a kiss.

Chapter 21

A Sense of Community

Overwhelmed with their feelings for each other, Clara and Jack stay at the lookout soaking up the view across Lake Phewa towards the mountains. They watch the early stars appear in the night sky. The teahouses lose their bright colours as the night darkens. They talk about their past, and possible futures, until Jack takes them back to the compound before it gets too cold.

Only having had a couple of panic attacks before, Clara knows that they really do knock the stuffing out of her. Anxious to make a great impression at her first day at work, unlike her last job in Wellington, she hits the sack early.

She sleeps soundly for the first half of the evening, but Clara wakes early in a hot sweat. She was having a weird nightmare about Fred Elliot.

What the fuck! Why can't I get him out of my mind?

She tries to go back to sleep and no matter how much mind-over-matter and how many positive affirmations she runs through her head, nothing works. Frustrated, she fumbles for the torch, gets up barefooted and quietly creeps over to the meditation room to meditate in the early morning darkness.

Feeling calmer, she returns to her room and collects her practical work clothes, before heading over to the shower block, for a hot shower to warm up.

To keep herself busy, she decides to do Jack's kitchen roster, and heads for the kitchen where she starts the breakfast preparation. She elects to make a pot of tea, to wean herself off all the coffee she has been living on lately. *Maybe the coffee triggered the panic attack. At least it wouldn't have helped.*

Just then a rumpled, kimono-clad Mary shuffles in, "Good morning Clara. Is the coffee on? I don't smell it."

"I can put one on, or there is a pot of tea ready now?"

"Tea, thanks. Isn't Jack meant to be on duty this morning?"

The door opens again, and this time Jack appears, "Hey where've you been? I came over to your room to wake you up for meditation and you weren't there? Have you forgotten already?"

"No, I haven't. I couldn't sleep so I got up early, meditated, and started YOUR kitchen duties. What about you? Skiving around at this time of the day?" Clara ribs.

Jack laughs, "Yep, you've got me there. Hasn't she, Mary?"

"You Kiwis are far too much first thing in the morning. A girl hasn't even had her first cuppa!" Mary runs her fingers through her unruly hair, "I must have a shower to wake up. Jack, I'll have one egg sunny side up when I get back, thanks."

Handing the egg slice to Jack, Clara orders, "I'll have two eggs on toast, thanks, and you can cook your own..."

"I was waiting for the *Once Were Warriors* line," Jack grins.

Simon limps in, takes a seat and pours himself a cup of tea, "Jolly good! Jolly good! A proper pot of tea. Wonders will never cease. How are we all this fine morning?"

"Great thanks, Simon," Clara replies. "I'm looking forward to getting stuck in today."

"Capital, capital. After that beastly storm, the weather has turned out rather well, hasn't it?" Simon observes over his tea cup.

"Any eggs today, Simon?" asks Jack.

Clara sits back and watches the growing camaraderie, chipping in a comment or two enjoying the light byplay between her new working family.

*****

The sound of a chainsaw pierces the silent mountain air, as Jack starts to dismantle the fallen teak tree piece-by-piece. Clara stands back with Mary and Simon, waiting for the signal to come in and clear the sawn debris away.

An hour later, a group of locals appear at the compound gates, waving to Simon, who hobbles over to investigate.

Dragging a large branch out with Mary, Clara sees Simon in discussion with the locals, and then they all approach the school room.

Clara calls to Jack, "Looks like we have company. Must be time for a break."

When they were all together, Simon explains, "This is Shekhar, the village Headman, and a few of the men they can spare from the fields. They have offered their assistance."

"Namaste, thank you Shekhar," Mary says with gratitude.

"We really appreciate it."

"That's our pleasure, Miss Mary. Our speaking English not so good, but we understand okay," Shekhar replies.

"Fantastic!" Jack enthuses. "Look Shekhar, if we can get a couple of your men to help me with the tree removal and maybe some of the team can start cleaning the broken furniture out of the class and take what's repairable over to the maintenance shed... Clara can show them where… that would be a great start."

Shekhar turns to his men and in rapid-fire Nepali, he directs the seven men to help.

After a solid morning's work, most of the clearance is completed. Mary and Simon, on kitchen duties, make a large pot of *kwati daal,* lentil stew, for lunch.

With everyone sitting around the outside of the kitchen, bowl in hand, enjoying lunch, Simon stands to address them.

"I say, I say, Shekhar, Prasad, Nimral, Yuki, Ram Bar, Kush, Milan and of course Krishna, we can't thank you enough for helping us today. Your contribution has been extremely valuable. By Jove, what with my gammy leg, we would still be cleaning up in a month's time, leaving us all in a terrible bind! What!" He pauses before continuing, "So we deeply thank you all and will reciprocate when you are in need. *Dhanyabad.*"

Shekhar rises, translating Simon's speech into Nepali, before turning to Simon. "*Dhanyabad* Simon, this is our gift to you for the village school, *dhanyabad.*"

Mary has a tear in her eye, she leans in whispering to Clara to explain, "*Dhanyabad* means thank you, and this is truly a huge gift of so much labour to us, as the village survives mostly on subsistence farming."

"A real community all helping each other." Clara smiles. "I'm so glad to be a part of this."

As each man finishes his lunch, they stack the bowls by the kitchen door, bow and wave before heading back to their homes and farms.

The team clean up the dishes and Jack says, "Well guys, as Simon said, they have saved us so much time. I'll check for structural issues this afternoon, and perhaps get a proper timeline from there."

"Do you need a hand with that?" Clara offers.

"No thanks. You guys have all worked so hard." Jack grins at them. "You deserve the afternoon off."

*****

In the late afternoon Jack searches many different nooks and crannies around the compound looking for Clara. He finds her in her new secret spot. "Is there room for two of us?"

"Sure. How do the structural repairs look? I'm just doing my journal and reflecting on stuff I wrote when I wasn't in such a good space."

Slipping in beside her, Jack snakes his arm around her waist, he gives her a quick peck on the cheek. "Repairs are not so good. It will depend on how long it takes to get the materials shipped up from Kathmandu. The windows will be the hardest part, getting the double glazing at this time of year. There could be a bit of a delay, at least two to three weeks."

"Have you told the others?" Clara asks.

"Yeah, poor Mary is a bit down about it, but Simon is trying an old contact of his in Muzaffarpur in India. We'll be able to board up the windows once the roof is repaired, but it will be cold and Mary isn't keen to open the school back up until the class room is fully restored."

"That's such a shame. Look, I know its early days, but I really love it here. It just makes my old life seem so meaningless. I can see me sticking around for quite a while," Clara predicts, as she snuggles into his chest.

"Good. You know we are not meant to drink on site here, but do you fancy putting on your new rags and heading into town? I think we have a lot to celebrate. You being here, with a job and loving it," Jack invites, then teases, "Oh, and of course us."

"Hmm a date? Sure thing, give me half an hour and I'll be ready," Clara smiles.

"Great, I'll meet you over at the kitchen."

Clara excitedly gets ready and after a few false starts, puts on her new bright purple harem pants – referred to as 'shit catchers' and a tight black top, bit of lippie and eye liner for old time sake, a squirt of perfume and heads on over with her bag and lightweight leather jacket slung over her shoulder.

"Wow, look at you. You are definitely ready to go. I have a surprise for you. I bought her two weeks back. Come have a look. I mean someone as classy as you can't keep cruising around in a school van," Jack teases.

"Flattery will always get you somewhere." Clara winks as she admires Jack from the corner of her eye, in his slim fitting jeans, black T-shirt and black biker's jacket.

They walk over to one of the many sheds and there is Jack's pride and joy stored away under a tarpaulin. He rips off the tarpaulin, revealing a bright red motor cycle. "Look at this. What do you think?"

"Wicked Jack! It's not a Harley Davidson. But very stylish," Clara comments enthusiastically.

"It's a 1961 Royal Enfield Super Meteor, a real beauty," Jack says proudly.

"Looks like I've got some competition," Clara ribs.

"You might yet," Jack winks at her smiling.

"Motorbikes are my favourite mode of transport. How did you know? You never had a bike in Wellywood?"

"Oh, a certain girl I know used to almost purr with excitement when a Harley would pass us in the car."

"I did not, did I?"

"Yes, you sure did," Jack laughs, before continuing, "Just imagine the adventures and places we'll be able to visit on this beast. Where does a certain young Kiwi girl fancy going for her Christmas holidays?"

"I don't care Jack as long as it is with you. I feel safe with you, so the sky's the limit. Surprise me, you set the itinerary," Clara ventures.

"Let's pop into town and see if we can find your old favourite haunts and make a plan. We'll do a bucket-list. What were those places you never saw last time that you want to see this time? Or which places did you love so much you want to return, but this time with me?" Jack asks.

Straddling the bike, Jack kick starts the engine into life, revving the Enfield as he backs her out.

The engine is throbbing and so is Clara. She can't wait to get on the back and push her body, firm and hard, against his. With an hour's daylight left, Jack puts Clara's helmet on for her and gives her his warm leather jacket to wear and they tear off down the hill. Clara thinks to herself, *I'm safe I've never felt safer. Life couldn't be better.*

The engine pulses as they sway to and fro with the corners down into the night life that awaits them below.

Chapter 22

Picnic and Party

Pulling the Enfield into the lookout, Jack parks his bike near the shore line. He produces a picnic blanket from his saddlebag for them to relax on, while taking in the spectacular view.

"Jack, you are a true romantic at heart. What other plans does my man of many talents have?" Clara hugs him.

"I thought going out on the town would be fun, but we can boogie the night away later. For now I want to look after you. I know you eat like a sparrow, and I know you don't dress for the weather, so I thought I would take it on myself to bring down these few extras. I hid them away in my saddlebags."

Wrapped up warm Clara sprawls out on a rug while Jack produces a simple romantic dinner of cooked chicken and salad, plus another rug to wrap up in, woollen mittens, hat and scarf.

Seeing all the effort he has gone to, Clara gets emotional

and unexpectedly starts crying.

"Hey, babe what's up? I thought this is what you wanted. A bit of romance." Jack reaches over and dries her tears for her.

Between sobs, Clara replies, "Of course I do, Jack. I'm just overwhelmed. I had almost given up hope for you and me. It seems too good to be true. Me here, back in Pokhara with you and with a dream job. I guess even for me things have happened so fast, my mind sometimes is still back in the dramas in Wellington."

"I get that Clara. You were there only a week ago. And so much has happened since. All the shit and trauma you have had to put up with. Not only recently, but basically for your whole life. Your family, work, everything. But we're not going to talk about it now. Tonight, is for now. We are living in the present. Okay? Now, help me dish this out. Show me your cuisine skills and posh this up. Make it look like we are dining in style."

"Everything about you and what you do is style, Jack. It just took me a few bad choices to realise that. But I'm never making the same mistakes again. This feels so right. Okay, I will do the kai. You do the wine."

"Deal," and Jack pops the small bottle of local Dandaghere red wine and pours it evenly into two plastic goblets. Clara decorates the plates and folds the napkins in a fancy fan shape style and presents them on the rug.

Jack gives her a goblet of the spicy sweet wine and gets on his knees to propose a toast. He looks deeply into her eyes, "Here's to the love of my life, Clara James, and the rest of our lives together."

Clara, taken aback, is not sure where this is going. She keeps her cool while she sips her wine, nods her approval and proposes her own toast. "I second that, and many more romantic, spontaneous rendezvous like this one. Maybe in other faraway places as well."

"Be careful what you ask for, Clara, you may just get it," Jack warns.

They fall silent and with their arms around each other look into the distance at the setting sun.

"I have a confession to make," Clara says finally.

Jack looks solemn and slightly disappointed. He jumps to conclusions, thinking *Oh no, not again, I thought all that stuff was behind us. What now?*

"Please don't think the worst of me. But last night I had a nightmare about Fred, and I realise that this PTSD may take a while to work through. I guess what I'm trying to say, is that I know what I want, which is you, but I may be a bit up and down at times. Oh, this isn't coming out right," Clara says frustrated.

"Take your time. I'm listening."

"Thanks, I know I can keep it together most of the time, but if I get triggered, I might need some support. I know it's a big ask, but can you be that support for me?" Clara asks.

"Clara, please listen. I want you to get this," Jack starts. "I know very little about therapy, but I suspect that as long as you are looking after yourself, which you are doing in the main, with all that exercise, meditation and reflection stuff you do, you will get better. Also I think getting into the teaching will be good for you."

"Thanks, I have to say I am a lot happier now, than I have been in a long time. I'm actually quite proud of myself. Especially the way I got on the plane and came over. I just knew it was the right thing to do."

"I'm really proud of you, as well. I notice you're not pushing back that wine as quickly as you normally would, either. Can't you see how much you're growing?"

There is silence for a few minutes and Clara looks at Jack closely. He looks like he has something on his mind, but is finding it hard to articulate it.

She puts her hand on his. "Jack a penny for your thoughts?"

"Yep, well, I've got a mad idea. You know how it's likely with the delays for roofing and windows, that the school will be closed for at least a few weeks, maybe even a couple of months. Once the term actually starts we will be right into it, so there will be no time to cruise around."

"What are you suggesting?"

"I think we'll have a few weeks up our sleeves before the double-glaze windows are even close to being ready. Is there anywhere in particular you would like to go while up in these parts of the woods?" Jack nods towards his bike.

"Of course, you know how much I've missed travelling. I mean being back in Wellington was great, but we are so isolated, and it takes so long to get anywhere. Once you get halfway around the world, there are so many options. So, what are you thinking, Jack? Here in Nepal?"

"No, I wasn't actually. I was thinking further afield. Somewhere you know, quite well and it's pretty at this time of year especially with the snow and lights and celebrations," Jack ventures.

"Snow, must be northern hemisphere, but could be anywhere. Come on give me a clue..."

"Okay a clue... Somewhere, I've never been but, you have..."

With excitement brewing, Clara replies, "Yes, I think I

know where you mean…, did you want to give one more clue so I don't make a dick of myself when I scream out what I think it is?"

Jack breaking into song, sings, "Dancing Queen, feel the beat…"

Clara cuts him off with a scream of joy, "Sweden! You want to go to Sweden!"

Rubbing his ear, Jack replies, "Remind me not to be too close when I surprise you. That was loud!"

"Oh Jack, *God Jul* with our dear friend *Tomten*, rolling in the snow, drinking lots of schnapps, mulled wine, seeing old friends…" an excited Clara reels off a list.

"Why not, babe, I'd love to see the northern lights and get to experience the place with you. Then I can understand your stories better."

"Oh my god, you aren't joking. A white Christmas in Sweden, Oh Jack that would be *jättebra*." She gives him a big hug. "I would love that so much."

"I thought you would. It's not that far, well it is, but not as far as from New Zealand. I've had a quick look at flights. If you like we could go via India. The flights are dead cheap, even though it is very last minute. What do you reckon?" Jack asks.

"I say book it. Yay! Let's book it now. How long can we go for?"

"To make it worthwhile say… two… maybe three weeks, I've already had a chat with Mary when I broke the news about the repair delay and she's okay with it."

"This is so exciting!" Clara exclaims, "Okay, okay… so tomorrow. Can we pop into town tomorrow and check it out? I can't wait to email all my old Swedish friends. Mind you, it is Christmas so they may be away with families. Speaking of which, where are you planning to have Christmas? In Stockholm, or somewhere else, and who with?"

"With you, of course! So anywhere you choose."

"We fly into Stockholm anyhow, so we could have a few nights there, see the sights and catch up with the crew who are still around. And then fly up north to *Umeå* and maybe stay at my friend Elisabeth's place, a sweet little summer house. Does that sound cool?"

"It does in a summer house…" Jack replies quizzically.

"Don't worry, most summer houses are well insulated these days," Clara reassures him.

"Sounds perfect then, it's settled!" Jack laughs seeing Clara's excitement.

Clara is so thrilled and so cold she starts dancing around the picnic rug pretending she is at Midsummer in Sweden and is dancing in a circle around the Maypole.

"Right young lady, it's definitely far too cold to be outside now. Are you still up for checking out one of the night clubs for a bit of a boogie before we head home?"

"You're not getting out of dancing tonight, Jack Fenton. Come on!"

Clara pinches herself, everything feels surreal. They rug up jump on the bike and head off to a local club to boogie the night away.

*****

One of Clara's old night clubs is still open, and they enjoy the music and dancing in the party room upstairs. Occasionally they retreat to the relative quiet of the bar below, for a drink and to make more plans.

Clara dashes off an email on her phone to her Swedish friend Elisabeth to ask what her plans are and they carry on the holiday planning between dances.

Just before midnight Jack pretends he has been in the toilet, but has quietly seen the DJ and made a request.

As the DJ announces the last song for the night, Jack stands and asks, "Would you make a man very happy and have this last waltz with me?"

As the tune of *Dancing Queen* comes through the speakers, Jack acts surprised, "What a coincidence!"

Clara laughs and joins him on the dance floor. "Coincidence indeed, you little trickster!"

Most of the crowd have left the floor as the song is too old for them to know it, although a few Australian tourists are doing the dance actions while mouthing to the lyrics.

In the middle of the floor, it is just Clara and Jack waltzing away the last of the night together. She whispers in his ear, "It's almost midnight Jack, I turn into a pumpkin then, so best you take me home."

They finish their waltz and grab their gear from the cloak room, putting their helmets on, before tearing off into the night back up the hill. Clara is so happy she is crying, tears are streaming down her face, freezing on her cheeks in the cold night air. She has always felt so safe in Jack's arms and especially with her arms around him on the bike. *Life is perfect, I don't know how it could get any better.*

Jack pulls into the lookout on the way home, and shuts the engine down. He turns to Clara and says, "Clara, I have one more surprise for you."

The excitement builds again, as she dismounts from the bike and undoes the helmet. "Okay, I'm ready and waiting. I don't think you could shock me or surprise me anymore, so go for it.”

Jack hangs both their helmets over the rear-view mirrors, then taking her hand leads her towards the lake.

“We’re not going swimming, are we?” Clara asks in disbelief.

“Clara, I love you. I trust you. I now know I want to be with you. In fact I want to be with you forever. It doesn’t matter to me that you can’t have children. It doesn’t matter to me what’s happened in the past. All I’m concerned about now is the present and our future together…” Jack begins.

Clara is nervous, she is not sure where this is going. “I’m sorry Jack, what are you…”

He puts his finger on her lips and responds, “Shh sweet one, it’s okay. It’s you that’s important; I didn’t realise how much I loved you until you came to Nepal. When you had that accident in Kathmandu, when you had that anxiety attack in Pokhara and when I saw you mucking in yesterday, hefting timber and everything. They were all turning points for me. This is taking longer than I thought, but I’ve been in denial.” He pauses to take a breath. “It’s so much easier to suck it up, and just be angry. I was angry with you, but the reason I felt so angry and betrayed was because of how much I loved you.”

Seeing the look of disbelief in her eyes, Jack goes on, “Yes I loved you back home, but here I have seen another side of you. The real Clara and I’m so proud of you, and I’m so in love with you. Clara…”

“Yes...” She is now focused completely on Jack.

Jack turns and points to the full moon sitting high over the mountains, lighting her face in its glow.

Jack gets down onto one knee and takes her hand in his. “Clara, Clara James, will you marry me?”

There is silence, yet again, as Clara says nothing. She is overcome with emotion, kneeling down to meet him, she finally replies, "Of course I will Jack. I would love to be Mrs Clara Fenton."

With the biggest grin on his face, Jack fumbles for a moment with his jeans pocket, and out comes a small three-gold Russian wedding ring which he slips onto her ring finger.

Jack stands and lifts her tiny frame off the ground and whirls her around. "Thank you, Clara, thank you. You have made me the happiest man in the world." He placed her back down on the ground. "Don't go anywhere. Stay there, I'll be back."

He returns rapidly with the same two wine goblets and the half empty bottle of wine, and picnic rug over his shoulder, "I think a glass is in order for this special occasion." Spreading the rug on the ground, they sip their wine, arms around each other and take in the spectacular starry view.

Clara is the first to speak, "I can't wait to tell the girls. Do we tell anyone here? I want to get on my phone now. It's 1.30 in the morning so it's almost 9am back home. The girls will be awake. I want to ring them."

"I think that's a grand idea, but I hate to be the party pooper. I think we both need sleep," Jack tries to be responsible.

Thinking briefly, Clara agrees, "Yeah, you're right of course, and we want to get up early tomorrow and check out flights to Sweden."

"Besides your mates might be in boring meetings and it would be awful to have to leave such good news as a message. Wait until their evening and catch them then,"

Jack suggests.

"Hey Jack, I just clicked. Do we have an engagement party here?" Clara asks.

"What do you want? Do you want to wait? Do you want to ring your mum? Have it in NZ?" Jack offers.

"My mother wouldn't even care. She would be too busy to cancel her hectic schedule to attend her daughter's wedding. I mean it's hard enough for her to come into Wellington from her retirement village, let alone fly to Kathmandu!"

"Why wait then? Do you want to skip the engagement and go straight to the wedding?"

Clara is so excited she can't take in all the options. "A wedding, an engagement, or both, maybe in Sweden?"

"Up to you to decide. That will give you something to think about overnight, won't it? Come on let's get back to the compound," Jack suggests.

An excited Clara keeps talking as they approach the bike. "Wedding plans, I'm not sure if we could organise a wedding so quickly in Sweden. But let's see what tomorrow and a couple of emails and phone calls bring."

"One last request." Jack stops when they reach the bike. "Now we are officially engaged will you come back to mine and stay the night?"

"Of course I will! Oh, I love the ring, Jack. I remember you looking for rings for me back in Wellington. That was very clever, the way you subtly got the size of my finger that day. You obviously never forgot that I love Russian wedding rings," Clara recalls.

They jump back onto the bike and make their way back to the compound, *my new home with my fiancé, can it get better than this?*

Chapter 23

Plans and Distractions

Jack is the first to be woken by the soft tapping at the door. It is Mary. She looks serious, so Jack decides to leave Clara to sleep and walks outside with her.

"Morning Mary, what's up?"

"I've just been into town to collect some supplies and I have a telegram for you. It looks serious, have you checked your email?"

"No. I can't get signal up here."

"Read the telegram. Let's go to the office. My laptop can get a faint signal from there," Mary encourages.

Jack opens the telegram. It reads:

JACK FENTON STOP
URGENT FAMILY DISASTER STOP
READ EMAIL STOP
SEND CLARA HOME SOONEST STOP
MAUDE JAMES END

"I can see why you woke me," Jack comments as they enter the office.

"Here Jack, log into your webmail account," Mary is concerned, offering her laptop.

Jack takes a seat and logs in, worried that he may have to break some bad news to Clara.

"How was your date last night?" Mary tries to break the sullen mood creeping over them.

"It went really well," Jack brightens, as he waits for the webmail to load. "I asked Clara to marry me and she said yes."

"Well congratulations! I hope this family thing isn't too bad. What a rollercoaster for Clara."

"Ah here it is," Jack says, before reading:

Dear Jack

I trust this will find you happy and well. I am sorry to write with such devastating news, but it's Clara's father, Frank. He has taken a turn for the worse. I didn't want to trouble you or Clara, but for some time now he has been very poorly.

As you know I am separated from Frank and due to no fault of my own. Clara I am afraid has inherited her father's genes, he is very stubborn and very impulsive and hasn't taken good care of himself since we separated. As a result, he was admitted to hospital and is now in critical care. The doctors say it does not look good.

*Clara should come home **immediately**. I don't think he will last until Christmas.*

Besides, Clara should never have gone to Nepal especially at this time of the year. Clara's sister and I are bearing up but we would appreciate all the support we can get right now.

Of course, this is most inconvenient. We are up in the Bay Of Islands and have only just started our holidays. While Frank is down in Palmerston North hospital. So, it would mean we would have to break our holidays early and I hate to think what the price of the airfares will be at this time of the year.

If Clara hadn't gone away so quickly, she could have represented the family in our absence. I mean she is her father's daughter and she has more in common with her father than Sabrina and I do.

You know how temperamental Clara is and I felt it was best to let you know this as I hate to think how Clara will over-react to this.

I am in two minds I am not sure if he is looking for attention or if this is the real deal this time. He's been threatening to kill himself for years. I think it's just attention he needs but we can't risk this.

I do appreciate your time Jack, I have faith in the way you will handle this. I am sure Clara won't have enough money to fly home, and I don't have any spare cash either. Frank hardly left me with any money after he ran off with his floozy. I really appreciate you delivering this message. I'm feeling pretty helpless nowadays, I think old age is creeping up on me but I know you have our family's interest at heart, so thank you in anticipation. Please send Clara home as soon as possible.

Best regards, Maude James

Jack sits in pensive mood, "Oh my god the cheek of

that woman. She is one heartless cold bitch. No wonder Frank traded her in for someone else. Mary, come and have a read."

He watches while Mary reads the email. "I don't know how he put up with her for so long. Clara told me that Frank left Maude over half his money and the whole house, but she still sued him for more. But more importantly how I am going to break this to Clara and not now. She's been through enough. God her mother is such a piece of work," Jack says with frustration.

Taking a moment to read the email, Mary sits back, "This doesn't stack up Jack."

"What do you mean, Mary?"

Thinking for a moment, Mary replies, "Jack, I wouldn't bother Clara with this until you have confirmed with the hospital in New Zealand what the actual story is. There are far too many inconsistencies in this message. From what both you and Clara have said about her mother, it sounds exactly like my ex's mother. She suffers from DNP or Destructive Narcissistic Parent syndrome and it looks like Clara's mother does too. There is clear evidence of that in that email. Please contact that hospital, talk to Frank if you can and get the real story."

*****

Jack takes Mary's advice and lets Clara sleep. He heads back to the kitchen to make a brew of coffee and then joins Mary back in the office. Borrowing her laptop, he googles the Palmerston North hospital, tapping the number into his phone, "I think I'll try the reception at the lookout. I'll do what you suggest and keep this between us until I find out more."

"I'm sorry Jack about springing that news on you. That's all you both need right now. You know Clara seems to be settling in well. I know it is early days, but she really is quite a resilient, brave young lady and I think you're both good for each other."

"Really, what do you mean?"

"Jack, I've seen another side to you since Clara has been here, and from where I'm sitting, you're growing a deeper more caring side."

"Thanks, Mary. I'd best get up the hill pronto before Clara wakes," Jack goes to the door.

"Don't worry I'll run interference for you. Gone for a walk to clear the head," Mary waves Jack off.

Checking his phone for a signal as he walks up the hill, Jack ponders on Mary's words, *Well, we are both growing, that's far better than where we were in Wellington, ah there's the signal!*

He dials the number while standing absolutely still and the phone makes the connection. "Hello?" Jack asks, "Can you hear me okay? I'm calling from Nepal… do you have a patient by the name of Frank James? I'm his son-in-law. I was hoping I could speak with him please?" Jack pauses, waiting for the reply, "… Well thanks anyway."

Shaking his head, Jack turns and heads back to the compound thinking, *why that absolute bitch!*

*****

Discovering the office empty, Jack walks over to the kitchen to find both Mary and Clara deep in discussion.

"… and that's when he popped the question." Clara

grins.

"So romantic," Mary replies, then seeing Jack enter the room, "Jack, who knew you had such talents?"

"Not a bad job, eh?" Jack smiles, then putting on an old- fashioned accent asks, "Now my fiancée, I was just thinking that I should contact your father to ask his permission for your hand."

"We're not in the 19th century, Jack. Besides I've already said yes."

"I know, babe, but I think your Dad would appreciate it. Would you have his number?"

"How sweet," Clara responds, grabbing her phone. She pulls up her contacts and hands her phone to Jack, "There you go, I'd love to see him, but it might have to wait for the next trip home to see his Coromandel pad."

"Thanks, babe," Jack taps the details into his phone, "I think I'll try the lookout for signal. So, he doesn't live in Palmy then?"

Looking confused, Clara replies, "No, why would you think that?"

"Just a random thought." Jack looks at Mary raising an eyebrow, "I'm off to do the old-fashioned thing, then."

*****

"Hello Frank, it's Jack Fenton, I'm calling on behalf of Clara from Nepal… How are you?" Jack smiles with relief that the signal is still strong enough for the call.

"Fine thanks, Jack. Clara has told me a little about you…has something happened to Clara?" Frank asks, the concern evident in his tone.

"No Frank, Clara is fine. "She had a bump to the head

in Kathmandu, but she's fine now."

"Okay, so to what do I owe the pleasure of this expensive call?"

"Straight to the point eh, Frank. I've done this a bit backwards, but I thought… well… I wanted to ask you for permission to marry your daughter…"

"As long as she said yes, you don't need my permission, Jack. But thank you for asking. It means a lot to an old fellow like me."

"Look, Frank, while I've got you, there's something else …"

*****

Returning to the kitchen and looking rather pleased with himself, Jack overhears the conversation between Clara and Mary.

Mary all smiles, asks, "I know we haven't known each other long, but…"

"Thanks Mary, I know it all seems a bit too quick and out-of-the-blue, but..."

"Ha! It may seem out-of-the-blue for most, but not for me, I could see this coming right from the beginning. When I saw you two at the hotel together, I knew you were suited for each other. You just needed the usual chain of life's events to push you together to make you realise that. Believe me, Clara, and I'm speaking from experience here, stubbornness and pride doesn't make you happy. They only hold you back, blocking you from real happiness and following what your heart truly desires. I should know…" Mary stares into space, a faraway look in her eyes.

Jack looks at her, asking softly, "Is there something

you want to share?"

"I just know my life would have panned out very differently if I hadn't been so stubborn and so god damn so-called independent. I would probably be living in New York, playing the happy wife and mother and career woman all swept up into one big over-complicated life. I don't regret what I've done, not now I'm here, but for many years I did. It was particularly hard going back home initially seeing the life I could have had and the woman who replaced me..." Mary shakes her head. "Right I've said enough. Now when is the wedding or should I say engagement?"

"We are still at the planning stage and heading into town today to check flights and send a couple of emails. Oh, and the other big thing, I forgot to mention is, we are thinking of going to Sweden," Jack grins broadly.

"Yes, I've emailed a friend in Stockholm to check the ins and outs of foreigners getting married there," Clara interjects.

"How exciting! My god you two don't let the grass grow under your feet, do you? A white Christmas and a white wedding. Well you have a lot to plan, so I won't hold you up. Nothing is going to be happening much here over the next few weeks, just the usual admin and paper work so there's nothing for you to worry about." Mary replies.

"Come on then, fiancé! Let's stop gassing and get into town," Clara encourages.

*****

As they walk back to Jack's room, hand-in-hand, Jack asks, "So my gorgeous fiancée, how are you this morning?"

Clara leans in for a kiss, before answering, "I'm great. I'm very excited. I can't believe I slept last night. My head was buzzing, but maybe I felt so cosy and contented in your arms, my body just relaxed and let me sleep."

Jack laughed, "Your body was certainly relaxed after I'd finished with you."

Opening the door, Jack sees his bed strewn with pages of writing. "Wow, you've been busy this morning. What's all the paperwork about?"

"Ah, just brainstorming some people I want to come to the wedding, where I want it, and the dates and the venue… and contingency plans, just in case the dates and venue I want aren't available." Clara rattles off her list. "But first Jack what's our time-frame? I'm assuming it's anytime from Boxing Day until about the fifth of January? Won't we have to be back by then?"

"Hey, you're way ahead of me. I haven't even looked at my diary. We can do more planning in town, but give me an outline of your thoughts. Let's come up with a basic itinerary and then we can show the boys down at Overland Encounters in town. So, who do you want to come? Anyone from New Zealand by any chance?"

Clara laughs, "Well no wedding would be complete without the Trinity Trio, so even though it's very unrealistic at such short notice, and with Freya and her new business, I thought I would go for gold and see if those two were free. I don't like my chances though. Oh Jack, there is so much to plan, where do we start?"

Jack takes her hand, "Look sweet one, don't sweat the small stuff. This is exciting to plan, but if it gets too much, let's not do the wedding yet. We can just have an informal engagement party and have the big day when we get home or in the summer months over here. There's lots of choice. Together we can conquer anything. Although I do like the sound of Sweden."

Jack looks up at the Annapurna Mountains and in his corny way does a Sir Edmund Hillary impersonation, with one hand on his hip and the other pointing to the mountains, he says, "Let's knock this bugger off," and he imitates trekking off up into the mountains.

Clara laughs and gathers her things together into her bag. "Okay, Tiger, I'll be ready in two minutes."

He looks at his watch, "I'd better get my skates on then."

*****

At the Overland Encounters office, Jack waves to his mate Ralph, thanking his lucky stars he is on. "Over here, babe. Ralph is very clever with the booking system and if there is a tricky booking, he can fix it!"

"Introductions, Jack?" Clara hints as they approach Ralph's counter.

"Namaste Ralph. How are you? This is my lady, Clara, Clara James… actually my fiancée," Jack stumbles.

"Congratulations sir, what an achievement. I see you have the ring to prove it. That is a stunning piece of jewellery," Ralph observes.

"Thanks, didn't he do well?" Clara beams proudly.

"Aye, he did at that. Okay, now what can I do for you two lovebirds. What exotic places are you thinking of travelling to? Everest, or one of our smaller treks?" Ralph looks at them expectantly.

"An exotic place… exotic to me," Jack explains, "but

we're thinking of Sweden, and we only have a couple of weeks to go there, see the place, get married and return for the start of the school term."

"Sweden, now that's a new one to me. I have never been to any of those Scandinavian countries." Ralph types rapidly on his keyboard and looks at his screen, "Right, so that will be flying into Arlanda airport. Bear with me while I have a look at the choice of airlines. When were you thinking of going?"

Clara cuts in, "Now. Today would be good."

Laughing, Jack adds, "Ralph, with this one, everything has to be done by yesterday."

Ralph smiles back, "This may take me a while with the IATA system running like a dog at this time of the year. Would you like to go off for a coffee somewhere and come back in say thirty minutes, and I'll give you a choice of itineraries. I don't want to get your hopes up. You know the whole world is flying at this time of year trying to get home to loved-ones and or family."

"Thanks Ralph, see you in about thirty," Jack replies as they head out into the street.

"Shall we go find Nugan's place, Jack?" Clara asks.

"It's just around the corner, this way," Jack leads.

"Oh my god, what am I going to wear?" Clara exclaims.

"Oh, I hadn't thought about that. Well I'm sure I could always hire a suit from somewhere, or at least borrow one for the day," Jack ponders as they walk down the unpaved street, "But as for a wedding dress? I've no idea."

"I wonder if Elisabeth can help? Maybe she can find a dress? Or I buy a simple white dress in Stockholm. Oh, look, there's my old hairdresser Vatsa and Remi's sewing shop! That gives me an idea." Clara exclaims. She points at a brightly painted shop, with a sign saying *Frock Work Orange Pokhara,* as they round the corner to the café.

"*Namaste* Nugan!" Clara greets as they walk inside.

"*Namaste* Miss Cla-ara and Mr Jack. The usual?" Nugan hands them two slips of paper with the morning's Wi-Fi code.

"Great thanks Nugan," Jack answers, "Where do… Oh, looks like we're sitting over there." Jack waves to Nugan and follows Clara to her table near the window. She has already started to load the Wi-Fi code into her tablet.

"No time to waste, lover boy. Do you want to have a look at some flights online, just in case Ralph's system is jammed?" Clara grins as she logs into her webmail.

Ignoring another email from her mother, Clara starts rapidly typing a joint email to her besties to save time:

Hi Girlies, it's me.

You will never guess, what has just happened!

Go on guess, I dare you!

Okay I will tell you I can't wait, we only have limited time to get organised!

Last night, and it was so romantic, Jack proposed to me!

Well no actually this morning, after midnight. We were in my favourite place at the lake lookout.

We had had a romantic picnic in the freezing cold then went and warmed up over a bit of a boogie at a club. We were cruising on his new baby, one sweet bike. It purrs and roars at the same time. It is one sexual beast. Anyhow on the way home he proposed. He even had a ring. Can you believe it? So, he must have planned it.

But anyhow, so there is a WEDDING to go to! ARE YOU AVAILABLE?

And now guess where?!

We are going to Sweden, hopefully in a couple of days, just for two weeks.

So girlies I know it is the wrong time of the year as its cold and dark, but remember how romantic Sweden is at this time of the year, with all the lights, the snow, everything looks so pretty. How about if I can organise a venue, just something small and simple could you come? I can't see myself getting married without you two as my bridesmaids.

Okay here's some ball park dates, so you can suss it out. Let's say tentatively between 30th December and 5th January. That way that gives you time to get over jet lag.

Now I know I'm probably dreaming as Freya you have just started your dream enterprise at Portobello but could you find someone to oversee it? I would love to see Zac and Charlie, so can all four of you come over?

I know it's a big ask, but it's for a good cause, I, Clara Bethnay James, am getting married to Jonathan Anthony Fenton. Oh, do I take his name, he takes mine or do the double-barrelled thing – I need my besties!

I'm pinching myself. I must away to book tickets.

Talk about seat of the pants! I don't even know what I'm going to wear!

Okay get back to me

Love you both

Flat White xx

"Right Jack that's the girls done. Now how are you getting on with flights? Any joy?" Clara is all business-like.

"I had a good look and as we only have a limited time, I don't like the options of flying into other airports and then waiting for a connection. It's also a bit risky." Jack looks up from the computer. "I've been reading the weather reports and watching the news over in Europe. There has been a shit load of snow falling in the UK, and Heathrow was snowbound the other day. All flights in and out had to be cancelled. I'm sure Stockholm wouldn't be any better off, but it's better to get stranded in Stockholm, than in the UK."

"Let's see what I can find." Clara, on a mission, starts swiftly typing on her tablet, swiping screens open and closed so fast, Jack sits back in amazement, sipping his coffee.

She looks at the different airlines, giving a running commentary to Jack as she scans the information, "Hey we can get Royal Nepalese Airlines from Kathmandu to Delhi, stay in Delhi a night or two then catch KLM from New Delhi to Stockholm. And there are a few seats available."

"Maybe, but they look like business class and we can't afford that," Jack comments as he reads her tablet upside-down.

"There is economy as well, I think. Well actually we could afford business class. I do have the money from my house. I can't quite understand their coding system and it keeps changing each time I refresh the screen. I think it's best if we get back to the travel agent. He'll be able to tap into stuff we don't have access to."

"Okay, let's get these coffees down us," Jack agrees.

As the couple walk back to the Overland Encounters office, Clara offers, "Jack, I know both of us are not earning money right now, but that doesn't matter. I'm happy to pay for business class. Let's not restrict ourselves if all economy seats are gone. Let that be my gift to you. Money should not get in the way of our happiness."

"Thanks for the offer Clara. I'll have to think about that. I don't feel right about taking money from a woman. That's not how I was bought up. Call me an old fart, a sexist pig, whatever, but I have always believed that the man should be the breadwinner and I should be looking after you."

"You do, Jack. You do look after me. But, you better sort out that old-fashioned attitude young man, as you're marrying a thoroughly modern woman. Besides, I'm here because of you. Hey, I've just had an idea for my wedding dress. Do you mind if I go and visit my old mate Vatsa at the hairdressers, his wife Remi makes these groovy outfits, I bet she's never been asked to make a wedding dress for the winter for a Scandinavian wedding? I promise I won't go to too much expense. Besides she won't have much time to sew something up, but I would love something with a bit of a Nepalese flavour. What do you think?"

"Sure, sweet one, it's your day."

"And everyone always forgets the groom. What are you going to wear? Come on, let's both go over and see what's cooking in the bride and groom department."

They discuss their requests for something stylish yet simple and in a relatively short time. After measuring both of them up, Remi has a brainwave, pulling out some colourful Nepalese scarfs to be woven into sashes for the girls and cummerbunds for the boys, promising to have them ready overnight.

An hour later they get back to the agents and Ralph

has worked his magic. "Fantastic timing, guys. It took me all that time, to come up with something. It wasn't easy, but you know I love a challenge. I can get you flying out of Delhi in two days' time, so you would have two Christmases, one in this continent and one on the plane. But I believe they celebrate Christmas the night before the 25th in Scandinavia, so you would miss Christmas over there."

"Yes of course," Jack says anxiously, "but more importantly how much will it cost? What class have you got us in?"

"Well that's the deal-breaker, I'm afraid. There's only business class available. But I have managed to get a good deal for you. I see Clara is a frequent traveller and she can use up some of her points. This basically means she would fly for the price of economy class, but Jack you would have to pay the full business class fare. What do you think?"

Clara jumps in, "Yes, that's perfectly fine. Do you take Visa?"

"Of course, we do," Ralph grins.

Jack is looking a little startled, but seeing the excitement on Clara's face, it is all worth it. Clara looks at him and he nods, "Yes, we'll take it. Thanks a lot." He bends over to kiss his new fiancée on the cheek.

"Great, I've held the booking. I'll confirm it now. Congratulations you two. You are out of here tomorrow with a stopover in Delhi. Does that give you enough time to organise everything?"

"We'd better get packed if we're flying out tomorrow," Jack answers in a daze.

"Come on Jack, what are we waiting for." Clara jumps for joy.

"You'll never have a dull moment with that one, Jack," Ralph observes, "Don't worry I'll have your tickets ready tomorrow morning before your flight."

Chapter 24

Leaving on a Jet Plane

Back at the school compound, Clara feels the need to be on her own. All the excitement and sudden changes in her life have been a bit too much, what with the wedding plans. She now needs time out to catch up with her reflection journal.

She collects her journal from her room and grabs a cold soft drink from the fridge in the kitchen before heading for her special place up on the observation deck. She is wrapped up well with her woollen hat and scarf, prepared for the cooler weather.

She opens her reflection journal and sees that she hasn't written in it for a little while, so she contemplates the last few days and is inspired and fired up enough to write some poetry, beginning with an easy one to get the creative juices flowing, before starting the one she wants to write about her engagement.

I love being in the mountain up so high
A definite bucket list before I die
Working with kids always sweet and kind
I'm so lucky what a find
Teaching English and storytelling
Listening to their tales, my eyes are welling
Having a coffee and pizza down in town
Meeting like-minded people all around
Lying in the sun reading a book
Beautiful mountains just take a look
Catching up on goss via emails we type
Getting the rundown with all the hype
Reducing my drinking to a healthy amount
Just a couple of glasses so I don't lose count.

Clara sips on her cold drink and looks out over the mountains toward the quaint-looking tea houses dotted along the countryside. She can see in the distance the donkeys who help the Sherpas carry the tourists' supplies.

She runs through everything she has been up to since coming to Pokhara - the times with Jack, but also the time spent on her previous visit to Nepal with Sven. On that occasion the organised treks were closed for the year and there was only a skeleton staff at the different adventure trekking companies. Her favourite Sherpa she had met while trekking with the English girls, was dancing at her night club, had taken her and Sven on their own personalised trek a few days later. It was fun to reminisce.

Then she thinks about her wedding dress accessories that were being made down at Frock Work Orange, Pokhara by Remi and had a slight panic. *What if they're not ready by the time we fly out tomorrow? What is my backup plan?*

Maggie's exercise comes to mind and Clara practises some of her CBT. She catches a thought right there and then before it transforms into a feeling and explodes into action, bringing on anxiety and a downward spiral.

Wow! It worked! Very proud for stopping the thought in mid-flow, Clara hastily records it in her journal.

She considers Jack's comment earlier about inviting her mother and sister, and runs through the likely scenarios. Knowing how tight her mother is, and how much control she has over her sister, Clara dismisses the idea. *They wouldn't come all this way to Nepal, let alone Sweden. I mean Mum refuses to use her free travel gold card to catch the bus or train in to see me in Wellington. So why would she hop on a plane to see me get married?*

Realising she is starting to spiral again, Clara goes back to more positive things that are in her control, like her engagement and upcoming wedding.

Oh my god I'm in a tiss
He's proposed I'm finally his
Jack Fenton has asked me for my hand
Now I know where I finally stand
I'm his girl and I'm wearing his ring
I'm so happy I want to sing
Fancy finding happiness all these miles away
Nepal is the place where I want to stay
I'm back doing my love of teaching
No more idle chat or that corporate preaching
Teaching kids who want to be taught
Not the usual shysters so easily bought

There's far less gossip and idle chatter
It's so nice to be appreciated by those who matter.

Her concentration is broken by Jack wandering over, "Found you again. All okay? I would have thought you'd be madly packing your bags."

"I will be in about ten minutes. Lots to do, eh? But exciting stuff. Hey, does Mary know we're going tomorrow?"

"Yep, sweet as. She would like to have a quick chat with you before we go." Jack continues, "I'm just drawing up my own invite list to see if anyone can come over at short notice."

"Okay, good luck. I won't be long." Clara re-reads her last poem with a smile on her face. *Right that's enough for today, I have definitely made up for not filling in my journal. Next, packing, or Mary? Hmm I wonder what Mary wants? I hope she's still okay with us leaving.*

She crosses the small courtyard towards the office, and realises just how much she has settled in. She only arrived a few days ago, but it now feels like home.

"Hey Clara, whatsup?" Mary greets Clara.

"Oh nothing much, just a trip, wedding dress and venue to arrange."

"Too funny. Anything I can do to help? I remember my wedding was such a big event, a lot of people, lots of stress not to mention a hell of a lot of money," Mary recalls.

"I didn't know you were married."

"No, well I don't exactly shout it from the roof tops. That was many lifetime's ago. I'm happily unmarried nowadays and that's the way it will stay," Mary says adamantly.

"Oh, so nothing between you and Simon?"

"Ha! Good one Clara! No, I don't go for the bookish Brit type," Mary laughs.

"So, what did you want to see me about?"

"I wanted to check with you, can you keep a secret from Jack?"

"Well that depends on what it is exactly. After our break-up and reuniting, I want to be totally honest with him from now on."

"Oh, it's a… wedding surprise," Mary reveals.

"Tell me more," Clara asks intrigued.

"Well, I had this idea…"

*****

Clara sees Jack emerging from his hut as she strides across the school yard towards her room. Waving, they start towards each other, when a little van speeds up the driveway coming to a sudden halt beside them.

Rolling down the window, Ralph leans out, "Hey guys, I've got something for you." Grinning, he hands them an envelope containing their tickets and passports.

"Mate! Thanks. I didn't expect these until tomorrow," Jack takes the envelope and hugs it.

"I pulled out all the stops to get them through today, just to be sure," Ralph beams.

"Wow, that's awesome," Clara adds her thanks.

"Do I get to kiss the bride-to-be?" Ralph asks cheekily.

"Steady on mate. We're Kiwis not Brit's," Jack grins.

Clara leans over and gives Ralph a quick peck on his cheek, "There you go Ralph. You're a star."

Jack shakes Ralph's hand, and with a quick wave, a beaming Ralph is gone and out-of-sight within seconds.

"Yay, that's going to save time tomorrow. Thank god for that, Jack. Now just for the wedding sashes and cummerbunds, before we head out in the morning."

"I'm just about packed, but I've got a few of your things from my room you may want to take," Jack says.

"Great, that means you can give me a hand. I want to be packed and sorted before I hit the hay tonight, or I won't sleep."

As they walk to Clara's room, Jack says "You know, babe, we can always use Sweden as a dress rehearsal and do a second wedding back home. What do you reckon? Are you up for two weddings? It will be a lot cheaper for the guests that way, instead of them flying all the way to Scandi. I'm not sure many people will want to leave sunny New Zealand at this time of year?"

"Of course. I'm okay about having two weddings. But does that mean we need to invite my dysfunctional toxic mother?"

"That's up to you. Life is about what you want to do, not about SHOULDS anymore. If it doesn't fit with you, don't force it," Jack advises.

"Thanks Jack," Clara turns and kisses him.

Leaning into the embrace, Jack returns her kiss passionately. Coming up for air Clara murmurs, "Steady on, Tiger, or we won't be ready tomorrow."

"Plenty of time for packing," Jack replies as he pulls Clara back into his arms.

*****

Sending Jack back to his own room to sleep, an excited Clara stays up half the night packing and repacking her bag, remembering she needs to leave enough room for her wedding accessories. Then she realises they are going business class and would be getting an extra weight allowance. Just when she thought she had it sorted, she clicked that on the domestic Nepalese flights she wouldn't be entitled to the extra weight, especially at this time of the year. Planes would be overflowing with other passenger's extra holiday luggage.

After a short and fitful sleep, Clara wakes, worrying that she has forgotten something else, like the right shoes to go with her colourful wedding sash, or that Remi would not be ready in time. In the end, feeling defeated, she walks over to the octagonal house and meditates.

Each time she does this, especially in the early hours of the morning, or the dead of the night when the rest of Nepal is sleeping, she gets more clarity. This night is no different. She feels so much better for meditating and comes back to her room and sleeps like a log for the rest of the night.

*****

"Oh, no, I can't wear this," Clara exclaims, after checking herself in the mirror. Scowling at the crow-lines around her eyes and on her forehead, Clara notices some new ones around her lips and then, aghast, notices her neck. "Oh my god, I can't wear a plunging neckline with these ostrich wrinkles on full display." Her face contorts as she tries to push and massage the lines from her neck, to no avail.

"What on earth are you doing to your neck? Is that a

girl's definition of a deep tissue massage?" Jack asks as he enters her room. "It looks like torture. Is it absolutely necessary?

Clearly embarrassed that she is caught, Clara thinks quickly and explains, "Ah… no, just ah… rubbing in some extra moisturiser for all the flights we're taking. You know how your skin gets dehydrated from being up that high for so long."

"Yeah, right, if you say so," Jack notes sceptically, "Have you eaten? We need to get our bags in the van. Mary's taking us to the airport."

"I might grab breakfast while we're in town collecting our accessories from Remi," Clara thinks out loud.

"By the way, sweet one, you're looking hot today," Jack says admiringly. "Looks like I'll be fighting off the other male passengers wanting to chat you up."

Clara decides against changing yet again, and throws the last of her items into her bag, "Right, that's me packed. Please put that bag on top. It's got space for the cummerbunds and sashes. And before you ask, yes I have already meditated."

"Funny, I didn't see you over there."

"I know. I did mine at two this morning, when I couldn't sleep. Nothing to worry about, just last-minute nerves," Clara explains.

"We can always catch up on our sleep on the plane." Jack hefts the bag from the floor.

*****

Looking at her watch, Mary calls, "I'll stay in the van, you have ten minutes max kids!"

"Thanks Mary," Jack says as he tries to keep up with Clara who has already exited the van before it came to a complete stand still.

"*Namaste* Vatsa, is Remi out the back?" Clara asks as she enters the barber shop.

"*Namaste* Clara, go on through… oh you have…"

"Sorry Vatsa, we're in a bit of a hurry. Got a plane to catch," Jack apologises as he follows in Clara's wake.

As Jack emerges into Frock Work Orange out the back, he is greeted by two women in tears, hugging each other.

"Oh Jack, look what magic Remi has done overnight!" Clara excitedly says, as she breaks the embrace and holds up one of the brightly coloured sashes.

"Perfect!" He pulls his wallet from his back jeans pocket, "I've got the cash. How much Remi?"

Jack sorts out the payment as Clara neatly folds the cummerbunds and sashes.

Remi wraps them in a turquoise silken scarf, "Here you are my friend. I want to see the photos when you get back," she demands.

Hugging one last time, Clara says, "You will be one of the first I visit on our return, I promise."

"Thanks again Remi, I don't want to be rude, but we have to go." Jack guides his fiancée towards the door.

*****

Mary tears into the airport drop-off lane, mounting the curb onto the pavement right outside the departure doors, narrowly missing one of the verandah posts. "Go, go, go!" she yells.

Jack explodes from the passenger's door with one bag

269

and the tickets in hand, racing for the check-in counter.

Clara and Mary race to the van side door, getting the rest of the luggage out onto the pavement.

"If it wasn't for that... never mind, look Clara, just go or you will miss your flight. Oh and please give this to Jack from me," Mary gives her an envelope and a quick hug.

"Thanks Mary, you're the best." Clara has a tear in her eye. As she turns to follow Jack, she spies an airport police man walking briskly their way, "Ah Mary, you better go too."

*****

With a sigh of relief, Jack slumps down onto the airport bench seat beside Clara. "That was a close call, babe, but we made it in time."

Clara fires up her tablet to check her emails. "I want to see if Elisabeth has replied."

"I think I'll just unwind." Jack closes his eyes.

Suddenly Clara's tablet starts pinging its familiar email alert. "Yay, Elisabeth, Sven, Freya and oh Mum. Damn what does she want? Elisabeth first."

Dear Clara,

Plans at this end are progressing. I've even found an adorable celebrant for you.

I need a copy of both your passports for the marriage licence. It normally takes about eight or nine weeks to get the licence, but I have a friend who can fast-track it.

My friend Ulrika has a gorgeous wedding dress she said you can borrow, you are both about the same size. Unless you have found one, let me know.

Do you have an invite list yet? The caterer wants to know numbers.

This is so exciting!

Let me know what flight you are on and I'll meet you at the airport.

Can't wait to see you and your man!

Puss och kram, E

Elbowing Jack in the ribs, Clara asks, "Hey Sleepyhead, give me your passport for a minute. Looks like I've got a wedding dress too." She snaps a couple of photos and emails them to Elisabeth immediately. Clara then checks her friends' emails:

Dear Clara,

Talk about synchronicity! You will never believe it but both Freya and I are on our way over to Stockholm! With our men! So we will definitely see you there!

Charlie and I would be delighted to come for your special day. Try stopping us.

What do you want us to wear? Sorry to be a bit presumptuous but are you having bridesmaids or is that something old-fashioned? Are there speeches? Who is making them? Has the wedding got a theme? Who did you manage to round up from the old days in Sweden?

Ok sorry about all the questions. I will send our flight details in the next email. We are flying into Arlanda to stay in Stockholm where we will be based.

Guess what? This is the first holiday Charlie has had in two years. He has been so pushed playing fill in detective here there and everywhere, he has accrued over three months of leave. So we will be coming for six weeks.

Dear old Bernard confessed to me that he has been having an affair with Katarina, and guess what! They will be over in Stockholm soon too!

Now that Charlie has arrested Margaret for Cat's murder, oh my, you wouldn't know that yet, we will fill you in when we get there!

I miss you I miss our chats, coffees and laughter.
Anyhow gal more news later.
Hey I have a poem for you,
Love Sven xx

POEM

Clara James you've finally hooked your man
Oh my god now a wedding for you to plan
You followed your man to unknown parts
Now pumping in time your two hearts
The stuff you've been through unbelievable
But now look where you are inconceivable
You chased your man to Kathmandu
Now just take a look at you two
Of course, I'm coming to your wedding
Fun and excitement, now watch this heading.

Clara wipes a tear from her eye as she thinks to herself, *Yep mate the feeling is mutual, I miss you heaps too.*
Opening Freya's email next, Clara reads:

Hey girlfriend,
How exciting!

We are really excited Zac has never been to Sweden so he's hyped up about it!

He just remembers all those ads on the tele from the old days where they used to have all those pretty blonde girls with fresh faces, shampooing their hair with spring water running down their faces. He thinks that every woman in Sweden looks like that, all blonde and blue eyed...

So where are you right now?

Have you got your speeches organised, the music, have you and Jack written your own personal vows?

Clara stops there she can't believe it, saying out loud, "Oh my god, with everything to plan I completely forgot to do our vows, our personal ones. Shit, how could I have forgotten?"

Jack puts his hand on hers, "Hey babe! Don't worry we have plenty of time to work those out, three flights remember?"

Clara takes a deep breath and calms down. "Thanks Jack, you're right. Hey, Sven and Freya can make it. I'll read more, then fill you in."

"Great, I'll know a couple of people coming then," Jack grins, leaning back into his seat.

"Cheeky." Clara continues reading the email:

What music are you going to have as you walk down the aisle?

Enough with the questions, the news here, Portobello is fab.

It's been hard work but all the tenants now have contracts all sorted.

Micco is still a real star running his alfresco dining out in the garden and will look after the restaurant and bar for us.

I have lots of clubs and associations coming using both the turret and the cellar downstairs in the basement. All sorts of quirky people, from the Romantic Writers to the Wednesday Wine tasters, and the Lowry Bay artists' association. Even Simon has booked one of the rooms for a new venture of his! Mind you I must admit it has got really quiet as it's almost Christmas and people are starting to go away.

Most people are still frazzled by the earthquake and those crazy scientists at the BS ministry are predicting there will be another one.

Zac's mum Zita has been great. She has offered to move in while we are away and play hostess.

Between Zita and Micco, I know Portobello is in safe hands while I do my assignment in Scandi.

In a nutshell, Dimitri my old boss at the Education Ministry has given me a six week assignment in Scandi looking at their school systems, the bonus will just about pay off the mortgage on Portobello!

I'll fill you in when we touchdown in Stockholm, email me your dates!

Ok girlie, will be in touch soon.

PS let me know what special NZ food you miss? Like the old days, remember when mum used to send us over Crunchie bars and flakes and all those packets of milk bottle lollies and chocolate fish. Let me know what you are dying to eat and I'll see if those Customs officers will let me bring them through.

Take care for now,

Love Freya xx

Getting nostalgic again Clara's mouth waters as she thinks of all those Kiwi chocolates and lollies.

Clara starts typing on her tablet:

Here you go E, one invite list:
Elisabeth and ??
Sven, Charlie, Freya, Zac
Saga and Reiner, Silke and Markus, Sheila and Bertill
Not forgetting of course, Jack and Clara
Might pay to cater for a few extras and see if Lars can make it too, it would be good to see him again after all these years.
Is it too much to ask for flowers at this time of year? And thank Ulrika for the loan of her dress at short notice, you are a star.
Love Flat White xx

Speaking out loud she said, "Shit I better check my Handelsbanken balance, to see if I still have some money in my old bank accounts."

Jack leans forward, "Clara, you know it is traditional for the bride's father to pay for everything, but under the circumstances, that would be in poor taste. How do you feel if I pay for everything?"

"That is very sweet. How about a good old-fashioned compromise? Let's go halves, eh?"

"That sounds very fair, babe. Let's roll with that," Jack agrees, rising from his seat, "I might just check how much longer before we board."

Okay, one more email to read:

Dear Clara

I won't be hypocritical and start this off by wishing you a Merry Christmas, because that's not why I am writing.

I want you back home!

Why haven't you responded to the urgent message I sent Jack?

I have just heard the most outrageous news from an unnamed source, but it appears you are racing off and getting married. Why?

At such short notice, you must be pregnant!

How irresponsible!

Do you not ever think about what an embarrassment you are to the family?

If you did you wouldn't be acting so immaturely and selfishly.

Why you have chosen to go over to Nepal at the coldest time of the year is beyond me? Then I hear you have sold your house for peanuts and are now working for peanuts in the middle of a mountain with all those roaming animals and such like.

No wonder you are always sick, if you gallivant half way around the world in third world countries like this.

I would much rather hear that you were on one of your shopping sprees in New York, London or Paris, than in the middle of a rundown village in the mountains of Nepal. I am sure Sir Edmund Hillary was a lot more equipped to do this sort of thing than you are.

When are you going to come to your senses and come home?

I can't be having this.

I am not getting any younger and your impulsive little actions are starting to take a great toll on my health.

I would appreciate if you could acknowledge this email and let me know that you have broken off the engagement immediately!

There is nothing wrong with Jack, but you know you can do much better.

Why can't you be more like your dear sister Sabrina?

Now come home on the next flight!

With ever increasing impatience,

Your mother

Tears of frustration and emotional pain, stream down her cheeks, *Fucking hell*, what a *headcase! No wonder I am as flawed as I am, with a mother like that. How the fuck am I meant to get ahead with my life with Mum playing the holier than holier act with me? It's all about her controlling me and my life. She can talk, leaving Dad like she did for that creep who ended up raping me... and she's always been in denial about that. Blaming me for his death or blaming Dad for everything, not taking responsibility for her own actions or happiness. She doesn't seem to realise it's not up to us to make her happy. It's an inside job. She just can't keep blaming me for everything. Why does she still do it?*

Jack seeing his fiancée in distress, comes flying back from the counter, "babe, what's up?!"

"Oh Jack, I got another fucked email from my head-case of a mother. God, does she know how to wind me up? Would you read it for me? Maybe I'm too sensitive and just get the wrong end of the stick. Maybe she does mean good after all and I just misinterpret her words…" Clara starts to second guess herself.

Jack reads the email. "No Clara, you haven't got it wrong. She is manipulating you, but then you have always known that, haven't you? She likes to control your life because her life has been so pathetic. She has to create drama, to add to her boring life and she hooks you in every time. Stop taking the bait. Don't reply to this. Leave it. Don't let this woman control you from the other side of the world. Clara if her life was that wonderful, she wouldn't give you another thought and you know that."

"You're right, I don't know why I keep taking the bait," Clara acknowledges. "Damn." She pauses. "What email to you is she going on about?"

"Sorry Clara, I should have told you about it," Jack apologises, then explains, "but I checked it out and it was bullshit. Your mother said that your Dad was in Palmerston North hospital on his death bed. I called the hospital to check it out, and they had never heard of him. That's why I asked for his phone number yesterday. He's fine in Coromandel."

"I can see why you checked. What a bitch, using any trick she can to break us up and get me back home under her influence." Clara's hands are trembling with rage.

Jack kneels in front of her, takes her shaking hands in his, and asks, "Now, my fair lady, are we going to let someone else destroy our happiness from a distance? Or are we going to enjoy this path we're on?"

"Full steam ahead, Tiger." Clara smiles.

A flight attendant calls from the counter, "Boarding now. All passengers to Kathmandu on flight…"

Chapter 25

Touchdown

Jack nudges Clara with his elbow, "Wakey, wakey, babe, nearly there."

The plane's PA crackles, as the Captain's voice announces, *Uppmärksamhet. Attention. Would all passengers return to your seats. We will be landing in Arlanda in 20 minutes. It is a cool minus 2 degrees in Stockholm this morning and adjust your watches, it is 5.15 on Christmas day. Merry Christmas everyone, or should I say God Jul and gott nytt år. Tack så mycket.*

Clara's face breaks into a smile as she hears the familiar Swedish language for the first time in years. "Well, my fiancé, are you ready for your Swedish adventure?"

"Bring it on. I'm ready for anything with you by my side," Jack replies enthusiastically, folding his tray table away.

"This is going to be so much fun. I wonder where Elisabeth has us staying," Clara ponders, as she repacks her bag.

"Under the seat please madam, *Tack*," an efficient hostess instructs as she checks the passengers.

Seeing the surprised look on Jack's face, Clara explains, "You get used to it, they aren't being rude. Okay here we go!"

*****

Standing at Customs and Immigration, the officer notices Clara's old work permit in her passport, stamping the page he hands the passport back to her and smiles, *"Wilkommen tilbaka Ms James and God Jul, Varsågod, tack så mycket, hej da."*

Clara beams a big smile. *"Du ocksa, hej da."*

Having no idea what they are saying, Jack leans in and teases, "I think that guy fancies you, Clara. Was he your type?"

Laughing Clara fires back, "A tad jealous, are we? Best stay on your toes then, lover boy. I always fall in love with their cute accent."

They walk through the sliding doors out into the airport. People frantically move from one side of the airport to another. Clara recognises the Swedish shop signs and points some out to Jack.

A stylishly fur-clad woman emerges from the crowd and runs up with her arms wide, "Clara! *Hej* Clara! *Wilkommen!*" She wraps Clara in her arms, and they hug each other tight.

"Hey thanks for meeting us, Elisabeth. It means a lot," Clara says.

Standing back Elisabeth asks, "And who is this good-looking man next to you? Are you going to introduce me?"

"Yes of course. Jack this is Elisabeth, Elisabeth meet my *sambo,* Jack," Clara proudly presents.

Elisabeth shakes Jack's hand in the formal Swedish way. "Please to meet you Yack."

Suppressing her laughter, Clara knows she can't take the piss out of the Swedish accent, just yet.

"Come on, let's get you to the *lägenhet.* I've borrowed a car from Lars. Don't laugh when you see it. It's an old Volvo, very slow, but practical for your bags. Public transport would be faster and cheaper, but hey I needed to welcome you to Sweden in style," Elisabeth laughs.

"Okay, lead the way, *älskling.*" Clara takes Jack's hand and they follow Elisabeth. Clara looks at her friend, as they walk past the shops towards the exit. "It's so good to see you, Elisabeth."

They walk passed a coffee bar and Clara sees the row of neatly displayed Swedish pastries in the window. She cries out excitedly, "Oh my god I can't walk passed a *kanelbullar!*"

Elisabeth laughs. "Come on then, you two. My treat as I bet you haven't got any *kronor* yet! Yack, you simply must try our *kanelbullar!*"

"Can I be cheeky and get a couple extra? No doubt you have the obligatory coffee flask in the car? Then we can munch away on these. I've told Jack all about the pastries, so he must try them all out," Clara says eagerly.

"*Ja visste,*" Elisabeth replies.

Elisabeth pays for the pastries and hands them out, "Enjoy, Yack!"

Biting into the appetising pastry, Jack comments, "Damn, that's delicious. Glad we got a couple."

"Yack, it is so good to finally meet you. I have heard so much about you from Clara. I never realised you two were that serious, so I am surprised, but excited. I can't wait for you to meet the rest of the friends." Elisabeth leads them out to the car park.

While Jack is loading the luggage into the back of the station wagon, Clara leans in close to Elisabeth, out of Jack's earshot asking, "Ah, let's not mention Lars, I haven't told him…"

"But you invited him…" Elisabeth starts.

"Shh, we'll talk later," Clara hisses as Jack closes the boot.

"You two take the front and catch up, I'll ride in the back and rest," Jack offers.

"Yack, what a gentleman." Elisabeth climbs into the left-hand driver's door.

The car ride into town takes a while, and Jack listens to the girls in the front seat nattering away for a while, but not following the Swenglish chat he switches off and takes in the scenery.

It is like a scene out of an American or European movie, with paddocks and tall trees covered in snow. The houses look gorgeous, like little chocolate box houses, painted mainly red or yellow, all wooden with sloping high-pitched roofs to catch the snow. Being a builder he is fascinated by the different styles.

Elisabeth turns, "All okay in the back seat, Yack? Can you hear yourself think over all the cackle we are making?"

He laughs. "Yes, I am used to it. I'm admiring your gorgeous houses. The houses and the backdrop look like a scene out of a romantic novel. I can't see any animals, though?"

"It is too cold with them right now with minus temperatures so they are all tucked away in those large buildings, I can't think of the word," Elisabeth struggles.

"Are you serious? They live in houses? Oh, a barn."

"Yes, they do, they would never survive the winter. It is only the wild animals like the moose and reindeer that roam the woods at this time of the year," Elisabeth explains.

"Moose? Reindeer?" Jack shakes his head in wonder.

"*Ja,* but they are mainly up north. You may see one or two where we are heading for the big day. Speaking of which Clara, I can't wait for you to try on Ulrika's dress."

The girls continue chatting all the way into Stockholm.

"So where are you taking us, Elisabeth?" Clara finally asks.

"Well you know the place. It's Bernard's old apartment in town," Elisabeth smiles.

"What! Not *Vasastan?* You are joking? Right in the heart of town. How the hell did you score that sweet number?" a surprised Clara exclaims.

Elisabeth puts her finger on her nose, "Ahh my sweet *flicka*, it's who you know, isn't it? Not what you know. I've been in and made sure it's not looking like a bachelor pad."

Emerging from one of the motorway tunnels into downtown Stockholm, they drive passed some of Clara's familiar old haunts, H & M, her favourite, *Åhléns*, seeing all the lights in the windows as part of the Christmas displays.

"Oh look, our coffee lounge is still there," Clara exclaims to Elisabeth. She points out to Jack, the well-lit coffee bar with the pastries displayed nicely in the windows, red-checked curtains and matching red-checked tablecloths on the tables.

They drive passed the *Vasa Real* school, a huge old

building on the corner and then turn onto *Vasagatan* and pull up on the cross roads by Bernard's old *lägenhet*.

"*Wilkommen hem, varsågod,* I have a door code, just punch that in and I will park the car. Yack, would you mind playing doorman and grabbing the suitcases from the trunk?"

"The trunk? Oh, you mean the boot."

"Apologies, Yack. My English teacher was American so I do use the odd American word. Boot. What a funny word, though. That's what I am wearing on my feet." Elisabeth looks confused.

"It sure is, eh?" Jack agrees.

They hop out, and dragging their cases behind them, Clara pushes the four-digit code on the building's security number pad. The door buzzes open. Jack walks in and comes to a complete halt, mouth ajar, staring, admiring the incredible old interior decor.

"This must be original. All this old wood-panelling, wide stairs, and look at the lift with the wrought iron surrounds. It's like something out of a thirties' movie." Jack is looking at the lift. "I thought that would be a museum piece by now? Surely it doesn't work?"

"It sure does, lover boy and we're about to take it," Clara replies.

"I'm not going in that." Jack pulls back. "It must be a health and safety risk."

"Don't be stupid. How else are we going to get these bags up the stairs? You're not thinking of putting your back out over some stupid safety concern. Now help me with these," Clara demands.

They haul the suitcases up the concrete steps to the lift and push the button. A resident is coming down to the ground floor and jumps out. He makes quick eye contact, and says, "*Hej*" and is off as quick as he arrived.

They stack their luggage in the lift, and Jack says quietly, "That wasn't exactly friendly was it?"

"Don't take it personally, the Swedes are very formal and if they don't know you, well… it is winter and they don't get a lot of sunlight." Clara explains, "You should be here in the summer time, when they are all out at the cutesy red summer houses on the islands. They are very friendly. Everyone is tanned and happy. It's just the weather. I mean take a look outside, would that make you happy?"

"The snow is beautiful and the countryside we just drove through was magical like a fairyland."

"Yeah, but it's also a pain in the arse, especially when it turns to black ice. I remember many a time ending up on my backside, while walking down this very road to catch the bus. Now that's a true health and safety hazard, not this old lift."

By the time they get in the lift Elisabeth calls from the door. "Wait for me. Let's go up together. Besides, I have got the keys. What have you been doing?"

"Remember how I was slightly culture shocked when I first came here? Well Jack is going through that initial stage where everything is a novelty." Clara explains.

"Like what?" Elisabeth mocks, "You must get snow."

"Oh, these old-fashioned lifts, the abrupt Swede we just encountered, you know that sort of NORMAL stuff." Clara continues, "Elisabeth you really should come out to New Zealand, then you will understand why we react the way we do."

"It is definitely on my list. Okay here's the key, let's see what awaits you inside?" She pushes the large double wooden doors, and they open into a large hallway with a wooden parquet floor. Elisabeth takes the lead walking up to another set of double wooden doors that lead to the open-plan dining room and lounge. Pointing, Elisabeth indicates, "Over there is the bedroom and en-suite, and there is the kitchen."

"It's fabulous, I must admit when Bernard had it, he never gave us a tour of the place. We were just here for drinks one night. It's perfect Elisabeth." Clara notices a vase of red and white amaryllis. "God knows where you got these from at this time of year. Thank you so much." Clara turns and gives her friend a big hug.

"From Spain, like everything else. Now in the refrigerator there is some food for you. Just the basics from ICA." Turning to hug Jack, Elisabeth advises, "I have parked on some resident's car park and you know us Swedes avoid conflict like the plague, so I should get going."

"Oh already?" Clara pouts.

"Also," Elisabeth continues, "I need to return the car to its rightful owner. Cars are such a pain in the arse in the city, the *Tunnelbana* is a much better mode of transport."

"But we have hardly caught up."

"Now none of that *älskling*. You will be jetlagged and probably wanting to rest for a few hours, have a shower… so how about I return later with some of the gang at seven or are you up to going out and checking out some of the old bars?" Elisabeth asks.

"Can I get back to you on that one? But yes, *klockan nitton* would be perfect." She goes to her friend and gives her another big hug, "*Tack ska du ha* for everything. It was wonderful to be greeted at the airport."

"You are welcome. Now settle in and I will see you later. Yack, a great pleasure. *Wilkommen* to Sweden." Elisabeth waves from the door.

Clara goes into the bedroom, kicks her shoes off and flops onto the bed. "Well, my fiancé, what do you think of Sweden so far?"

"I'm blown away. I don't think I've ever been anywhere like this ever." Jack looks out the window and notices that it is very gloomy, and raining. The glistening pavements, dark and wet like the sky. There are rows and rows of four to six level apartments in every direction. The architecture is gorgeous and he can't help admiring the elegance and the age of the buildings. Some have turrets in their corners, and others have small balconies.

He can hear the traffic and people below, as they scurry to and fro. A couple of leafless trees line the pavements. There is no greenery anywhere, just white snow, slowly melting away with the rain that is falling harder and harder. He opens the window, and feels the cold bite to the air, and after a few breaths decides that fresh air is not a good idea at this time.

Clara calls from the bed, "Let's have a shower and rest for a while. I want you to be in top form when you meet some of the others later. It's going to be a bit social for the next few days, so best be prepared for it."

"Yeah, sounds like a good idea. Any chance of a snack before we hit the sack?"

In a husky voice, Clara asks, "What sort of sustenance do you have in mind? Me or the foodstuff variety?"

"Well Miss James, I'll have both, if they're on offer," Jack replies, quickly removing his travel clothes.

They snuggle up together, and as Jack caresses Clara's

white porcelain skin. "Has anyone told you how gorgeous you are? You are like a fairy princess surrounded by the fairy lights and grand castles around here. Will you be my princess and complete the picture?"

"*Ja visste, Yack, Ja visste for alltid...*"

*****

Clara arranges the glasses and snacks on the table, ready for their guests. She looks over as her fiancé emerges from the bedroom, doing up the buttons on his shirt sleeve. "Jack can you put some music on please?"

"Sure, babe. This place looks set for a party." Jack hears chatter and foreign voices out in the corridor. "Is that the guests? Why aren't they coming in?"

"It's a Swedish thing. They are always exactly on time. If they arrive early, they believe it's rude to knock on the door a minute early, so they will walk around the block, or hang out in the corridor until the exact time."

Looking at his watch, Jack eyes Clara up, "So we still have a couple of minutes..."

"Steady on, Tiger!" Clara laughs as he takes her in his arms for a passionate kiss.

She breaks off first. "You're so naughty! Now I've got one minute to fix my lippie!" Clara laughs, and races back to the bedroom.

"Is this music okay?" Jack calls as he starts the CD, and smooth jazz sounds trickle from the speakers.

"That's perfect," Clara says coming back into the lounge. The doorbell rings and she heads to answer it.

Elisabeth leads the pack, "*Hej älskling, hur mår du?*" Lots of hugging and kissing and exchanging of presents and wine. Jack hears lots of *Tack så mycket*, and *varsågod*, finding it hilarious and a little intimidating. He listens but does not understand it all and sheepishly gets up and stands in the background by the door leading to the lounge.

The gang notice him and quieten down. They stand there, staring at him expectantly.

Clara suddenly realises what the awkward silence is all about. *It's clearly Jack's good looks, but they are also waiting for the expected formal introductions.* "Jack I would like you to meet some of my old friends. This is Saga…"

One by one she introduces them as they walk in single-file, pause to shake his hand and then proceed down the hallway breaking back into their light conversation.

The night goes off well. Jack becomes acquainted with some Swedish customs, which he finds distinctly different. Talking with Elisabeth towards the end of the night, he asks, "So how did you get to know Clara?"

"I met her first when she came to visit my cousin, Samantha in Stockholm, too many years ago. Clara stayed in our flat and we just, how do you say… hit it off."

"Oh, you and Sven are cousins!" Jack exclaims, "Now you mention it, I can see some similarity in your features."

"Yes, did you not know? Anyway, oh, before I forget, Clara!" Elisabeth calls.

"Coming! Excuse me Saga," Clara breaks away from her friend to join them.

"I got a text on the way over here. The family has made the next two weeks free for the wedding up in *Skeppsvik*, as they are down south for another family gathering, so we are now all go!" Elisabeth relates.

Hugging her friend, Clara exclaims, *"Fantastisk!"*

"Where's *Skeppsvik?*" Jack asks.

"About an hour's flight north of here. It will take longer to drive from *Umeå* to *Skeppsvik*," Elisabeth answers. "So we are flying up in a couple of days, then we can get everything prepared for the guests."

"Good. I've got a friend coming over, too, can we add one more to the catering?" Jack asks.

"Sure," Elisabeth replies.

"Who's coming Jack?" Clara asks.

"Ah, a relative…" Jack starts.

"*Ursäkta mig*, but we are leaving now," Saga interrupts formally.

Signalling the end of the party as the gang makes their farewells complimenting and thanking both Clara and Jack.

*****

The next two days are full-on, as Jack was warned, meeting many of Clara's old friends. In-between they get to have some time by themselves to do some sightseeing.

They take the *tunnelbana* and visit the ABBA museum, walk along *Strandvägen* and looked at the huge gin palaces parked up for the winter. They sit in coffee shops around red-checked table cloths and drink copious cups of coffee looking at each other over candlelit tables; they overdose on *mazarines* and *kanelbullar*. They do all Clara's favourite department stores, even taking a ferry out to one of the islands in the archipelago.

Stockholm is renowned for its huge archipelago of 30,000 plus islands where a lot of families for many generations have owned cute little red *stuga* summer houses. Legend would have it that the ABBA boys Benny and Bjorn still have their traditional family summer houses where they composed some of their best music out there.

A lot of the summerhouses look deserted and locked up. All the lovely outdoor summer furniture is tucked away on verandahs and inside, and all you can see are forlorn deserted houses, grey rock where usually there are glamorous Swedes draped over them, sunbathing worshipping the sun. There are a few Swedish flags still up full mast and blowing in the wind, but basically it is bare and barren. It is good to show Jack the islands though, so he can imagine what it would be like in a few months' time over the Swedish summer.

Clara and Jack, despite the weather, have a great time exploring new and old haunts around the city. Jack loves looking at all the old Volvos and Saabs that still frequent the streets, as well as the historic architecture of the palace and the old buildings in *Gamla Stan*. Jack wishes he could stay longer, but their flight is leaving that afternoon and it is time to pack and leave.

Back at the apartment, Clara leaves it in pristine condition, better than she found it.

Elisabeth has already returned to *Umeå* to get the wedding plans under way, so they catch a bus out to *Arlanda*. The idea of catching a train does interest Jack, but it would take too long and this is easier, quicker and surprisingly enough cheaper.

*****

They catch a SAS (Scandinavian Airline Services) plane up to *Umeå* and Elisabeth is there to meet them as before.

More hugs and kisses and Elisabeth leads them over to a nearby café, "Let's have a sit down coffee and *mazarine*."

"At this rate I'll never fit into my wedding dress," Clara laughs.

As they chat over the wedding details, Jack notices Elisabeth is a little distracted. He asks, "Are we pressed for time Elisabeth?"

"Ah… no, why do you ask, Yack?"

"It's just I've seen you looking at your watch a lot."

Elisabeth breaks into a big smile, "Well I have a surprise for you both."

Clara and Jack focus on Elisabeth and Clara asks, "Do we have to guess?"

Suddenly there are shrieks of delight from over their shoulders.

"Look, there she is!" a familiar voice calls.

Clara turns to see her besties running towards her.

"Flat White!" Freya, the fastest, wraps Clara in a huge hug, tears rolling down her cheeks. She is followed closely by Sven also in tears.

Elisabeth stands to greet Sven, "*Hej kusin!*" More hugs, handshakes and kisses ensue as the crowd make their introductions. Charlie is meeting Jack for the first time and they shake hands firmly, before Zac goes in for a man hug.

Elisabeth admires the men and says, "What's with these hunky Kiwi men you girls all have? I think I will come to New Zealand sooner than planned."

"That's a great idea. You should meet Rex," Sven suggests. "He's one good-looking copper and he's available."

They all laugh and talk animatedly for the next few minutes.

Elisabeth, standing back, says, "Come on you Kiwis, the minivan is outside. We can catch up on the way there. It's about a half hour, but we need to shop on the way and I don't want to drive out there in the dark."

*****

They shop around *Umeå* buying up supplies of everything as there is only a small ICA shop at *Skeppsvik* and then drive out to the summer house. It still looks the same to Clara. There are a couple of alterations, but still, as Jack would say chocolate-box like. The three houses all slightly smaller than the other are still there, positioned well to get maximum views of the lake. The little sauna house is up and running. They drag in their food supplies, salmon, bread, cheeses, a huge stock of *kanelbullar* and *mazarines*, butter, milk, yoghurt, cereal, chicken, and especially flown-in fruit and vegetables.

With an hour of daylight left they walk around the outside of the summer houses and through the woods which border onto the house. Everything is exactly the same. It brings back happy memories to the girls who had spent many a long weekend up there, especially for Sven as she had spent quite a bit of time working for *Handelsbanken* in the *Umeå* branch and actually lived in the house and commuted each day.

Sven always on the lookout for a quiet retreat would spend hours sitting on the lawn looking out over the water or inside by the fire during the winter, writing poetry and reading. It was here that she learnt most of her Swedish, as being so remote she very seldom received visitors. The summer house was a perfect place for study and solitude.

Jack smiles when he sees the sauna, "So, will we be using that Swedish style, then? A bit of a romp in the snow, then straight into the sauna and out again into the lake of course downing schnapps to help us keep warm?"

Teasing Sven cuts in, "Only in true Swedish style, of course."

Getting the joke, Freya adds, "I would say when in Sweden do as the Swedes do, so of course, yes."

Charlie, guessing something was up, asks, "So what exactly do you mean by *True Swedish Style?*"

Sven turns to Elisabeth holding her finger to her lips, "Not a word *kusin.*"

Smiling, Elisabeth says, "Okay, Clara, let's go. It's five o'clock and the celebrant said he would meet us at the *kyrka* then."

"We'll stay and unpack and keep these boys out of trouble," Freya says.

*****

The two girls get into the borrowed family fur-lined moon-boots waiting at the door, put on thick fur coats and walk down the snow-covered road to the cutesy picture-book little church.

"It's even more gorgeous than I remember. I never ever dreamed that I would get married here. I think I came once for a service, but I never thought..." Clara's mind wanders off when an old rusty Saab rounds the corner.

"*Hej tjena Kurt, laggit?*" Elisabeth asks.

The girls walk up to a middle-aged, funky-looking man. Clara says to herself, *hmm one very groovy celebrant; I think I could handle him doing the service? Not a typical*

Swede at all.

Kurt has mousey hair, a goaty, John Denver look alike glasses and is wearing jeans, tall snow boots and a big thick heavy sheepskin jacket.

"*Hej* Elisabeth, Clara, congratulations. Let's get inside before you freeze to death. We don't want our little South Pacific flower catching a cold from our glorious Scandinavian weather, do we?" He puts his arm on her shoulders to guide her into the church. Clara can't help noticing that Kurt's gaze lingers on Elisabeth.

Once inside, Clara gasps at the beauty. Every window is stained glass. Old-fashioned wooden pews are in neat rows, wooden panels line the walls, and a little altar sits at the front. It smells musty, as if it hasn't been opened up for a while.

"Did you not have a service here on Christmas Eve? Clara asks. "I thought the village would have been jumping."

"No I am afraid nothing jumps out this way, especially not at this time of the year. But I am sure you will change that in the next few days. Now Clara I will show you a rough outline of what I usually do and please change, delete whatever you want and naturally add your personality and flavour where you want. Have you written your own vows? Any poems perhaps?"

Clara blushes, "Ha, I knew you were going to suggest that. With all the mad rush, I have only jotted some ideas down on the plane. The beauty of getting here a few day's early it gives us plenty of time to write something and work together. Are you around over the next wee while?"

"Yes, my dear. I live here. I may go into *Umeå* to get supplies, but you are right, we have plenty of time to make this the most perfect wedding *Skeppsvik* has ever seen. I have to say I have never married a New Zealand bride before. This is a first and I am very excited. Now music. Do you want the old-fashioned organ up the back, or something a bit jazzier? You know we have slides and a more up-to-date music system now." Kurt grins at them.

"Wow Kurt, you come with everything. You really are the one-stop shop every bride dreams of," Elisabeth gushes.

"Thanks so much, Elisabeth. I can't believe I am back here for my wedding. You have been a star to get this all sorted," Clara says genuinely.

The three continue to work with the ceremony selections and after a half hour of looking at the church and the hall and discussing table configurations and decorations, Clara and Elisabeth farewell Kurt and head back to the cottage.

Jack has a roaring fire going and, with Sven, they have the sauna heated, all ready for the evening shenanigans. He asks, "How did it go? Is he a boring minister?"

Clara laughs and winks at Elisabeth. "No, surprisingly, not at all."

Elisabeth sighs, "You will never change will you, Flat White? You are so naughty."

"Yes naughty, but innocent, I've got the right man with me, right here by my side. I would never do anything to jeopardise our relationship. A little innocent banter with some novelty eye-candy, does no one any harm. As long as you window shop and don't buy. Besides I think he only has eyes for you," Clara explains.

Elisabeth blushes slightly. "What? You have lost me. Not another one of your weird Kiwi sayings?"

"Yes, sorry, I'm playing with words. Right looks like

Jack and I have a bit of work to do, like writing our vows."

"Hmm I think I understand what you mean now, so on that note, I will leave you lovebirds to it. As you English-speaking people, say, Two's company and three's a… how do the French say it, *ménage a trois.*" Elisabeth winks.

Clara laughs. "*Touche!* Well done!"

"And what time are we gathering for the '*Swedish Style*' sauna?" Elisabeth teases.

Chapter 26

Gott Nytt År

They share the three houses between them. Clara and Jack have the smallest one-bedroom place to themselves. The four other Kiwis are holed up in the two-bedroom house and Elisabeth is in the large home, which will accommodate the Stockholm gang when they arrive.

The days fly by in a flurry of wedding preparations. In between the gang explore in and around the village, take plenty of walks, and evening saunas, where they catch up on each other's news.

Filing into the sauna, Jack comments as he disrobes, "I dunno about you guys, but this 'Swedish Style' takes a bit of getting used to for a boy from Eketahuna."

"Hmm, he's hardly a boy," Elisabeth comments quietly as she elbows Clara.

"Steady on Elisabeth, besides I thought I saw you eyeing up Kurt at the church the other day," teases Clara.

"Oh, what's this?" Sven pricks up her ears.

Blushing, Elisabeth protests, "We are just good friends."

Clara laughs and continues in a mocking tone, "I was quite embarrassed. They couldn't keep their hands off each other."

"Flat White, that's just not true," Elisabeth objects.

Freya asks gently, "Are you sure you wouldn't be tempted? Kurt is one good-looking minister."

"Well… let's not rush into anything," Elisabeth softens.

"Anyone for a drink?" Zac asks.

"Let's try one of those local lagers we picked up today," Charlie replies, "but serve the girls first."

With drinks in hand, Clara proposes a toast, "Thanks again for everyone coming over to celebrate with us. Here's to a happy New Year, *Skål!*"

"*Skål*," they all chorus.

Sven is the first to speak, "Flat White, is there anyone you want that isn't here, like family?"

"What girl wouldn't want her Dad to walk her down the aisle?" Clara replies. "But I've only just found him, and it's too short notice. Of course, Sabrina, but she's with Mum up in the Bay of Islands."

"Not your psycho mother, then?" Sven teases.

"Fuck, no way! You know she tried to have me committed once," Clara replies.

"I can't say I've heard this one, babe," Jack pricks up his ears. "Let's hear it."

"It was just before I went to boarding school and Mum dragged me along with Fred. Dad was out of town," Clara recalls. "I just thought I was going to the doctor for a check-up, but this psychiatrist was asking all these weird questions. I remember Mum answering them all on my behalf, until he sent Mum and Fred out of the room."

"You didn't tell us about this, Flat White," Freya says. "What happened next?"

"Well, the shrink was really nice to me. He asked me questions about Mum, so I told him how I saw things…" Clara goes quiet, remembering.

"And…" Elisabeth prompts.

"And when Mum and Fred came back, he told them there was nothing wrong with me. But he wanted to make an appointment with Mum."

"Fucking bitch! I knew she was a psycho," Sven spits.

Charlie elbows the boys on either side of him, nodding towards Sven, "Remind me never to cross that one."

"So did she go?" Freya asks.

"Of course not. It's a shame really. If she had, who knows how life would have turned out," Clara reflects philosophically. "For one, we wouldn't have met at boarding school."

Breaking the mood, Jack proposes, "Here's to our boarding-school girls, *Skål!*"

*****

They gather together for breakfast at the big house. Elisabeth brings the coffee pot out to the dining table. "So Flat White, one more day of freedom. Are we going out for drinks tonight?"

"I'm in two minds about that."

"I'll be taking the Stockholm crowd out tonight, but can you be here around midday?" Elisabeth asks.

"Sure, why?"

"I'm bringing out Olaf from the *ålderdomshem*. He has a small gift for you."

"Of course. I'll be here." Clara wells up.

"Yay *Farfar* Olaf! Oh, Charlie, you will have to be on your best behaviour," Sven says excitedly.

"Why's that?" Charlie asks.

"See that hunting rifle up there?" Sven points above the fireplace. "That's his and he still uses it!"

"Damn, I thought that was for show." Charlie is shocked. He leaves the table to inspect the rifle.

"He's coming tomorrow, isn't he, Elisabeth?" Clara queries, "Any of the rest of the family?"

"Olaf will be, but sorry no, the rest are down south in *Malmö* at another family reunion," Elisabeth answers. "Olaf can't travel far these days."

"Hey guys, you wanna have a look at this?" Charlie calls from the fireplace.

"Take that outside, please, I don't like guns being played with inside the house," Sven calls.

The three men walk out onto the porch, closing the door behind them.

"Oh thank god for that, I thought they would never go," Freya breathes a sigh of relief.

"Trouble with one of the happy couples?" Elisabeth asks.

"No Elisabeth. Look I'm not being rude. It's great, this new boyfriend, fiancé thing we have going on here, but seriously! They are such a bunch of introverts, aren't they?" an exasperated Freya replies.

The girls burst out laughing, and Sven explains, "I heard Zac snoring from our room, might pay to have a nap this arvo Fin."

"I guess it's a male thing, but sometimes I just want to get into third gear and ready for the next topic and they are still fumbling around in neutral and stuck on a topic five conversations before," Freya vents.

Sven laughs, "You're hilarious, Freya. Sometimes you two are like an old married couple already, but I guess that's because you've known each other all your lives. Don't get me wrong, I see the way you guys look at each other, but it's still hilarious watching you finishing each other's sentences."

Clara chips in, "And being so brutally honest with each other."

"Well, I'm not there yet." Sven replies wistfully. "I guess it's because I found my true love, then being so immature and jealous at the time, lost it and it's taken me decades to get it back. So, I'm treading more carefully."

"Right, Flat White, while the boys are outside, can you please explain why on earth you invited Lars to the wedding?" Elisabeth puts Clara on the spot.

"You didn't!" Sven says shocked.

"Your ex? What were you thinking Flat White?" Freya asks.

Clara looks a little bashful and replies in a small voice, "Um, it seemed like a good idea at the time."

"Clara, I'm going to be straight with you," Elisabeth states, "Lars was pretty cut-up when you returned to New Zealand. I think it will only reopen old wounds."

"I didn't think of that," Clara sighs. "I just thought he might like to see that we can move on and find happiness."

"Geez, Flat White, this could all go tits up if he comes," Elisabeth warns. "He was besotted with you."

Sven recalls, "Elisabeth and I spent many hours at

his *lägenhet,* getting him to lay off the booze and to eat properly. Poor Lars was a mess for some time."

"I didn't know that," Clara admits. "I stayed in touch with him, and he said he would come out to Wellington, but he never did. Then he stopped returning my emails and wouldn't answer his phone."

"Oh, he didn't tell us that he was going to Wellington, did he Elisabeth?" Sven asks.

"No, I don't recall that, but I know there was a lot of pressure from his family for him to stay at *Handelsbanken,*" Elisabeth informs them.

"God, I remember meeting his parents. They were so conservative," Freya chips in.

"They were half the problem when we were a couple, especially the father, always banging on about religion," Clara recalls. "Okay, okay it was a bad idea to invite him, but I didn't mean to hurt him. He's such a nice guy."

"So, what are you going to do?" Elisabeth asks.

"Do you have his phone number? Should I phone him?" Clara asks.

"Yeah, probably that's best," Sven agrees.

"I just hope he's not already on his way," Elisabeth states, handing Clara her phone.

Clara takes the phone and walks away from the table, waiting for the phone to connect, "It's gone to voicemail… Hi Lars, Clara here. Hey, I didn't mean to upset you, but please phone me back. It would be good to talk…"

Looking back at her girlfriend, Freya says, "Good on you, Flat White. Let's hope he phones and doesn't arrive with Saga and the crew."

*****

Resting up before lunch in their summer house, Clara looks through her journal and the words she wrote over a month ago. She comments out loud, "So much has happened in such a short time, but it seems a million lifetime's ago."

Jack looks up from the Scandi crime novel he is reading, "All okay there, my sweet one?"

"No. I'm feeling a bit of a prat. I'm flicking through my journal and I just can't believe some of the stuff I've written. What a state I was in. No wonder you walked out on me."

"Would you like to share any of that stuff with me? It might make me understand more what you went through. You know, Clara, you don't exactly wear your emotions on your sleeve. You are a pretty good actress. I had no idea what was going on for you. To me it looked like you were having a ball." Jack shakes his head as he puts his novel down. "But I must admit some nights towards the end it was like watching Amy Winehouse's demons on stage unfold. I just couldn't stick around and watch. I realise now, that if I didn't care I could have stuck around, but I cared too much. I mean, I didn't even know you were in therapy."

"I know Jack. I'm great in covering up everything. You know it's still hard being so open."

"So, do you want to share some of your works of art? I'm all ears if you want…"

"I'm a bit embarrassed, so one sign of a yawn Jack Fenton and I am snapping the book shut, and that's it. Okay, here's the first one from early November…"

The shrink is okay so I will give it a go
But I'm okay, that I know

I'll do what the doctor says I must do
Labelling feelings that's something new
I'll go for the sessions she has prescribed
Discussing my feelings in detail described
Changing the negative stories in my head
Replacing them with new ones I think instead
Trying this new mindfulness app
Breathing and all sorts of nonsensical crap
I'm not sure this new age stuff is for me
But I'll give it a go I'll wait and see.

"I'd forgotten how anti I was going to a shrink," Clara comments, finding another poem, "Oh, here's one from the weekend at Waitarere Beach before the earthquake…"

The Trinity Trio finally reunite
Talking away half the night
So many stories they need to tell
Another drink oh what the hell
Too much has happened good and bad
Hilariously funny and extremely sad
I for a change had the most to say
Freya's been talking half the day
Firstly my job goes up in smoke
Hardly the time to laugh and joke
Getting caught on the Judge's bench
Then sacked by an HR evil wench
Selling my house on a whim
A ditzy moment feeling dim
Out of work and nowhere to live
What else have I got to truly give?

"Man, I was desperate then. That's when I hit rock bottom. I never thought I would be able to pick myself back up again. How the hell did I get through this?"

Gently Jack answers, "You have two solid friends Clara. So, you didn't see the signs?"

"Well unbeknown to me I was crumbling for ages. I was so busy putting on airs and graces and drinking, I didn't know I was numbing the pain. I just thought I was having the time of my life. But I wasn't. I was band-aiding everything. I was miserably unhappy and thought I had everything, but instead I had nothing and even when I was with people I was incredibly lonely," Clara reveals.

Turning the page Clara starts crying when she sees the next poem. "Jack, I promise I started with him while we were having time out. I'm not that much of a bitch."

Taking a deep breath, Jack replies, "Okay go on. You know the vows we wrote for tomorrow say we have no secrets from each other and no lies. So, let's get it all out now…"

Oh my god, my life is full of lies
Who's been watching me, all those spies?
I should have known cameras were in that room
My life is now all doom and gloom
The camera I know never lies
It's now time to break all ties
I've done wrong, I must admit
Oh my god I don't give a shit
I loved Jack I never knew
I've fucked up. I've made a blue
And now there's no turning back

I've lost my true love I'm so sorry Jack.

Jack reaches over to hold both her hands, "I know you're sorry, babe. You have told me a million times, but I do know you are sorry. Besides, it must be so hard to go back and read all of that. You're one very brave woman, Clara James and that's one of the reasons why I'm marrying you. I mean, who goes to therapy and faces their demons, then writes about it and goes back and reads and reflects on it. That's big stuff. Having the guts to fly to Nepal and apologise to me in person. That's just amazing." Jack compliments.

Clara looks up sheepishly, "Thanks, but Jack I have never gone to therapy before. I thought it was for nutcases or those yummy mummies who felt they needed a therapist as their latest fashion accessory. I know I've got a way to go yet, and if it wasn't for my mates I wouldn't have got this far. I truly feel blessed and I am so grateful. I've always had everything I wanted but felt empty. Now everything I value belongs in here," Clara says as she points to her heart.

"Can I let you into a little secret, babe?" Jack asks.

"Sure."

Jack begins, "Okay, my turn to confess. Like you I always felt the big flash car, the house and job was really important and it defined me. Then I wondered why I was so unhappy. Hey, in my defence I'm just a bloke, so I slowly realised that they were all nice things to have, but not what makes you really happy."

"Go on, lover boy, I like it when you're being real," Clara urges.

"Well, I saw an advert on my social media about being of service in Nepal. By then the rumours of your affair were just starting, so I took a punt and got on a plane. I was running away from New Zealand, but also from myself and my own social conditioning. I guess coming to Nepal made me see the light. And then you texted saying you were coming over."

"I knew you weren't happy about it, but I had to see you at least one more time."

"I know, babe. My head was saying, stay away, but my heart, well, it felt right and I took the risk and it paid off. I admit I didn't want to meet you at Kathmandu airport that day. I was still feeling bitter, but that was male ego. My heart felt differently. You know I think I loved you right from the first time I laid eyes on you on the wharf that day. Did you see me eyeing you up?"

"Not at first. You were hiding behind your sunnies and the sun was in my eyes so I couldn't see you clearly. But once we got to the bar, each time I looked your way, we caught each other's eye. It was so funny. You know the first time is okay, then the second, well maybe it's a coincidence, but when you lock eyes a third and fourth time, then it means business. You looked so handsome in that suit and tie. It was such a formal occasion, wasn't it and I was all dolled up in my flash gears," Clara remembers.

Jack laughs, "As I recall it didn't take long to rip those flash gears off, did it?"

Blushing Clara remembers their first night of passion, then changes the subject, "Thanks for being open with me, Jack. Now where are you sleeping tonight?"

"You know me, I still like to do some things the right way. We know it's not good luck if I see you in your wedding dress before the ceremony. So, I'm staying with the gang at Elisabeth's house. Speaking of which, I'd best pack my gear and get over there." Jack gets up off the couch.

Clara pulls him back towards her. "Not so fast, Tiger…"

*****

Jack is laughing with Zac as he passes him a beer. Charlie joins them, "Right brothers, let's get this party started. Who's on the sounds?"

Jack points towards the stereo. "It's over there. I gave Elisabeth a hand to wire the speakers out to the covered porch. She put a local band on. Some Swedish sounding jazz trio."

"I just happen to have a playlist from home that will get us dancing," Charlie replies, "I got it from your Samoan mates, Zac."

"Paulo and Isaia? Fantastic! Who needs a wedding as an excuse to have a party? We have the New Year to celebrate and see in," Zac replies.

*****

Two familiar faces enter the room. Clara exclaims, "*Hej* Katarina! *Hej* Bernard! Wow you made it all the way from little old Wellywood. This is a great surprise. It's so great you could come."

"Apologies for being late, Clara." Bernard gives her a kiss on the cheek and hands her a small present. "My fault, I took a wrong turn. Poor Katarina is most embarrassed we are late."

"*Så ledsen* Clara," a mortified Katarina apologises.

Clara holds Katarina tight, saying, "It's okay Katarina, really."

"*Tack så mycket*, I bought this from home for you," Katarina says as she hands Clara a box, saying excitedly, "Go on open it."

Clara tears the paper from the box and opens one end, "Wow, you know my favourite! A bottle of Daniel le Bruin."

"I thought you may like that tomorrow morning while you are getting prepared. Oh, Flat White, I'm so happy for you." Katarina beams.

"Now where are those friends of yours? I'd like a report on their assignment." Bernard winks.

"They never did tell me that story…" Clara begins.

Kurt and Elisabeth are up dancing together with Saga and a few others. While Freya is lining up shot glasses of schnapps, along the kitchen bar, Sven and her grandfather Olaf are sitting by the fire catching up on family news.

****

Later in the evening Clara walks over to Jack, "Hey, lover boy, care to walk your fiancée home? I'm going to turn in early for some beauty sleep."

"Your wish is my command, my dear," Jack replies doing an elaborate bow. He takes her arm, and they quietly leave the party to cross the snow-covered ground towards their *stuga*.

As they get close to the summer house, they can hear the countdown followed by cries of *Gott nytt år* and *Skål*.

Pulling her in for a kiss Jack whispers, "Happy New Year fiancée."

Clara melts into his arms, enjoying the moment. She opens her eyes, and suddenly breaks the kiss. "Oh look Jack! Look!"

Turning, Jack sees the northern lights for the first time, the fluorescent greens and blue colours dancing in the night sky.

"How magical." Jack stares in wonderment, as the couple stand mesmerised by nature's light show.

Chapter 27

New Year, New Beginnings

Shading her eyes from the sun shining on the lake waters, Clara admires the tree branches painted white with last night's freshly fallen snow, as she walks flanked by her friends, Sven and Freya.

"I didn't picture us recovering from a New Year's hangover in *Skeppsvik* when we stayed at the Waitarere bach a month ago," Sven says.

"How many shots did you have last night?" Freya asks.

"Far too many, once *Farfar* Olaf left," Sven replies massaging her temples.

"The question is my friends, when is the next wedding?" Clara asks cheekily.

"I'm not rushing into anything this year," Freya replies, "I've got to concentrate on building a regular income at Portobello."

"Neither am I. It's still early days with Charlie. Don't get me wrong, he's great, but this time around I'm taking it slow," Sven relates.

"Well girls, this is beautiful, and the cold has given us all that 'rosy red' cheek look, so let's head back and see if Elisabeth's hairdresser has arrived." With her heart filled with happiness Clara thinks, *the setting is picture perfect for our wedding especially for a South Pacific Belle, so far away from home with my chums right beside me. Just the way we always have been since our school days as the Trinity Trio all those decades ago.*

"Wow, Flat White I still can't believe this is happening, the wedding. You and Jack. It's so surreal and so is the whole setting, like something out of a fairy tale," Freya comments.

"Exactly, I keep having to pinch myself," Clara responds. "I feel so blessed, so lucky. I'm on the other side of the world with my two best friends and my soon-to-be husband, and my two best friends' men. Here we are in the middle of nowhere. No one could have predicted this."

Freya slaps her forehead, "I plain forgot, Flat White, I've got some mail for you, in my makeup bag."

Approaching the *stuga*, Sven sees a car parked up and comments, "The hairdresser must have arrived girls. Hang on a minute…"

"Shh," Freya whispers urgently.

Their stealthy approach muffled by the snow the girls walk in and surprise Elisabeth and her guest. Elisabeth is in a deep embrace with Kurt. Suddenly they need to break their passionate kiss, both looking a little embarrassed. Elisabeth hastily protests, "It's ah…"

"Not what it looks like?" Clara finishes Elisabeth's sentence.

"*Kusin!* Go, you good thing! And as for you, you

Danish rogue. Do we get an explanation?" Sven crosses her arms, tapping her foot doing her best impression of a stern parental figure.

"Ah caught out." Kurt smiles, then slipping his arm around Elisabeth's waist, he explains unapologetically, "How can I resist this *Vackra Svenska kvinnor*, this beautiful Swedish woman? From the first time we met to arrange this wedding, I knew we had a connection and it's just built steadily from then."

"Well congratulations you two," Clara says.

"I think it's going to be one of those days," Freya laughs.

"So, any cold feet, Clara?" Kurt asks.

"No, I know this is the real deal. Here's the hairdresser now," Clara replies as another car pulls up.

"Good, I'd best go and make sure your fiancé is ready, *ses snart*, see you all soon," Kurt farewells, then leans in for a final passionate kiss. "Especially you *käresta*."

*****

Rummaging in her make up bag, Freya triumphantly holds the envelope aloft, "I've found it! Here you go Clara." She passes the golden envelope with the pretty red waxed seal to Clara. "Flat White, Leo wanted to give you something. I only just remembered in time. It was you talking about PREDICTIONS that triggered my memory. Open it when you are ready, and if you want to share let us know how accurate the contents are to the actual events. You may want to open it after the wedding. It's up to you. He said, only you would know when to open it."

Clara takes the envelope and hesitates. "You know I

initially thought I would want to read it, but no, I don't need to. I'm happy to put it in a safe place, and look at it some other time."

"Dear Leo, the guy is a natural and he so looks the part with his long Jesus-like hair, beard, rosy red cheeks and big brown eyes," Sven says dreamily. "I really must go and see Leo again to get a 'top up'."

Freya comes back with, "You will be joining a line, Sven, He's become quite the icon, with woman of all ages swarming at his feet."

The girls continue to talk about Leo and the other characters at Portobello, telling Elisabeth and Karin the hairdresser all about it.

Elisabeth's phone beeps. Checking it, she turns to Clara passing her phone, "It's for you."

Clara reads the message from Lars out loud, *Hey Clara, thanks for the invite, but I am unable to get up to Umeå this weekend, but all the best, have a great day, you deserve it, take care, Lars.*

Clara feels grateful. "Always the gentleman, but that is a relief." Becoming emotional, Clara continues, "Who could have predicted this special day. This is why so many people are so grossly unhappy, because when you are little you grow up thinking that a knight in shining armour is going to come riding along and sweep you up in his arms before taking you to his fairy tale castle in the sky."

Sven replies gently, "Guess what Clara? Sometimes fairy tales do come true. Especially to those like you who have had it rough but learnt from it and came out the other side. Why? Because you followed your heart and did what you felt was right inside, instead of living the BS life from the past."

"Look at us three." Sven agrees. "What were the chances that we were all going to stay in touch? Reunite all those years later after school on our OE over here of all places, then return home and go through an earthquake, a couple of murders, legal battles, bad career choices, psychopathic narcissistic mothers, you name it." She is on a roll. "But then we all end up with our men. And it's all happened now in the last few weeks!"

"I think even Leo couldn't have possibly predicted all that?" Freya cuts in.

Sven continues, "But you see miracles do happen. And you don't have to pinch yourself, because it really is happening and we have all created this. The three of us have never stood back for too long and taken crap. We've carved our own dirt tracks, instead of following the trusty well-worn path that most people follow."

"Yes and carving our own dirt track has come at a price," Clara adds.

"Of course, it has. Do you think pioneers find it easy?" Sven hasn't finished yet. "Do you think Edmund Hillary or Peter Jackson found it easy? Hell no. They took risks, but they followed their dreams, their goals, they were true to themselves. They went through rejections, hardships, that's what makes their achievements so special. Do you want to be a boring soul-less shallow person who can say at 65 when they retire, Oh I never took a risk in my life, but I managed to make it to my pension day without putting a foot wrong and towing the line?"

Clara gets the bubbles out from the fridge, "Wow, not another deep and meaningful! I love it when we have these real conversations. Yeah girls we have all come a long way with our trials and tribulations, but I wouldn't change it for the world. Right who's first to propose a toast?"

Freya looks at Clara, "Here's to judges and how helpful they can be in solving cases and getting me back my business. Here's to all the sharks with lipstick, snakes in suits, and scorpions in stilettos that created the obstacles and setbacks, that eventually led us to the pot of gold at the end of the rainbow. Here's to Flat White, for having the balls and the heart to get her to where we stand today—the wedding of a lifetime. Here's to Clara James."

They lift their glasses, "*Skål, Lycka till.*"

Sven takes over, "Yes Clara, my darling. You have been the most infuriating, flighty, pretentious friend a mate could ever have. But I never gave up on you, even though I tried so many times to divorce you. I knew that you were really made of good stuff deep inside, even though you hid it well, so well that most people never saw it. That was their loss. We knew who you really were. Here's to Clara James."

"*Skål,*" everyone raises their glasses again.

Clara goes to propose a toast but is just too overwhelmed with happiness. She sits down and composes herself.

"I will make this short," she sobs. "But I am the happiest I have ever been. I have learnt so much about myself in the last few weeks. I am so grateful for all the shit that has happened in my life that has bought me to this moment right here, right now. I also know that if it wasn't for all your help, I wouldn't be here. So here's to all of you!"

The girls clink their glasses. "*Skål!*"

✶✶✶✶✶

After Karin the hairdresser leaves, Elisabeth runs

around fussing with their last-minute hair and makeup changes, arranging the flowers. Taking photos for the pre-wedding shots. Elisabeth saying to everyone, "Come let's get a fun photo with you in the snow, we will be quick!"

Walking outside, Freya sees Jack jump into the Black Volvo, quickly standing in front of Clara blocking her view. She says, "Shit, Stop. Thank god for that. Clara it would have been bad luck you seeing him before the wedding."

The Volvo takes off down the road, Sven asking, "Where is he going? Must be some last minute thing to sort?"

Clara thinks to herself *why on earth is Jack in the wedding car taking off from the house and in a different direction to the church?* Looking at her watch, Clara shakes her head, "I can't believe he's taken off like that with only minutes to go before we're meant to leave the house."

They all start giggling as they are literally and physically in the middle of the woods. There are no neighbours, cars, people for miles, just their three little houses and everyone having already left for the wedding.

"Shit we are stranded. Oh my god what a nightmare!" Elisabeth panics.

"That will teach us for being so laissez-faire and starting on the bubbles too soon." Sven advises. "Shit I'm meant to be the responsible one. Let's get back inside out of the cold. I'll grab my phone and call Charlie and see what's going on."

*****

Disconnecting the call, Sven relays, "So Jack had forgotten the rings, that's why he was taking the car. The driver will be back soon to pick us up."

They hear the old Volvo approaching and the girls get their gear together.

There is a knock at the door.

Clara lets out a little scream, "Oh my god, oh my god, quickly, we aren't quite ready."

"Yes we are more than ready, remember your breathing. Just breathe girl, you'll be fine. It's just the chauffeur. He is ready to take you." Freya soothes.

Clara responds, "I'm so glad I'm not going on my own, I need you guys for moral support. You are my family…"

A surprised Sven opens the door, as the driver wearing a dark suit enters the room, removing his hat, his soft firm voice announces, "I am your family Clara."

Clara can't believe she is hearing this familiar voice. She pinches herself for the 98th time that day. She turns to look at the others. "It can't be."

Freya having no idea what is going on, looks up in bewilderment to see Sven with a huge smile, tears running down her face.

Blinking back tears, Clara whispers, "Daddy, is that really you?"

"Of course, it is my dear," Frank replies smiling, as he dabs his handkerchief at his own welling eyes.

Rushing towards her father, Clara throws her arms around him, "What the hell are you doing here?"

Fiercely returning her hug, Frank replies, "I believe my daughter is getting married today."

"My wedding you are here for my wedding!" Clara exclaims excitedly.

Holding her at arm's length, looking her up and down, admiring the brightly coloured Nepalese sashes and flowers against the white wedding dress, Frank praises, "Gigi, you look fabulous!"

"Daddy come in, come and sit down. I need to know how you got here. What's the real story?"

Frank enters and looks around the room. He opens his arms to Sven, "My you have grown a lot since the school days, haven't you? Still slim and ever so pretty."

"Thank you Mr James," Sven replies, "and this is my cousin Elisabeth."

"Ah the wedding organiser, apologies if I've messed up the catering numbers, Elisabeth," Frank says.

"I'm sure we will cope Mr James," a teary-eyed Elisabeth replies.

Turning to Freya, Frank hugs her. "You look exactly the same, too, Freya. Maybe a little taller, but the same as I remember you that day you won those running races at the School Sports tournament." Shaking his head, "Gosh it is frightening. It seems just the other day you three were sharing a dorm together. Do you think it was worthwhile after all that money and homesickness and rebelliousness that went on?"

"Of course it was Mr James. We wouldn't all be standing here now, if we hadn't all gone to that school," Freya replies.

"Hmm but none of you followed the rules, did you?" Frank chuckles.

"We're not here because we followed the school's stuffy rules and curriculum. It was because we broke them all and created our own. We were Rebels WITH a cause." Freya explains.

Sven grabs another glass and tops everyone up, "Okay one more toast for the road. Raise your glasses folks.

Here's to Rebels WITH A CAUSE!"

Just as they clink their glasses they hear the church bells down the road ringing out.

"Oh that's so romantic," Freya says with more tears running down her face.

Elisabeth races around with tissues and make up, trying to repair their mascara lines on the girls' cheeks, "Now stop with the tears! Or we will never get to the *kyrka!*"

"Well my little Cinderella, your carriage awaits," Frank says pointing outside.

Clara is so excited. "My dad made it. He came all the way from New Zealand. Who is the luckiest girl in the world?"

"Come along Clara, a girl mustn't be too late for her wedding now, must she." Frank urges. "Especially now I have had the privilege of meeting the good-looking groom."

"You've met Jack? How could you have met Jack?" Clara asks.

"Who do you think was behind all this?" Frank queries with a twinkle in his eye.

"Oh, isn't he the best!" Clara exclaims.

Walking his daughter arm-in-arm out to the wedding car, Frank turns to the others, "Come along you lot! I've got a bride to give away."

Slutet
The End

You are cordially invited to join our regular newsletter to learn more about the author's upcoming releases, entertaining blog posts, competitions, giveaways and much, much more at:

www.bachdoctorpress.com

or follow us on our Facebook page:

Hinemura Ellison and Ted Hughes

GLOSSARY

Acronyms

Bach	Holiday Home
FAA	Federal Aviation Authority
Flagrante delicto	Caught in the act
JAB	Justice Advisory Board
Mint	Good condition (Slang)
Munted	Wrecked (Slang)
Perv	To look at lecherously
Porte cochère	Main Hotel car entrance
PTSD	Post Traumatic Stress Disorder
Scarper	To flee, to leave
Tarted up	Dressed up (to the nines)
TESOL	Teaching English as a Second Language

Māori Dictionary

Aroha mai	Apologies, sorry
Ata mārie	Good morning
Atua	Māori Gods and Goddesses
E hika!	Heck! For goodness sake!
E noho rā	Goodbye (to someone staying)
Iwi	Tribe
Ka kite āno	Goodbye (informal)
Kakato	To be pleasant of taste
Kia kaha	Be brave, be strong
Kia ora	Hello, greetings, good health
Mōkarakara	Aroma, savoury, appetising
Ngāi Tahu	(Kai Tahu)South Island Tribe
Rongoā	Māori medicine

Tena Koe	Hello, greetings (singular)
Tēnā rawa atu koe	Thank you very much

Nepali Dictionary

Dhanyabad	Thank you
Namaste	Hello/Goodbye
Subha din	Have a nice day
Swagatam	Welcome

Swedish Dictionary

Åhléns	Swedish Department Store
Ålderdomshem	Retirement Home
Älskling	Darling
Arlanda	International Airport Stockholm
Du också	You too, also
Fantastisk	Fantastic, amazing, incredible
Farfar	Grandfather
Flicka	Girl
Gamla Stan	'The old Town' Stockholm
God Jul	Merry Christmas
Gott nytt år	Happy New Year
Handelsbanken	Swedish Bank
Hej	Hello
Hej da	Bye
Hej tjena	Hello (Slang)
Hem	Home
Hur mår du?	How are you?
Ja	Yes
Ja visst	Yes sure, of course
Jättebra	Very good, excellent
Kanelbullar	Swedish cinnamon pastry
Kanske, en liten	Maybe a little
Käresta	Darling
Klockan nitton	Seven o'clock (1900 hours)
Kronor	Swedish currency SEK
Kusin	Cousin

Kyrka	Church
Lägenhet	Apartment
Laggit	How are you (Slang)
Lycka till	Good luck
Malmö	Swedish City
Mazarine	Swedish almond pastry
Så ledsen	So sorry
Sambo	Partner
Ses snart	See you soon
Skål	Cheers
Skeppsvik	Swedish lakeside village
Slutet	The End
Smultronställe	Hidden secret special place
Strandvägen	A prestigious street in Stockholm
Stuga	Cottage, cabin, small red house
Tack	Thanks
Tack så mycket	Thank you very much
Tack ska du ha	Thank you very much
Tillbaka	Return, back
Tomten	House Gnome, Santa
Tunnelbana	Stockholm's underground train
Umeå	Swedish University town
Uppmärksamhet	Attention
Ursäkta mig	Excuse me
Vackra Svenska kvinnor	Beautiful Swedish woman
Varsågod	You're welcome, there you go
Vasagatan	A street in Stockholm CBD
Vasastan	Exclusive Stockholm suburb
Vasa Real school	A school in Stockholm
Wilkommen	Welcome

Main Characters

Clara James	AKA Flat White
Freya	Clara's bestie
Sven	Clara's bestie
Edward	Sven's cat
Jack Fenton	Flat White's boyfriend
Maude James	Clara's Mum
Sabrina James	Clara's Sister
Yvonne Wakefield	HR Manager JAB
Agnes	JAB Secretary
Laurie	JAB Security
Judge Martin Jacobsen	High Court Judge
Kirsty	Real Estate Agent
Maggie	Clinical Psychologist
Bernard Johnson	Department Chief Executive Big Super Ministry
Margaret Johnson	Bernard's wife and Department Chief Executive
Mystery Man	Police Commissioner
Fred Elliot	James' family friend
Nigel	Recruiting BS Ministry
Patricia Bentley	Maude's skiing friend
Bianca	HR Margaret's Ministry
Jasmine	Barista
Prendergast	Dodgy Lawyer
Donald Church	Property Developer
Cathryn Tennyson	HR Director, BS Ministry
Claudia	Ministry employee
Taylor	Ministry employee
Megan	Ministry employee
Emily	BS Ministry IT Temp
Chris	BS Ministry IT Temp
Tom	Trendy Private Eye
Leo	Petone Palm Reader
Frank (Francis) James	Clara's Dad
Angus Robinson	Retired Police Officer
Peg Robinson	Hospice Nurse
Zita Nilson	Freya's Mum
Sean	Flight Attendant

Courtney	Flight Crew Team Leader
Mary	School Doctor and Director
Simon	School Director
Girvesh Thapa	Pokhara Police Officer
Nugan Devkota	Pokhara Café shop owner
Shekhar	Khapaudi Village Head man
Ralph	Overland Encounters agent
Remi	Seamstress Pokhara
Vatsa	Hair dresser
Elisabeth Svensson	Clara's Friend and Sven's Cousin
Saga	Stockholm friend
Kurt	Danish Minister
Olaf Svensson	Sven and Elisabeth's Grandfather
Katarina	Bernard's Secretary
Lars	Clara's Ex
Karin	Hairdresser, Skeppsvik

Also available from the Bach Doctor Press:

Sharks With Lipstick

Book 1 – Trinity Trilogy

Hinemura Ellison and Ted Hughes

Freshly back from Europe with a new job, Samantha Svensson (Sven) reconnects with her old friends while managing a new role within the Big Super Ministry – where everyone is busy playing their own internal political games.

After the HR Director ends up dead on the same train that Sven was on, suspicions abound, not least from the chief investigating police officer, Charlie Rogers, who happens to be her ex and is still incredibly damned hot!

With Wellington still reeling after a recent big earthquake, Sven must use all her canny resourcefulness to clear her name and identify the killer within their midst.

Available via Amazon: https://www.amazon.com/dp/B07HXVV9QN

Snakes In Suits

Book 2 – Trinity Trilogy

Hinemura Ellison and Ted Hughes

Freya returns to Wellington to restore her inheritance, 'Portobello', an Art Deco building in Petone, to her former glory. Only to find dubious dealings with various Snakes in Suits, Lawyers, Bankers, the Council and an unscrupulous property developer who will stop at nothing, even murder, to get what he wants - 'Portobello'.

Freya fights back with the help of her childhood friend Zac - who just happens to be drop dead gorgeous, and Simon her cute Bank manager who is also competing for her attention.

Reuniting with her besties Sven and Clara, together they navigate their chaotic lives, a massive earthquake and help each other to find love and to solve the murders that plague them.

Book Two in the Trinity Trilogy following on from Sharks With Lipstick

Available via Amazon: https://www.amazon.com/dp/0473494426

Check out more information at: www.bachdoctorpress.com

Follow Hinemura's Blog at: www.hinemuramusings.wordpress.com

More books available from the Bach Doctor Press:

Concealment

M.W. Innes-Jones

Our genes: will they be our hope or our undoing?
Three centuries from now humanity has made its last stand ⌐ a city high in the Swiss Alps, a place of safety and security from a deadly past. This is the reality of Nathanial Paquette's life and it has been this way for the whole of his sheltered twenty-three years. But with a knock at the

family's apartment door everything changes. Now he must face an uncertain future and unexpected truth – he is genetically altered, and what really matters is what lies hidden within his blood.

Together with eleven others, Paquette finds not only does he have to navigate the competing agendas of the city's ruling council and a corrupt man of science, but survive the rigorous training he and his fellow recruits find themselves faced with.

It's a world where friendships are forged, enemies are made, and death awaits – ever wanting to become everyone's new best friend.

Concealment – book one of a six part series which follows Nathanial and his fellow internees through a world of deception and lies. Where the dark underbelly of power and science meet, threatening at every turn.

Available via Amazon: https://www.amazon.com /dp/ B07FTT8PNW

Revelation

M.W. Innes-Jones

Nathanial and those left of the original twelve may have made it to the end of phase one of their training, but will they all make it to the start of the second, let alone finish it?

Book Two, the chess board becomes deadlier; Professor Redmond sharpens his game and the council's fractious nature starts to unravel.

Against this, Nathanial must act to survive Chris' retribution while treading carefully not to become a statistic for the mystery informant who is killing the remaining eight, one by one. And what has this all to do with the cryptic question Commander Reed gave Nathanial to figure out?

In the end the real question is; of those who are left standing, which side will they be on?

Revelation is where lines are drawn, death knocks, and deception awaits to strike from the most unlikely of places.

Book Two in M.W. Innes-Jones' sweeping epic six book saga, the Engelberg Records, set in the Swiss Alps, which follows Nathanial and his friends fight for survival.

Available via Amazon: https://www.amazon.com/dp/B084LRP4TQ/